The Baghdad Chameleon

A fictional story based around
true events

I0674967

Also by David Balderstone
A Road From Damascus

'Balderstone's novel is about people, land and
displacement. It traces the lives of one-time Jerusalem
friends and neighbours, the Palestinian Habeebs and the
Jewish Avrahams as war, politics and ideology separate
them, and then makes their paths cross again. Balderstone
has the cadences and the speeches they enwrap just right
too…Above all he gets the people of the region right.'
The Age, Melbourne

DAVID BALDERSTONE

The Baghdad Chameleon

**THE
POPPY
PRESS**
AUSTRALIA

ISBN 978-0-646-57495-0

The cover image depicts playing cards developed by the US military following the 2003 invasion of Iraq to help troops identify the most wanted members of Saddam Hussein's government.

National Library of Australia
Cataloguing-in-Publication entry
Author: Balderstone, David.
Title: The Baghdad Chameleon / by David Balderstone.
ISBN: 9780646574950 (pbk.)
Subjects: Iraq War, 2003---Fiction.
            Businessmen--Australia--Fiction.
            Business--Middle East--Fiction.
Dewey Number: A823.3

Published by
The Poppy Press AUSTRALIA
(Corporate Affairs Office Victoria, business name registration number 1064567K)
P.O.B 850, Parkville, Victoria, 3052, Australia
poppypress@bigpond.com

In memory of Wasef Al Taher, a skilled
international translator, and an informed and
amusing raconteur

For suggestions and advice, the author is extremely
grateful to Don Gibb, Peter & Louise Hoobin, Robert
Killick, Jane Moon, David Wadham, Robyn Wallace, and
– as always – Susan Balderstone. Mistakes are the fault of
the author.

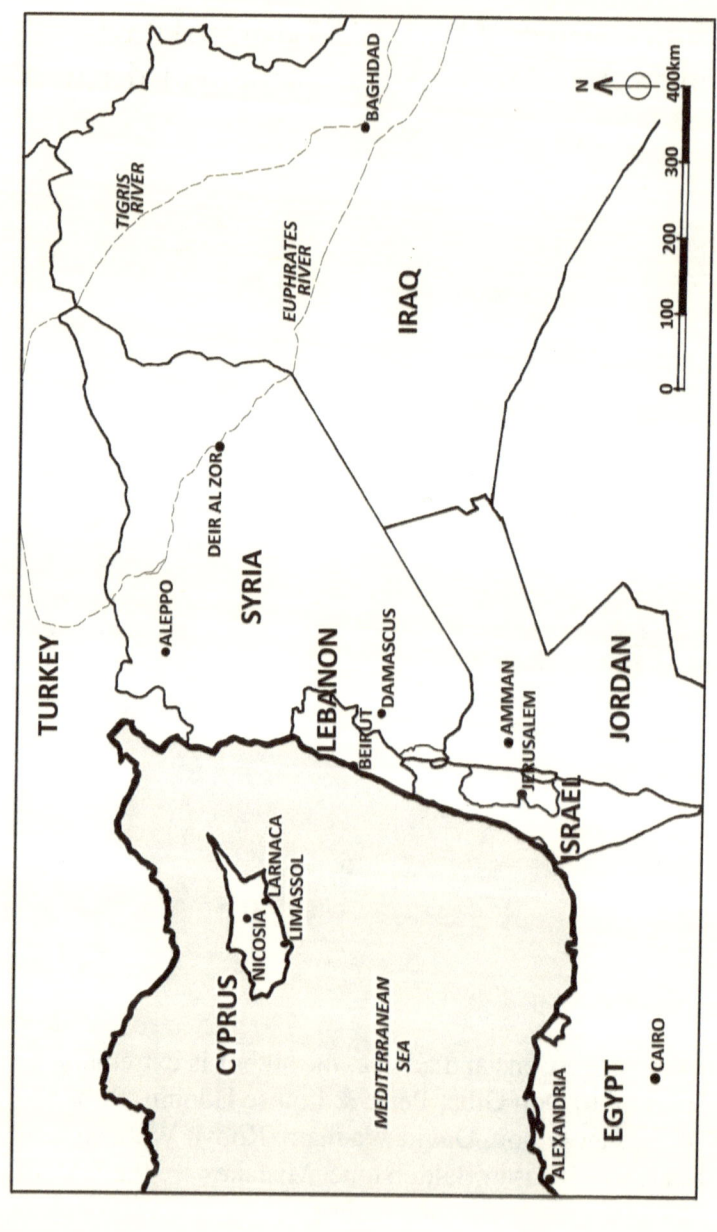

1

A light evening breeze off the Mediterranean did little to ease Scot Wallace's irritation as he strode the tree-lined esplanade skirting Limassol Bay. If he'd known how the evening would end, he would never have set off for the party. He'd have bowed to gut feeling.

Scot had good reason for apprehension, reluctance. Just before leaving his apartment, he'd received a mystery phone call. It was more than a nuisance call. There was silence on the end of the line, then raucous but muffled laughter, something akin to jeering. Then the sound of a gunshot rang out down the line, leaving Scot's left ear ringing, momentarily deaf.

Even before the phone call, Scot resented accepting the invitation. It had become a chore. As he turned into a narrow side street of shops and businesses, some with blue-painted cast-iron balconies, shutters were coming down at the close of trading. The pavement – still warm after a flawless sunny day – was busy with business people, tourists, and local Cypriots seeking bars and restaurants.

Scot had been looking forward to tonight's party. That was before Ahmad Kareem was invited. Ever since he'd met the Iraqi in Baghdad during the last year of Saddam Hussein's regime, Kareem had proved to be manipulative, an opportunistic turncoat, a likely looter of Iraq's money and antiquities – and, most recently, a blackmailer.

And yet, Alexander – the party's host – had still invited Kareem, declaring he found the Iraqi interesting.

There was more to that relationship than Scot was being told.

A couple of hundred metres along the street, people were greeting each other beneath a neon sign flashing 'Club Downtown'. It was a gathering of friends and acquaintances rather than the usual evening mix of diners and clubbers. Scot caught a reflected glimpse of himself in a shop window. His short black hair was looking limp, and his light fawn slacks a touch crumpled, but his neatly ironed blue-striped shirt lifted his tired image. He felt old tonight – much older than his years. Then, almost miraculously, his mood lifted. He hesitated outside a small music store where a CD was booming. It was the Beatles, a remastered recording. 'Yesterday, all my troubles seemed so far away…' He went inside, but not to buy. For a while at least he'd listen, and reclaim the enthusiasm of his youth. Back then, as far as he could recall, he'd no troubles at all. Now, though, troubles didn't seem so far away. He shuffled through a stack of CDs for a while to prolong the feeling of rejuvenation.

As Scot approached the crowd outside Club Downtown, Ahmad Kareem stood out from the crowd, with his Russian friend Boris who, it was claimed, oversaw investments in Cyprus for one or two Moscow-based oligarchs.

'You shall never guess, my friend Scot, what I have for my friend Alexander,' Kareem declared. He held up a small parcel wrapped in silver paper and bound with narrow red, white and blue ribbon supporting a card made from the image of the Union Jack. 'It's a memento of the time he spent in Iraq.'

'Do you think he wants reminding?' Scot spoke dismissively. 'He didn't choose to visit. Remember?'

Ahmad Kareem ignored Scot and led Boris to the restaurant entrance, where Alexander Belfort-Smith was greeting guests. The Iraqi lavishly kissed the host on both cheeks, first the right then the left. Then Boris followed. Alex looked uncomfortable and was relieved when Scot opted for a handshake.

Alex's partner Dimitri welcomed the Iraqi and the Russian.

Nodding a greeting to Dimitri, Scot grabbed the chance to get away and pushed past the three politely, heading for the bar. As he stood surveying the gathering, nodding occasionally to someone he recognised, he marvelled again at the building's transformation. Before Alex and Dimitri opened the restaurant, it was a small shoe-repair shop and factory. Now, bare stone walls, a fireplace, and pine tables replaced the smell of leather and old shoes. A stone arch divided the restaurant and a dance floor.

The reason for the party was Alex had been awarded an OBE by the Queen. Ever since the award was announced, Alex had been less than forthcoming about the reason he'd been made an Officer of the Order of the British Empire for 'services to the community and nation'. Those in the dark about Alex's moonlighting, both Cypriots and expatriates alike, must have guessed now that there was a lot more to Alexander Belfort-Smith than owning a restaurant on Cyprus. It was a good restaurant, but hardly a service to the British Empire. Most British expatriates knew about Alex's army dismissal, and believed his government service had ended there. Now they would wonder and gossip.

Scot was glad the Englishman had turned disgrace into vindication. In fact 'triumph' may not be too strong a word. Alex had been a rising star in the army, when – just a few years before Britain overturned an armed services ban on homosexuals in January 2000 – he was sacked for being gay.

But just why Alex would choose to include Kareem in the celebration was beyond Scot's comprehension. It was a British award after all, with limited meaning to those outside the UK or Commonwealth. There was a history to Scot's views. He'd been a victim of Kareem's manipulation. So much so he had to swear himself to silence for fear of being accused a conspirator in the Iraqi's schemes. The Middle East was an area of the world teeming with truths, half-truths, and outright lies and once trapped, Scot – like others, including world powers – could never escape.

Since jubilant crowds had pulled down the statue of the former disgraced Iraqi leader after the American-led invasion, Kareem had changed colour like a lizard in order to protect himself. He'd even discarded his lush crop of dark hair for a shaved scalp. His invitation to the party was testament to his success, even if enemies had been made along the way. Some British officials – and Alex, it seemed – believed that deep down the Iraqi knew the difference between good and evil, and had opted for good. In Washington, Kareem seemed to be appreciated too and rewarded with a part-time consultancy with a right-wing think tank.

The olive-skinned Dimitri tapped a spoon against a wine glass. Dressed in black slacks and an aqua blue long-sleeved T-shirt, he looked at Alex with fondness, reflecting the fact they were more than business partners.

Alex spoke from beneath the stone arch in the middle of the party. 'Friends! Your attention please! Well, let's get the formalities over and done with ... then we can enjoy the evening.'

Nothing was disclosed about why he'd been awarded an OBE, but the speech was mercifully brief. Afterwards, Ahmad Kareem insisted that 'his great friend Alex' open the small silver-wrapped parcel. Alex reluctantly obliged, and what emerged drew blank silence from most, but a loud gasp of stunned recognition from a few. It was an intricately-engraved black stone cylinder seal. It was almost certainly Babylonian, dating from around 1800 BC. Judging by his uneasy look of dawning recognition, Alex recognised its significance. Perhaps he'd read the same magazine as Scot, and knew hundreds of such seals had been looted from the Baghdad museum after the fall of Saddam Hussein.

The guests were mainly strangers to Scot, so the party provided a chance for reflection on both Alex and Ahmad Kareem, and how their lives intersected, along with his own as a journalist turned trader. As a Cyprus-based reporter, he'd written about the humiliated Alexander Belfort-Smith, but had never met the soldier until after Scot had swapped journalism for a business dealing with Arabs and Israelis. And Kareem? It was not until he'd established his business that the Iraqi entered Scot's life. As so often before, Scot recalled his first meeting with Kareem in Baghdad, less than a year before Saddam fell. Kareem, then of the Iraqi Interior Ministry, hadn't let on, but with hindsight he'd obviously thought there was a good chance the regime would fall, and planned to secure a bolt-hole, an escape route for looted Iraqi money, and eventually himself. With clarity not present at the time, Scot now believed that right from day one the Iraqi had set out to trap him – and he'd succeeded. For Kareem, it had been an each-way bet. If he were right and Saddam fell, then he'd secured his future. And if he were wrong? Then the regime would think he was continuing to do his good and bloody work, and even worthy of promotion.

Scot glimpsed the six-foot tall Alexander bending to whisper in Dimitri's ear. Like the youthful Cypriot, Alexander wore dark slacks. Their aqua blue tops matched, but the Englishman's was a collared shirt, not a

T-shirt. In his early forties, Alex had a full crop of blond hair, with some distinguished grey above the ears.

Scot remembered their first meeting. Mutual recognition had been immediate – although they'd never personally met. For Scot, it was an inevitable encounter he'd been dreading. And for Alexander Belfort-Smith, retired army officer, the meeting appeared to be just as unwelcome. Scot had been the messenger – and not the perpetrator of the outrage. But when face to face with Alexander, he felt some blame. At least the army discharge may have remained secret, or within the closed walls of the military establishment, if it had not been for Scot's story splashed over a London tabloid.

They'd met outside the Club Downtown before renovations were complete and open for business. Scot recognised Alexander from the photograph, which accompanied his newspaper story. Even though Alexander sported a white T-shirt and blue jeans rather than military uniform, Scot knew immediately it was the Englishman he'd written about. It was mid afternoon, and the street was quiet with many of the shops and businesses closed. People were at home resting from the heat, or playing cards in coffee shops. The bustle would return for late afternoon and evening trading with people and traffic choking the narrow street, and then Scot could have crossed to the other side like a bad Samaritan. But there was no place to hide now. Short of turning back like a scared rabbit, the encounter couldn't be avoided. So he'd smiled cautiously, and nodded half-heartedly. There was just enough movement of the head to acknowledge Alexander's presence, but hopefully insufficient to draw any more than a cursory response.

The minimalist tactic failed. Alexander Belfort-Smith said, not aggressively, but without any friendliness either: 'You're Scot Wallace, aren't you?' The question was delivered in the parade-ground style of a British World War II movie. After Scot nodded, Alex continued aggressively: 'The tabloid journalist?'

'No more. I've a small business now, trading.'

Since then, Scot had become more than a good friend to the Brit, who answered to both Alexander and Alex without, it seemed, any preference.

Grabbing another drink from the bar, Scot looked back to the crowd, noticing Alex and Kareem chatting enthusiastically with a few Brits. The Iraqi even slapped Alex on the back in a gesture of friendliness. Then, one by one, the Brits shook the Iraqi by the hand, but without any enthusiasm. As Alex and Ahmad Kareem broke away, the Brits muttered to each other. The body language was that of puzzlement and surprise. Definitely surprise. Scot's curiosity was overridden by weariness; he'd wait to find out if there was anything worth knowing. Limassol was small enough to be certain of him finding out eventually.

Around midnight, as guests were leaving more boisterous and mellow than they'd arrived, Kareem suggested to Scot they walk together. Scot gave a sigh of reluctance. Since their first fateful meeting in Baghdad, Kareem, who'd only recently arrived on Cyprus, had wreaked confusion on his financial affairs, and personal life as well. He wanted to distance himself from the Iraqi. But Kareem insisted: 'I have something to tell you. It is so exciting. You'll love to hear.' After further hesitation from Scot, the Iraqi persisted: 'I have something for you … something you want.'

Outside the restaurant, the evening sea breeze had overwhelmed the residual pavement heat. It was a pleasant night. From the shadows somewhere along the deserted shopping street came the clunk of a motorcycle gear engaging. Hearing the noise, but nothing more, Scot and Ahmad Kareem hesitated on the pavement about twenty metres from Club Downtown. Then the bike started roaring, and suddenly the machine was accelerating towards them.

The leather-jacketed motorcyclist crouched forward towards the handlebars, his pillion rider – jeans clamped either side of the bike – sat up, his left arm steadying his right hand holding a handgun. As the bike approached, his hands and helmet turned towards them. Two shots were fired in quick succession and the pillion rider, job completed, leant forward grabbing the rider's jacket. The bike accelerated more, the front wheel lifting off the road in something of a victory salute.

The sound of the shots, and the motorcycle speeding away into the darkness, brought Alex and party stragglers rushing from the restaurant. They looked on in horror as two bodies lay slumped on the ground. One had been thrown back against the wall of a shop, and left with a glazed smile on his face. The other had fallen, his head resting on the other victim's legs. Blood oozed across the pavement. As the crowd milled around, someone leant over in an amateurish attempt to check for any sign of life.

A siren could be heard louder and louder, and then the flashing lights of an ambulance turned into the street. It screeched to a stop just near the victims. The paramedics pushed the onlookers away, and checked the crumpled men. One by one, they carefully lifted Scot and Ahmad Kareem on to stretchers and into the ambulance. The rear doors of the ambulance were half shut. With the lights on, the paramedics could be seen checking one stretcher and then the other. One ambulance man then stepped from the rear of the vehicle, and – signalling to the onlookers – crossed his fingers before jumping into the driver's seat.

'It's obviously touch and go,' Alex said to the small crowd. With lights still flashing but the siren silent, the ambulance left the scene slowly, cautiously.

2

Some years earlier

Shaded by palm trees beside the mighty Tigris, Scot paced the gravel path of the hotel garden. He felt exhausted after the sixteen-hour road trip to Baghdad from the Jordanian capital Amman. A quick shower and a change into a lightweight fawn suit and blue tie had relieved his tiredness just briefly. But it wasn't just the trip causing weariness, it was the unexpected nature of the demand by the people from Saddam Hussein's Interior Ministry.

Before leaving Limassol, it hadn't worried Scot too much. But now, in the Iraqi capital, the demand seemed sinister, even threatening. 'We have a proposal we would be grateful to discuss with you, and Mr Kareem demands your attendance in Baghdad.' The words the Iraqi official had uttered on the telephone to Limassol echoed through Scot's head as he lit a cigarette.

As he'd built trade with the Iraqis in the face of sanctions, Scot had learnt not to be too surprised by requests from Baghdad. However, his usual client was the Trade Department, and all contact was made through his friend, Sadeq Ramadi, a streetwise Baghdadi trader whose recognised knowledge of international business had apparently made him immune to the frequent purges of the Iraqi bureaucracy. Unlike this Mr Kareem, Sadeq Ramadi demanded nothing. Rather, he was gentle and polite and couched requests to his few trusted foreign friends like Scot in terms such as 'If it would not be a great deal of trouble'. Sure, in a sense, it was the same as a demand. Refusing would mean sacrificing very lucrative ongoing commissions, and the likelihood his name would be dropped from Sadeq Ramadi's list of reliable trading friends. But this Mr Kareem *demands* attendance in Baghdad!

A barge loaded with bags of what looked like cement plied down the centre of the river, its wake sending a couple of black-clad washerwomen scurrying up the opposite bank. Scot was momentarily distracted, but his thoughts kept returning to Mr Kareem. He knew that Interior Ministries in countries like Iraq were involved with internal security matters, a thought that rekindled a latent, but long-held fear about the risks attached to this lucrative trade. As the scorecard stood at present, several foreign businessmen were languishing in Iraqi gaols for alleged spying and breaches of currency regulations. Scot tried reassuring himself that the Interior Ministry wouldn't go to the trouble of summoning potential hostages to Baghdad. There was a pool of potential candidates for trumped-up charges sitting all day in the lobbies of Baghdad's hotels: businessmen endlessly waiting for appointments. Scot tried telephoning Sadeq Ramadi as soon as he'd checked into his room. There was no reply at his Trade Department office, and the home number kept ringing on unanswered. That heightened Scot's paranoia.

Scot stubbed out his cigarette on the gravel, and looked across the river to where the women in black had resumed scrubbing their washing. It was a sight he wondered if he'd see once Turkey completed their dams upstream on the Tigris. From behind, a courteous voice broke into his daydream. 'Now I think your name is Mr Wallace.'

Scot swung around to see a well-built man of around forty years with a shock of dark hair groomed backwards, and a heavy, neatly trimmed moustache favoured by cadres of the ruling Baath Party.

'Yes, I'm Scot Wallace,' he said, in a tone of paranoid hope rather than courtesy.

The Iraqi took his hand, and shook it in a solid, friendly manner.

'I'm so glad you could find the time to come to Baghdad at such short notice. I'm Ahmad Kareem of the Interior Ministry. I thought it might be best if I came down and picked you up personally.'

'That's very kind of you.' Scot spoke with a sense of relief, guessing the 'demand' must have been due to the limited English vocabulary of the official who'd telephoned Limassol. Ahmad Kareem waited as Scot collected a brown briefcase from reception, and then led the way to a black Mercedes at the entrance of the hotel. The driver ignited the engine immediately he saw Kareem emerge from the hotel's revolving door.

'After you,' Kareem said as he ushered Scot into the back seat behind the driver.

'Well, it's always interesting coming to Baghdad.'

'Interesting! I appreciate your choice of words, Mr Wallace.'

Even after the few words they'd exchanged, Scot realised his new Iraqi acquaintance was smart and certainly no slouch languishing in an Interior Ministry career. He was as sharp as the creases ironed in the dark trousers of his suit. The chauffeured car, his confident manner, his deliberate courtesy indicated Kareem was extremely senior. And senior officials in the Interior Ministry were invariably highly trusted by the regime's ruling elite. This was a source of relief and concern. Relief that he was not some middle-level thug implementing orders and demands he didn't understand nor dare to question. But concern that while many businessmen craved relationships with bureaucrats close to seats of power, he was more comfortable with functional

friendships like the one he had with Sadeq Ramadi. Scot
always figured, the higher the profile, the greater the
danger, personal and financial.

After crossing the Tigris River, the black Mercedes
cruised along the palm-lined embankment before turning
sharply left into the compound of a six-storey concrete
office building of the type favoured by architects and
engineers during the era of Soviet influence. A couple of
guards carrying Kalashnikov sub-machine guns registered
recognition on their faces, and the vehicle manoeuvred
through a zigzag barricade and roared down a ramp into an
almost empty underground car park. Ahmad Kareem led
the way across the darkness to a small airless lift, and
pushed the button for level five. Not a word was spoken as
the lift clanked upwards, and the doors groaned open. 'I
shall lead the way, Mr Wallace,' Kareem said coldly, but
not discourteously.

The floor of the building felt empty. The room they
entered was in virtual darkness except for a glimmer of
light entering blue-painted glass windows crisscrossed
with white tape to reduce shattering if war returned.
Kareem fumbled for the light switch, indicating it wasn't
his usual office. An elaborate chandelier revealed a large
desk, empty except for a telephone, an ashtray, and an old-
fashioned electric bell button mounted on a small panel of
stained wood. The room must have been at the corner of
the building because as well as the blue-painted window
on the left, there was a roller shutter blacking out a second
window behind the desk. Kareem moved over and pulled
the shutter's strap. It lifted halfway up the window before
jamming.

'Well, that's better than nothing. It's nearly dark
anyway.'

As well as the desk and its chair, there were four large
club chairs, two on either wall. Heavy deep-red curtains

embroidered with gold bordered the two windows, and an elaborately carved cabinet beside the door completed the furnishings. A stern portrait of Saddam Hussein faced the blue windows from the right-hand wall.

Kareem gestured to one of the club chairs and Scot sat. The Iraqi stood behind the desk chair before offering 'tea or perhaps whisky?'

It seemed to Scot that in the empty building neither would be easily available, but he said half-heartedly: 'Perhaps, a whisky?'

The Iraqi bent over, opened a desk drawer, and produced a litre bottle of Johnny Walker Black Label. Then he gently pressed the electric bell before dryly contributing the comment, 'Aged in a Baghdad bunker!'

Despite the apparent emptiness of the building, a weathered man dressed in blue fatigues appeared at the door. Kareem spoke quietly in Arabic, and the man nodded and disappeared. The Iraqi had said little more than 'Well, let's get down to business' before the weathered man returned with ice and two glasses and then retreated. Kareem handed Scot a whisky before sitting.

'Well, once again, welcome to Baghdad. With the unfair sanctions against us, these are difficult times for my country, but we hope to see you here much more, *inshallah*.'

'God willing,' Scot echoed. 'Cheers.'

'I have seen your file, Mr Wallace, and you have done much good work for the people of Iraq. We appreciate that.'

Scot nodded quizzically, his eyes tightening suspiciously.

'And these days, we accept that people like you travel freely to the Zionist state.' Mr Kareem half-smiled before going on. 'Of course, there are still some people high up in our government who'd like to treat those foreigners who visit Israel as spies. But they are in a minority. Their views don't get taken – shall I say? – too seriously. Usually.'

Kareem's use of the word 'usually' hung in the air, and reverberated around Scot's head, releasing a stream of sweat from his brow. Heart pounding wildly, his mind delivered a kaleidoscope of alarmist messages. Iraqi gaols. Even gallows. And doubts that anyone would have an interest in trading anything for his freedom.

Mr Kareem seemed to be asking for confirmation that he visited Israel. He might know, but it seemed he wanted the fact spelled out in words. Scot took a deep breath, trying to regain composure and remembered an old salesman's trick that had served him well over the years. When faced with a difficult question, take a deep breath and count to three before uttering a word. Don't blurt. Conscious of Kareem's piercing eyes, he counted one, two, three, and then said: 'Another touch of whisky, please?'

Kareem exhaled, and his left cheek broke its tautness revealing just the hint of a smile. It was as if Ahmad Kareem recognised Scot's trick of defusing the situation. He then inhaled noisily, but not angrily, and said: 'A touch more whisky? Certainly, my friend.'

Having knocked around the Middle East for close to two decades, Scot knew not to take 'my friend' too literally. Like the word 'welcome', it couldn't be taken at face value. Enemies could be friends, and both could be welcomed, but not necessarily welcome. 'Thank you,' Scot said, accepting the whisky.

'It's one of my dreams to visit the Holy City of Jerusalem one day, but it seems you are reluctant to feed my fantasy with your personal impressions,' the Iraqi said. 'You are – shall I say – cunning, Mr Wallace. You remind me of captains of American nuclear warships; neither confirming nor denying what arms they have aboard.'

Kareem then seemed to relax a touch, and added: 'And that's the type of person we in Iraq like to deal with … people who have the confidence to keep things to themselves. Yes, we like to deal with people like you, Mr Wallace.'

Scot could feel a request – as yet unasked – hanging in the air. And it wasn't going to be a simple request, either.

'We like and trust you so much, Mr Wallace, that we'd appreciate you opening a small bank account on Cyprus for us. In your name, of course.'

For a split second, Scot was relieved the subject of Israel had been abandoned. Then the enormity of the request struck. Money laundering initially sprung to mind. Then, payments to Iraqi agents? Even worse, Iraqi terrorists? Scot was far from averse to money, but this was seriously dangerous.

'It would be a kind of petty cash account.' Then, without waiting for Scot's assent, the Iraqi drew a wad of bank notes out of the back pocket of his trousers and began counting them out on to the table beside him. 'Wahed, two, tres…' The multi-lingual count continued until 'Fifty'. 'Five thousand American dollars. As I said, a small bank account.'

Scot measured his words carefully. 'Wouldn't it be better to have an Iraqi national open the account for you?'

Mr Kareem looked at Scot as if observing someone somewhat retarded. As if Scot had missed the blindingly obvious. Which he hadn't. There had been many rumours of senior officials and army officers defecting with large amounts of government money. The regime couldn't trust its own people.

'No, we have to be discreet, and careful. It is not that we cannot trust our own citizens, but rather that we can't always trust outsiders either. Whereas Iraq's dealings with you lead us to believe, Mr Wallace, that we can – shall I say – sleep easily.'

The repeated quaintness of Kareem's language provided Scot with an opportunity to change the subject. 'You speak very good English.'

'I spent five years with an Iraqi company in London.' The words spoken, Kareem's eyes resumed fixing Scot with impatience.

'It's not that I wouldn't like to,' said Scot, 'but it's a big responsibility. I'm little more than a visitor in Cyprus. A resident yes, but a visitor. I could be refused entry even when I return, or allowed to return but then expelled a month later.'

'I don't think so, Mr Wallace. You're an Australian ... Welcome everywhere: Iraq, Iran, Cuba, *even* Israel. Such freedom!'

'Australia is an ally of America!' Scot had never bragged about that alliance before, but was immediately enthused. 'It's an ally of the great Satan.'

Undeterred, the Iraqi sneered.

Scot rolled his eyes towards the ceiling, weighing up whether to say yes or no. He then eyeballed Mr Kareem. The Iraqi must have sensed crunch time had come. He reached down to his sock and retrieved a 9mm. Beretta handgun and placed it on the pile of American dollars as if a paperweight was needed. As there was hardly a breath of air in the room, the charade could only be taken as a warning.

Scot decided it would be easier to say yes, and worry about the consequences after leaving Iraq. So he nodded and mouthed 'Okay'.

'Excellent, my friend,' said Kareem, unscrewing the top of the whisky bottle. Then, as if at last free to pick up on an earlier topic, he said: 'Yes, loved our years in London.' His eyes went almost misty as he described walking in Hyde Park, on Hampstead Heath, and visiting the Tower of London.

Scot chuckled inwardly as he speculated what an Iraqi Interior Ministry official might have learned at the Tower.

'Of course, there is nowhere quite like Baghdad,' said Mr Kareem.

'Certainly isn't!'

As they sipped their Scotches, Kareem gave instructions about the bank account. He handed over a business card, and pointed to an email address. Not an Iraqi email address, but an Italian one. 'Once you have established the account, email the details to me at this address. It will be forwarded to me.'

Scot nodded, wondering what he'd let himself in for.

'Well, I'll drop you back to the hotel'.

They drove back to the hotel by a different route, via Firdos, or Paradise Square – Baghdad's main square. As Scot looked out at the recently erected statue of Saddam Hussein, he wondered if Kareem's aim was to underline the egotistic and ruthless power of the regime. The sheer twelve-metre height and massive weight of the floodlit statue, and Saddam's depicted attitude, appeared a warning to Iraqis and visitors alike. Saddam Hussein and his regime were to be revered, respected, and feared. The leader's arm, reaching out from high above the square, was not so much a limb of protection, but one of infinite reach.

Heavy traffic slowed the black Mercedes. Scot watched the sidewalks crammed with shoppers mingling amongst fruit and vegetables, bags of rice and piles of bread. From a slowly revolving gas-fired *shawarma* or *guss* cooker, a man was slicing meat and selling it in wraps of Arabic bread. Suddenly, Kareem's conversation took a new and surprising tack.

'Mr Wallace, would it be too much trouble to find me a villa on Cyprus where I can escape the summer heat of Baghdad?'

It took a while for Scot's mind to change gears. Kareem remained silent during the long hesitation. 'Many apartments and villas are for rent on Cyprus. Tourism is the island's main business. You'd have no trouble finding what you want through any travel agent.'

'No, I want to buy a villa.'

'Yes, well that's easy. Many foreigners – particularly British – live permanently on Cyprus, and there are plenty of agents ready to take your money. There are developments all around the coast. Europeans love the sun.'

'Yes I know all that,' Kareem said. 'But I want something special. Something in the mountains maybe. Somewhere isolated where I can escape the bustle of Baghdad.'

'Not my line of business,' Scot said.

'It could be though. I think you'd know just the type of place I am looking for having lived so long on the island. Maybe three or four bedrooms, a swimming pool, and plenty of trees all around. Something tasteful, but not too ostentatious. I hate ostentation.'

Scot looked at Kareem first out of the side of his eye and then straight on. Had the Iraqi taken leave of his senses, was he dreaming, or securing a bolthole outside the country? Perhaps he believes the increasingly aggressive statements from Washington will become reality and the Iraqi regime will once again come under direct military attack. Already the US President was saying that 'Saddam Hussein and his outlaw regime' posed a grave threat and that disarmament was a must. That must be Kareem's motivation. He couldn't be thinking of holidaying at this time of increasing crisis? It'd hardly be appreciated if one of Saddam's Interior Ministry lieutenants declared, 'Well, boss, I'm off on holiday for a few weeks.' He'd be lucky to make it out of the country alive.

'Well?'

'It's not my line of business. And what I consider good taste and lack of ostentation may not be yours. You'd probably end up hating any place I found. Find an agent, or an Iraqi, for that job.'

'No, I want you … You'd be discreet, I'm sure.' He then hesitated. 'And I'll make it worth your while. After all, you do things for money, don't you?' It was not really a question. 'That's your life.'

The Mercedes pulled into the driveway of the hotel.

'Well, I'll look around,' Scot said, 'but that's all. Try other people as well.'

'Goodbye Mr Wallace, I'm looking forward to hearing once you've opened the bank account. And four bedrooms definitely, not three. And two at least should have en-suite facilities.'

As Scot collected his key at reception, the duty manager said: 'So, you're a VIP, Mr Wallace? We must look after you the very best we can.'

Scot responded not with words, but a puzzled look instead.

'Well, any friend of Mr Kareem is a VIP as far as we're concerned.'

This increased Scot Wallace's concern about his new relationship with the Interior Ministry, and the bank account request. Request? No, demand would be a more apt description. And why was Mr Kareem so clearly not using his usual office? Scot felt like skipping dinner and going to bed. The meeting had induced even more exhaustion. However, he'd been asked a favour. Upon learning about the trip to Baghdad, Alexander Belfort-Smith had insisted Scot deliver a gift. Now, Scot thought about 'forgetting' the request. He could say that phone number was never answered, or continually engaged.

Then curiosity won. Alexander had arrived at the Limassol apartment a couple of hours before Scot left for the airport. He'd brought a letter, and a book on French Impressionist artists. Alex seemed determined to get the letter and book to Baghdad, insisting that it was a dear friend who was dying of AIDS. Even then, Scot had felt he was being leant upon with base emotional blackmail. The feeling had returned – along with considerable tension – when Iraqi officials had scrutinised every page of the book at the Rutba customs post. It was as if they believed it might contain some subversive material, or perhaps coded messages. However, the worst was over now. Delivering the letter and book would be the easy part. So he telephoned, and an hour later found himself sitting in a courtyard, which had an artistic ambience probably unimaginable to most Iraqis.

The centrepiece of the courtyard was a hexagonal pond raised about a foot above the ground. The interior of the pond was tiled blue giving the water a shimmering appearance, which added an illusion of coolness to the warm evening. A reddish-orange vine clung to the house, which had been entered off an unimposing dusty street of shopfronts. The courtyard was an oasis of peace and tranquillity. Intricately carved capitals, long missing their supporting columns, were placed around the walls on the stone-paved floor. Like a curriculum vitae, they gave an instant indication of the owner's professional background.

'Yes, archaeology is my profession, but I became involved in tourism due to bureaucratic amalgamation.' Adnan Bashir was older than Scot had imagined – around fifty-five, at a guess – although Alexander hadn't given any details. Bashir was avuncular in appearance with a pot belly and balding head. 'I'm in antiquities and tourism. But tourism's been a bit lean recently.' He raised his eyebrows sharply as if to underline the understatement.

The Iraqi offered tea or coffee. Scot opted for the stimulation of coffee. Adnan Bashir walked to a wall opposite the entrance to the courtyard, and shouted in Arabic through a ventilator. As way of explanation, he said: 'One of the attractions of this house is that the people who have the shop right next to my entrance supply my tea and coffee.' He then gestured to Scot to sit.

'So how do you know Alexander Belfort-Smith?'

'I don't.' With tightened lips, the Iraqi added: 'He was a friend – an acquaintance – of my son, my late son. I'm Abu Adnan.'

A young man, a teenager, in a flowing white *dishdasha*, entered the courtyard, carrying a tray with a copper pot, and two small coffee cups.

'*Shukran.*' Bashir spoke profusely and enthusiastically to the young man, who nodded and smiled with neighbourly friendship.

Adnan Bashir looked back at Scot and resumed where he'd left off. 'Adnan died six weeks ago tomorrow.' A mist appeared to develop in the Iraqi's eyes, and he gazed towards the starry sky. 'Have you ever lost someone near and dear?'

Scot nodded, but didn't elaborate. He just didn't like talking to strangers about Lisa. No one else could really understand.

The Iraqi bowed his head momentarily, respectfully, as if his visitor was someone with the credentials to understand. 'So you know what it's like to wake up everyday and rediscover the world has changed.'

Scot nodded.

'Life goes on, they say, and it does. Move on, people say. But it's easier said than done.'

Scot found it odd to be talking about death and loss with an Iraqi he'd just met. And it was even stranger to be sitting in an elegant courtyard of a city suffering from years of international sanctions and now threatened by military attack. In a way it was easier to be away from familiar surroundings, where the insights of well-meaning friends were predictable and repetitive. 'I ran away from it,' said Scot, explaining his move to Cyprus. 'Or tried to...'

They both sat quietly, sipping coffee, under the canopy of the Middle Eastern heavens. They were bonded in silence.

Scot spoke first. 'Maybe you'd like the book anyway?'

The Iraqi looked at the book closely. 'My son often talked of his time in Paris. I'll keep it on his bookshelves as a memento of someone who loved life so much.' After a hesitation, he added something of a reflection: 'Maybe too much.' Adnan Bashir looked around the courtyard pensively before adding, 'The cause of death is not something I can talk about. Iraqis are in a state of denial'.

Scot indicated understanding, but said nothing. Instead his mind drifted to the newspaper stories he'd written about Alexander's dismissal from the army. He looked at the Iraqi and pondered whether to ask if he knew Mr Kareem of the Interior Ministry. But he thought better of it, assessing the question could arouse suspicions and require too many explanations – especially after the hotel manager's oblique comments. So instead he mentioned the name of his usual Iraqi business contact, Sadeq Ramadi.

'Of the Trade Department? Of course. He keeps behind the scenes, but we in the ministries know how important he is.'

Scot was pleased. It confirmed Sadeq was well respected. Also, he hoped, it gave himself a touch of credibility in a city where foreign shysters and opportunists were common. It seemed to open a door. 'Some time I must take you to a favourite archaeological site where I escape.'

Scot explained he was leaving Baghdad for Amman and Cyprus in the morning. 'Next time maybe'.

As they shook hands, Adnan Bashir asked how long Scot had known Alexander Belfort-Smith, and said, 'You must be close friends.'

Scot shrugged off the rhetorical question with a nod. A real answer would take time.

3

Dusk was descending over the port of Limassol as Scot's taxi approached the city along the motorway from Larnaca airport. The bustling streets looked welcoming after Baghdad, and Scot resolved to forget about Kareem's bank account for a couple of days.

In a state of weariness induced by travel, Scot daydreamed as the taxi manoeuvred through the evening peak-hour traffic. The taxi dodged motorbikes and scooters, and braked suddenly a couple of times to screech a signal to wayward pedestrians. Scot thought about his meeting with Adnan Bashir. With all the suffering faced by the Iraqi people, what sympathy would the Iraqi have received for a son dying of AIDS? Or was no one told? Scot guessed Bashir's son must have been gay, but only because of his association with Alex. How did Alex know Adnan's son? As the taxi turned along the esplanade towards his apartment, Scot planned to go to the Club Downtown for dinner, and get Alex to answer that question – and credit for delivering the book.

He thanked the driver, retrieved his bag from the taxi's boot, and headed for the lift. A light brown shoe prevented the elevator door from closing. It belonged to the building's manager, a title that was something of a misnomer as Nikos was very much part-time. At a guess he was in his mid-thirties, and judging by his dress and demeanour seemed somewhat confused about whether he was a tourist or a worker in the city. Nikos owed his position to the fact he was the landlord's cousin. 'Scot, is this yours?' He displayed a small leather-bound notebook – the size of a pocket diary.

'Thanks, where'd you find it?'

'Near the door of the building. Two days ago.'

'My door?'

'No. No. No,' he said pointing to the street entrance. 'It was on the footpath.'

'Must have dropped it. Thanks'

As the lift rose, Scot's heart began to race. No, he wouldn't have been carrying the notebook. It always remained in the drawer beside his computer. He opened the door to his apartment, and his worst fears were realised. Desk and filing cabinet drawers were open, and papers strewn across the floor. The computer was on, the ball on the screensaver bouncing around aimlessly.

Cupboards were open in the kitchen, but nothing appeared disturbed. Except, the whisky bottle. The level of spirits appeared to be lower than he remembered. But he couldn't be sure of that!

The bedrooms looked untouched.

Returning to the lounge cum office area of his two-bedroom flat overlooking the bay, Scot gathered papers off the floor. They were all from just one or two files from a top drawer of the filing cabinet. Perhaps, they'd been thrown across the floor for appearance, rather than frustration at not finding what had been sought?

Thoughts jumped to the little black notebook. Was that what the intruder had been looking for? Amongst contacts' telephone and fax numbers and email addresses, it contained amateurishly encrypted PIN numbers for credit cards, and – he remembered as an afterthought – his password for his internet banking accounts. He rushed to the computer to go online. Signing in to his bank accounts he was relieved to find they'd not been accessed since the last time he'd visited the site – a day before leaving for Baghdad.

He poured a large drink. Following the meeting with Kareem, the break-in was the last straw. Scot was exhausted; he felt his lips twinge and wondered whether the tragedy in his life had eroded coping mechanisms. Certainly, it had sharpened his daydreams and frequent nightmares. Scot closed his eyes. A car skidded on a wet freeway, and rolled over and over. It was imagination because all Scot had ever seen was a police photograph of the car, crushed beyond belief, resting on its side beside an overpass pylon.

Shaking himself from his daydream with a mouthful of whisky, Scot recalled Adnan Bashir's parting words in Baghdad regarding Alexander. *You must be close friends.* Scot fumbled through papers and newspaper cuttings in the bottom drawer of his desk. His back tightened with a tinge of guilt as he found the clipping he was seeking and laid it on the desk, flattening the old folds with the side of his clenched fist. He leant over the paper with eyes closed before daring to read his own work of a few years earlier. The front-page article screamed in bold black type: '**ARMY OUTS GAY MAJOR**'. Below the heading, the tabloid trumpeted: 'By Scot Wallace, our Special Correspondent in Nicosia'.

Even today, years later, it was the byline Scot was least proud of during his years as a journalist. In all honesty, he counted the story as one of the factors persuading him to leave journalism. Scot's own story was straightforward enough, he noted to himself as a way of alleviating his long-felt guilt. 'An Army rising star, Major Alexander Belfort-Smith, has been stripped of his commission and discharged from the Army after admitting being gay.' The initial source for the exclusive story had been an older officer on the same British Sovereign Base at Episkopi, just west of Limassol. Scot guessed the older officer, whose career had been languishing for some years due to occasional bouts of excessive drinking, acted out of jealousy of the up and rising major. Even this older soldier had admitted Belfort-Smith was an efficient officer well liked by his troops.

Scot slid open the glass door, and stepped into the moonlight on the balcony overlooking Limassol Bay. A few ageing, rusting ships were anchored off shore. A small white cruise liner, which ferried high-paying tourists between Cyprus, the Greek islands, and the Holy Land ports of Egypt and Israel, provided a pristine contrast to the older cargo ships dripping rust from every porthole, vent and opening. Scot loved his balcony perched five floors above the tree-lined esplanade. Slumping into a deckchair, Scot ran his fingers through his short black hair. His mind was taunted still by the story of Alexander's discharge. Soldiers have to expect to have their careers cut short, but not in such an unfair and devious way. Friendly fire never delivered hurt in such a ferocious way. For all Alexander had ever done was confide in a person he thought he could trust. It was a visiting chaplain who betrayed him. The irony of the whole tawdry episode was that the confession would never have been made if Alexander had not been such a loyal and conscientious officer. A boyfriend, and long-time lover, had been nearing death in London after a long battle with AIDS. Hearing the news that death was fast approaching, Alexander was desperate, still hoping his friend would live a couple more weeks so he could get leave. At that time a major British military exercise was about to get underway on Cyprus and Alexander couldn't with any conscience seek leave to visit London; he had to be with his men. Knowing him better now, Scot knew it would never have occurred to the then boyish-looking

Major Belfort-Smith to concoct the idea it was one of his parents facing death. He'd probably have got away with it, but it wasn't Alexander's style. So he went to see the chaplain for consolation and compassion. In the peace of the vestry, he told the truth, and admitted being gay. Within a week, Alexander was summoned to London for an interview with the army's special investigators. Over the next few weeks the process ground towards the inevitable discharge. An unshakeable boyhood dream ended.

After the newspaper article about the 'outing' was published, Scot was asked to dinner at the Episkopi home of his source, who hadn't been named in the article. Scot found it hard judging how much of what he heard that evening was documented truth, and how much gossip. But he remembered being surprised about the rigorous process leading to Alexander's discharge. Feeling he'd already done quite enough damage, he didn't pass on a word to his London newspaper. Sometimes messengers feel guilt, even if they don't deserve blame.

After topping up his whisky, Scot relived the evening at Episkopi. He'd arrived at the British garrison right on 8 p.m., but it took a few minutes to find the house. It was ten past the hour by the time he pressed the button by the door that set off a multi-toned chime. Lionel London answered with a profuse greeting, and led the way into the living area. The room was furnished with Cyprus cane chairs with cushions brightened by Liberty-style print covers. On shelves and the sideboard were knick-knacks obviously gathered from postings in Brunei, Gibraltar and Oman. Double doors were open on to a small terrace, where a table for three was set for dinner. A pleasant evening breeze blew in from sea. It was all rather stylish and comfortable and a world away from military brochures and promotional material depicting an infantry officer's life either daubed with mud camouflage or in full dress uniform at a regimental dinner. 'You've spent most of your career abroad,' noted Scot as they looked out towards the darkened sea.

'A couple of years in Northern Ireland. And in London for a time with the Ministry of Defence.'

From behind came a woman's voice. 'But Cyprus has been our favourite posting, hasn't it, Lionel?'

Scot turned to be welcomed by Lilly London, who was dressed rather smartly in white slacks and a deep green silk shirt. 'Haven't seen you for ages, Scot. We were always going to meet at a restaurant near your apartment in Limassol.'

'We still must,' said Scot, somewhat apologetically.

Lionel tugged at his blue cravat, and quizzically indicated towards a jug of Brandy Sour. 'Or gin, whisky or beer?' They all settled for the Brandy Sour. Lilly passed around some Cyprus olives and octopus on imported pumpernickel.

There was a largish photograph on the bookshelves of a handsome young woman. 'Your daughter?'

'Yes, Debbie … a few years ago now,' said Lilly, a tinge of worry creeping across her face.

Lionel attempted to explain his wife's concern. 'She did very well at the London School of Economics, but is now over in Iraq, working with the Kurds mainly, for an NGO.'

'I rather hoped she'd work in the City. She certainly achieved the qualifications. And she'd then have some real money to live on.'

Scot looked at the photograph more closely. She was certainly a beautiful woman. The photograph was black and white, but her hair looked blond or light brown. She looked healthy and suntanned. Maybe it had been taken in Cyprus. Scot offered an explanation for her choice of work. 'Well, I suppose growing up with parents living an exotic life, she's attracted to adventure.' Or was it flattery of the kind journalists lavish on contacts?

Lilly butted in firmly. 'It wasn't at all exotic in Northern Ireland!'

After some talk about the heat of the summer, and changes being made to some buildings on the base, Lionel got up from his seat and moved outside, lighting the candle on the dinner table. They settled down with a chilled bottle of Cyprus white wine, and Lilly's summer specialty, tomato and cucumber gazpacho. Despite the evening warmth, there was an unmistakable Englishness about the setting. Episkopi – along with the other sovereign bases – remained British sovereign real estate under the 1960 agreement giving Cyprus independence. Covering ninety-eight square miles, the bases enabled the UK to continue a military presence in the strategic East Mediterranean, close to the trouble spots of the Middle East. The pleasant breeze became a talking point before Lionel pointed across the road. 'Alexander used to live just across there ... not two hundred yards away.'

'Used to see him a lot. Dreadful thing,' said Lilly.

'It's a pity it got so much publicity,' said Lionel. 'Not blaming you, of course.' An outsider would be oblivious to the fact Lionel was the principal source of the publicity. Perhaps he'd broken some rule about leaking information to the press, and now, while sitting on British sovereign territory, didn't want to admit the fact even to himself. Did Lilly know of her husband's part? Probably not, Scot guessed, assessing Lilly as an army wife long practised in upholding loyalty, not only to her husband, but to the military as well. She'd be horrified perhaps about Lionel's role, especially as the story may not have seen the light of day without his efforts. Alexander would have remained mute, and the force commander would never have offered a comment.

'Alex took our Debbie to a regimental dinner once. She was out on holiday at the time, and I think quite liked him,' Lilly said. 'And to think I was worried it would lead to her being married to the army as well.'

'Lilly has enjoyed the life, really.' Lionel spoke as if well used to assuring people his wife was loyal to the service.

'Yes, but a new house to decorate every couple of years. It's not normal Lionel!' She wasn't arguing, but just making the point he'd a lot for which to be grateful.

'Quite.' There was a brief moment of silence and reflection. 'But not long to go now.'

'You're retiring?'

'In a few months,' Lionel said. 'It will certainly be a change, but we're looking forward to returning to England. I hope to do some consulting.' Then – perhaps deflecting attention away from his somewhat uncertain future without brass bands – Lionel returned to the subject of Alexander. 'He was well liked by his troops.'

'And that's all that counts,' Lilly said determinedly, apparently disapproving of the ban. At least, in this case, involving someone she clearly liked. 'He did well in all his postings …'

'Including BDILS,' Lionel added.

'BDILS?' asked Scot.

'British Defence Intelligence Liaison Service North America.'

Scot was surprised. 'So he worked with American intelligence?'

'In a liaison capacity, yes, and the procedure for clearance and scrutiny for those jobs is rather rigorous.'

Scot speculated aloud. 'So the Americans and British intelligence didn't know about his homosexuality?'

'Or didn't care.' Lilly spoke acerbically.

A cacophony of multi-toned car horns wakened Scot from the semi-dream of his dinner at Episkopi years before. Deciding there was little he could do about the break-in until the morning, he closed the drawers, and closed down the computer. He'd fill in Alex on his trip to Baghdad – and about the death of Adnan Bashir's son.

Dimitri was at the door of Club Downtown. He led Scot to his regular table beside the stone arch dividing the restaurant. It was later than Scot had thought, and the music was getting under way. Ordering a beer, he asked with raised eyebrows, 'Alexander?'

'He's away for a few days,' Dimitri said.

'I'd hoped to see him. I have some news from Baghdad.'

Dimitri shrugged, with a kind of 'what can I do?' sort of look. It was clear he wasn't going to elaborate on Alexander's whereabouts.

Scot had a light dinner before heading back home. He decided that after speaking to his bank and insurance company in the morning, he'd drive to the mountains for a couple of nights of cool alpine air. He had friends to visit in the village of Kakopetria, and they'd have some ideas about finding a villa for Ahmad Kareem.

4

Scot parked at the top of the old mountain village of Kakopetria – a hamlet of stone and mud-brick houses built between the island's only two permanently flowing streams. Gradually the old houses were being restored as Cypriots and a few foreigners became aware of the historic value of the enclave, which just twenty years before was being abandoned in favour of newer houses the other side of the streams. As so often on summer days, the surrounding pine-covered mountains were tinged with blue drawn from the brilliant clear sky. The main cobbled street – just wide enough for one vehicle – ran down the spine of the steep hill formed by the fast flowing rivers. From either side, narrow lanes – just wide enough for donkeys and villagers – led off and wound around the old houses. Passing under a balcony built across the street, then past the home of a bishop, Scot ignored women selling their home-made jams and preserves and pottery as he walked down the cobbles towards the Linos Inn. Once a hotbed of conspiracy in the fight for independence from the British, the old village – at 2,500 feet above sea level – was now a summer retreat for people escaping the heat of Nicosia and Limassol.

Turning into the courtyard of the inn, Scot instantly noticed Alexander Belfort-Smith sitting at a table with two men. Sipping coffee, they were talking earnestly, punctuating their discussion with hand gestures. So intent was the chatter that Scot decided to check in before interrupting. Fleetingly though, he wondered why Dimitri had been so coy about Alex's whereabouts.

He was shown to a large room overlooking the cobbled street leading down the village. Like most of the other rooms in the inn, it was furnished with either replica or genuine antique furniture. He could never quite decide. The phone though was easier to pick. It was 'replica ancient', and made in Italy, according to the label underneath. He telephoned his friends, who owned The Mill Hotel and Restaurant, to tell them he was in the village, and would be coming to lunch, then returned to the courtyard for coffee.

Alex and his friends were still in deep discussion, so Scot took a table on the opposite wall. It was a spot Alex couldn't fail to notice – sooner or later – when one of the party finally drew for breath. It was sooner rather than later, but much less effusive than Scot had expected. Alex merely raised a hand of recognition and mouthed an unspoken word and resumed talking to his mates. It was hardly the recognition Scot had expected after he'd carried the book to Baghdad.

He wandered down the cobbles to The Mill. As he turned off the main street, and headed down the stone steps to the stream, Scot looked across the deep and narrow valley to the monastery-like building clinging to the opposite hill. Built to blend in with the historic nature of the old village, it often baffled tourists who thought it must have been an historic monastery. Scot knew better. He'd seen it grow out of the narrow slice of land and up the hill in the 1980s. He crossed the restored stone bridge and sat at a table under a shady tree beside the original historic mill before taking the lift to the restaurant.

Sitting on the restaurant veranda – high above the lush greenery and rushing stream – Scot couldn't help hearing the increasingly raised voices at the next table. Suddenly, a few drops of water dampened his cheek, and he looked up to see a dark-haired man stand up abruptly, mop his face with a large handkerchief, and storm off towards the lift.

He left behind a woman of around thirty, with blond hair and a bright green T-shirt. As she refilled her glass from the earthenware water jug, her hand trembled slightly. Her eyes caught Scot's, and she spoke softly, with a European – perhaps Russian – accent. 'I'm so sorry, sir'.

'Don't worry, I was a bit hot anyway,' Scot said, smiling sympathetically. 'Not sir, please, my name's Scot.'

A waiter rushed to the woman offering sympathy, and carefully replaced the wet tablecloth. A tear slipped down the woman's cheek. Scot tried to hide his inner amusement. This beautiful, tearfully vulnerable woman having just drenched her companion with a glass of water drew sympathy, whereas her partner, who had been the victim of the attack, was demonised. His side of the story was not worth considering!

Tyres screeched from the car park below as the cad sped off.

Scot felt like building on the brief encounter with the woman. But a Cypriot man, who'd apparently been dining alone, stifled that idea by sympathetically talking with her before offering to share his wine.

After a lunch of grilled trout, Scot wandered to the village square in the hope of seeing an old friend, whose job as a taxi driver meant he knew all the gossip in the village. He might just know if there were any villa developments under way in the area.

'Course. There are many villa developments all across the island, but not so many in this area.' The taxi driver was sitting sipping a small cup of Cypriot coffee and reading a local newspaper. The table was shaded by the square's canopy of plane trees. 'Most of the developments around here are for private clients from Nicosia. They like to escape to the cool weather for weekends. Four bedrooms, two with bathrooms, that is a big house.' He put his paper down and offered Scot a coffee. 'Maybe though, I know something. I was driving someone to Larnaca airport two days ago, and they couldn't stop talking about this villa just built on a road to Ayios Nicolaos Monastery. Maybe it's true, but maybe not, but the passenger said the owner had run out of money and building stopped. The owner had trouble with his business, and his wife left him. Maybe he's looking for a buyer.'

The taxi driver lifted his mobile phone off the table and dialled. The talk went on for a couple of minutes, and the phone was put back on the table. 'A friend thinks it may be for sale, but it doesn't have a swimming pool. There could be space for one though. There is a lot of land around the house and plenty of trees. Where is your friend from? Who wants this house?'

'He lives in Baghdad,' Scot said.

'No wonder he wants to move to Cyprus. My friend thinks the owner has an agent in Limassol who is trying to sell the property. But he probably wants a lot of money. Too greedy those Limassol agents are.'

'Well, I could talk to him in Limassol.'

The taxi driver scribbled the agent's name and phone number on a scrap of paper. 'But I could take you to see the building. Now if you like.'

They headed off in the driver's silver Mercedes. Winding around the old village, the taxi then took a narrow road through an avenue of fig trees and under a long pergola from which grapes were drooping from lush vines. They arrived at an isolated villa of ochre-coloured rendered concrete walls and a terracotta-tiled roof. It had large windows overlooking a large paved terrace that looked directly down the fertile Solea Valley towards the distant sea. The villa was built on an old orchard watered by a narrow concrete channel flowing through the property. Many fruit trees remained around the house, and the property was surrounded by pine trees. Although only five or ten minutes drive from Kakopetria, it had a feeling of isolation. Swinging his pointed finger in an arc around the property, the taxi driver said: 'Freedom fighters against the British used to hide in these mountains.'

The house was locked, but they wandered around the garden. All rooms looked out on to the old fruit trees. 'Well, it might be okay,' Scot said.

'Don't be too keen if you talk to the agent,' the taxi driver advised. 'Tell him there are many problems with the building. That's the way we do business on Cyprus. And tell him a swimming pool would have to be built.' The taxi driver hesitated, shaking his head slowly. 'It's sad for the owner. His house is finished, but he can't move in. He has to sell. It's a tragedy.'

They drove back to the square in Kakopetria, and Scot – after thanking the taxi driver – made his way up the steep cobbled street to the Linos Inn.

It was not until the evening that Alexander appeared again. As Scot sat reading the *Cyprus Weekly* in the courtyard, Alex approached, his two friends in tow.

'Surprised to see you,' said Alex.

He then introduced Brad Birmington and Rick Jordan. Shaking Scot's hand firmly, they uttered 'hello' with American accents. They then moved to another table. Alex hadn't enquired about Scot's trip to Baghdad, nor asked whether the present had been delivered. Feeling jilted, Scot settled back into the newspaper. It may have been the article about the arrest of three men and a woman having sex on a beach near Limassol that sparked a thought. Was Alex having a wild weekend away from the Club Downtown, a *ménage à trois* with his two American friends? That may explain Dimitri's abrupt demeanour.

The next morning, just as Scot was finishing breakfast, one of Alex's two companions – the one named Rick – came over to his table, and began with some polite small talk.

'Good morning. Sleep well?'

'It's one of the reasons I come up to the village, actually. Very well … And you?'

'Yeah. The altitude of the place sure makes a difference. After Athens, it's great to sleep without needing aircon.'

'How long are you staying?'

'Fly out of Larnaca tomorrow, unfortunately. And you?'

'Back to Limassol tomorrow morning.'

'Alex says you're in business down there.'

Although reluctant to be too nosy, Scot was about to ask what Rick did in Athens. He didn't get an opportunity, though, as Rick looked up distracted. 'Well, my friends have finally arrived.' And with a tap on Scot's shoulder added 'Good to talk'. He was gone as suddenly as he'd arrived, joining Alexander and Brad at a table almost as far from Scot as possible in the confines of the courtyard. Judging by the intensity of their discussion, Alex and his two companions were clearly on business. They didn't have the relaxed demeanour of tourists nor the hardworking attitude of visitors determined to seek out every antiquities site. They both wore pale colour cotton slacks. Rick was somewhat overweight – a physique exacerbated by his blue T-shirt – and Brad sported a short-sleeved check shirt with two breast pockets, which were overloaded with pens, a notebook, and what could have been a wallet.

Later, as Scot was having a late afternoon drink in the shade of the trees by the old mill beside the stream, Rick ambled across the stone bridge. 'Can I join you? That beer sure looks great.' He sat without waiting for a reply, drew the waiter's attention and ordered a beer. He drew a business card from the pocket of his blue-check shirt.

Scot read the card. 'Richard X. Jordan, Associate Cultural Attaché, Embassy of the United States of America, Athens.'

The title was enough to convince Scot the idea fermenting in his mind was correct. Almost certainly, Rick and Brad were contacts from Alex's days attached to American intelligence. The only thing against this rushed theory was Rick's title. It was a cliché to think the CIA would give him the cover of 'Cultural Attaché'. Also, why meet in Kakopetria? And, in view of Alex's sacking, would he be interested in moonlighting either for Britain or America?

'What's the X stand for?'

'Most people ask that, or guess Xavier. Believe it or not, though, the answer is Xanadu. My parents – although you wouldn't know it today – were flower people and poets in the early sixties, and – so I'm told – conceived me around the time they came across Coleridge's poem *Kubla Khan*. Xanadu was the name Coleridge had given Shang-tu – summer capital of the Mongol emperors of China.'

Scot was beginning to wish he hadn't asked, and was learning more than he needed to know. 'It's a good story, anyway.'

'Sure is ... And it seems to have given me a wanderlust.' He exploded with something between a cough and a laugh. 'And I gather from Alex you're not someone who likes to be tied down in one particular place. Travel a lot.'

'For business, yes.'

'Import export?'

Scot nodded, but got the distinct feeling Rick had been fully briefed on his business and perhaps about his recent trip to Baghdad too. So he put Rick out of his misery. 'Just been to Baghdad'.

'Really?' Rick expressed the amount of surprise one would expect if he'd been told that his mother was a woman. 'Must be fascinating. One of the advantages of having an Australian passport ... go anywhere.'

Scot fumbled for a cigarette, feeling a bit apprehensive about what might come next. The 'go anywhere' had triggered memories of Ahmad Kareem, and the kind of request – or demand – made by the Iraqi was something he didn't want repeated.

'How freely can you travel in Iraq? Do you ever go north?'

'I only see the people I need to see.' That was a bit of a lie as he hadn't wanted to see Kareem at all.

'Suppose your contacts are mainly in the Trade Department,' the American commented.

'Mainly.' And then, a touch impishly, he added: 'Not in the Cultural Ministry, anyway.'

Rick smiled reluctantly. 'The three of us are eating at The Mill tonight ...' Rick said, pointing up to the restaurant's balcony. 'Like to join us?'

Scot couldn't think of an instant excuse that would stand up in a small village, so accepted.

'We're meeting around eight.'

5

Driving through the pine forest clinging to Cyprus's Mount Olympus, Scot joined the Nicosia to Troodos mountain highway just above Kakopetria. In the summer heat, the signs warning of icy conditions could be ignored. At a saddle of the range, he avoided the turn to the right, which led to the mountain's top, and headed down to Limassol. Thoughts kept flashing back to the previous evening and dinner with Alexander and the two Americans. He particularly recalled Rick's parting comments: 'Must keep in touch' and 'Look forward to hearing more about your travels'. Innocent enough. Even complimentary! But Scot, already snared by Ahmad Kareem, was wary of being embroiled in new machinations. Bugger it though, they hadn't asked anything of him, nor enquired too deeply into his business. They'd just asked superficial questions about his business and travels. The type of queries anyone would ask if trying to be polite – and impress. Perhaps that was the problem. Perhaps they'd tried – and succeeded – being a little too courteous!

Why had he got so little in return? He'd learnt about Xanadu, but was no wiser about their roles in life, nor about why the threesome had gathered in Kakopetria for three days. It did seem, though, that Alexander appeared uncomfortable that Scot – an outsider – had been invited to dinner. Alex had been decidedly aloof. Perhaps he was fearful something would slip out about his friend stricken by AIDS in Baghdad. Even that he had a friend in Baghdad! Whatever the reason, it had been enough to inhibit Scot from mentioning Adnan's death, or the meeting with his charming father.

When Scot arrived back at his esplanade apartment, Nikos was making one of his rare shows of being on duty near the entrance. 'Nice time in Kakopetria?' Scot just nodded with a smile, and headed for the lift. Over the past couple of days, he'd considered ignoring Kareem's request for a bank account. Cyprus was far enough away from Iraq for that to be an option. Maybe the Iraqi would forget too. The Interior Ministry would have enough on its plate to forget about one small operator named Scot Wallace.

Wishful thinking! The fax machine – in his absence – had stymied that option. Scot removed the paper from the tray and read the message from Baghdad. It was from his Trade Department contact, Sadeq Ramadi, and written in his old-style cablese with its spelled out punctuation. Sadeq Ramadi was far from IT rich. In fact he'd never moved beyond the days of cable. It was part of his charm that his words never even reflected the telex leap forward, let alone fax machines and email.

However, the message remained clear enough: HOPE ALL WELL STOP KAREEM SENDS REGARDS STOP HE HOPES YOU CAN CONTINUE BUSINESS LINKS REGARDS RAMADI.

Scot laughed. The abruptness of cablese accentuated the threat rather than diminished it. Open the bloody bank account and email the details or you'll do no more trading with Iraq, it could have said. But it would have lacked panache and verged on the threatening. The cablese, on the other hand, was succinct, polite, and to the point.

Scot's other accounts were held at the Bank of Cyprus, but he decided to open this new account at the Aphrodite Bank just around the corner. Despite the bureaucracy involved in opening an account at a new bank, he thought it wise to keep this account completely separate from his own. The bank's staff was very polite, but miffed he didn't want a credit card attached to the account. They were pleased, however, that he was accustomed to internet banking and arranged all the details and temporary password on the spot. The branch manager insisted Scot share coffee in his office, and waxed lyrical about the advantages of Cyprus – and Limassol in particular – as a centre for doing business in the Middle East. He was surprised Scot was opening the account with just $5,000 American dollars, which led to the admission that he did have other accounts at another Cyprus bank.

'Well, I'm sure you'll decide to bring all the business to Aphrodite in due course,' the manager said as he bade farewell to Scot.

That task over, Scot headed back to his flat and emailed the details of the new account to Mr Kareem's Italian address. He couldn't resist adding a message in capital letters, and hoped Mr Kareem understood that it was said by some to be bad email etiquette to use upper-case letters – the equivalent of shouting. 'LOOK FORWARD TO FURTHER BUSINESS STOP.'

While online, Scot checked his bank accounts. Surprise, then alarm, struck as his password let him into the home page summarising his main account and Visa card. The top right-hand corner stated the accounts had been accessed just two days earlier. But he'd been in Kakopetria and certainly hadn't looked at his accounts. He clicked on the main account opening the details. There were no unusual transactions. Then he repeated the procedure with his Visa account. Again, nothing had changed. No money had gone in or out of either account, but the online statements said they'd been accessed. Scot thought about his little black notebook. The amateurishly encrypted password had been cracked. He altered the passwords online.

Scot rested his head in his hands, elbows on the desk. The meeting with Kareem had sparked paranoia. Nothing seemed straightforward anymore. Business with Iraq now depended upon the Iraqi Interior Ministry, and Alexander was more than met the eye.

He felt so alone. It was at times like these that he'd like to share with someone the strange happenings that – one by one – appeared to be encroaching upon his life. But there was nobody. No one to say something like 'Don't worry … these things happen'. No matter how unhelpful such advice would be, it would be better than letting incidents ferment in the mind. He laughed at his loneliness. Well, he could hardly share the situation with Nikos. He wouldn't understand. And Alexander Belfort-Smith? He didn't appear in a sharing mood! *How had he come to be so vulnerable?* With no one to turn to, he noticed dusk was starting to fall. So he grabbed a beer and a packet of Royals and headed to the balcony. The evening traffic. The pedestrians on the esplanade below. The ships languishing. And the smaller boats coming back to shore. That would revive his spirits. It always did.

Scot clutched his balcony rail with both hands and looked out over the hazy sea. He could hear singing coming from the water, and saw a brightly lit tour boat returning to the harbour. On the horizon, there was a large yacht, its white sails catching the evening breeze, making its way back to port. Nearer to shore, three or four rusting cargo ships were languishing on the lazy summer sea. They were badly lit, almost a hazard. In contrast, there was the white-painted cruise liner, using all its lights to persuade shore-bound tourists of the romance of cruising the Mediterranean. Straight down below Scot's balcony was a mixture of locals and tourists relaxing at café and restaurant tables after another hot day. On the road, traffic was heavy as the business day came to an end.

Scot fantasized the balcony gave him a view of his world, or workplace – the Middle East. All he could see was languid water stretching out to the horizon. But he knew what lay beyond: his game board. Not the religious sites and antiquities which fascinated most foreigners, but rather the ports and border crossings of the Levant, and the customs officials of each country. These officials were as important to Scot as government ministers. More important, in fact. It wouldn't be any use having good government and business contacts if the customs officials weren't onside. It would be like a cigarette without a light.

Perhaps to convince himself he was totally in control of his game board, Scot braced himself against the tubular balcony rail as if on the bridge of a ship in heavy seas. Remnants of perspiration glued his palms to the rail, as his nicotine-stained fingers clutched for security. A couple of inches short of six feet, Scot wasn't overly tall by the standards of his homeland – Australia. But the balcony rail always seemed low, particularly when watching his mellowed guests swaying after accepting too much hospitality. Although fit and just a touch overweight, Scot envied the youthful, lithe fitness of the last of the day's windsurfers as they packed up their kit before heading home. Envy and bouts of loneliness were elements of Scot's life since he'd settled back in Cyprus after nearly a year in Australia – a visit ending in tragedy. Therefore, he put all the effort he could muster into his import-export work.

Scot knew he couldn't compete with the big players in the game, so constantly looked for niche markets and trades. More often than not, they provided a good return for a one-man operation, but not enough for a big corporation carrying exorbitant overheads. And they were too shadowy for government agencies facing the scrutiny of parliaments. Since setting up business, he'd been pleased by how much scope that left for him. Maybe it shouldn't have surprised, because the small ports of the area provided opportunities for shady business. And international sanctions begged to be broken. He often reassured himself that he didn't trade in arms or drugs. Pharmaceuticals yes, but illicit drugs – heroin, marijuana and opium – were never even considered. He sometimes thought it wouldn't be too difficult, but had never been tempted, a consequence of his conservative middle-class upbringing. Anyway, his business provided a good enough return without becoming outright immoral. His life was a game as much as a business, but a very important game indeed. He needed the money. Circumventing inter-national laws and embargoes concerned him occasionally, but mainly in case a transaction went wrong. People would get these things whether or not he helped! Some of the sanctions were more immoral than his trades, so guilt never really came into his calculations. The upside of loneliness was he didn't have to share secrets.

Scot had time to analyse the background to his newly found ethics and often did. He'd been left alone, and his life's plan shattered, so damn the small illegalities and shadiness. Most rules had been made by people enjoying balanced and comfortable lives. Despite this, they designed regulations and embargoes that harmed ordinary people more than the targets of their schemes. Perhaps, that was because of their balanced and comfortable lives? Maybe they were stricken with boredom, and stretched out to some exotic sphere of influence just for the sake of adventure. Or perhaps they were addicted to power, which they found not to be in sufficient supply in their own home cities.

Anyway, every regulation and embargo had its victims – and beneficiaries. The beneficiaries included the many senior officials in the countries of the Middle East, who seemed to be immune to regulation; certainly, averse to it. No one ever suggested Saddam Hussein's lifestyle suffered because of the long embargoes against his Iraq. So why shouldn't Scot Wallace join in a game that was already in play? The thing about this game was the more you played – even on a small scale – the more you were accepted. He was often invited to diplomatic parties in Nicosia, or businessmen's extravagant social displays of wealth, exactly because of his business. A tipsy high commissioner from one Commonwealth country had introduced him to a group of friends at a party as 'my business friend who sails close to the wind'. Far from taking it as a slur, Scot thought it gave a stamp of legitimacy.

He looked at his watch. It was approaching 7 p.m. Leaving the sliding door open to draw in the evening sea breeze, he went to the small kitchen to collect a beer and some cheese biscuits before returning to his cane lounge chair near the balcony. Reaching across the glass-topped table beside the chair, he retrieved the remote control and thumbed the 'on' button, just in time for the TV across the room to announce the hour in Greenwich Mean Time. He was addicted to the BBC World Television, and CNN, partly because he was alone so much in the evenings, and partly because of his media background. It was good for business too. A lateral thinker when it came to trade, he often gleaned the germ of an idea from some story emanating out of the region. Perhaps it was a fanciful thought, but he wondered whether his knowledge of current affairs gave him an edge over others, who were tied up with families and social commitments. Tonight's headlines covered a summit in London, fighting in East Africa, a bomb outrage in Jerusalem, and a major earthquake. Horrifying as they were, natural disasters rarely interested Scot. There seemed so little you could do

in the face of such catastrophes. Aid agencies and
governments did as much as they could – which often
wasn't very much or efficient – and there was little left
over for the independent entrepreneur. He preferred
situations and deals, which could be resolved and sealed
through eyeballing the players. Well, not exactly true. He
often recalled how he'd developed his business contacts in
Tel Aviv. It was the result of an act of God. In the wake of
a big earthquake in Iran, he'd transported surplus Israeli
army tents to Tehran for distribution by the Iranian Red
Crescent. He never visited the earthquake area, but had
seen the images of misery on television. So, for
humanitarian reasons, he'd only covered his own costs and
taken no profit. But the deal had its rewards. It led to
meeting with a senior Israeli army officer, who had a
cousin whose wife's family had an import/export trading
business. Scot floated an idea at the family's home on the
beachfront north of Tel Aviv that Iran might prove to be a
good export market. They were far from strict orthodox
Jews, but they almost choked on their beers in laughter as
if watching a Woody Allen film. The youthful head of the
family company said he liked the idea, adding something
about not having any objections to dealing with the
mullahs of Tehran, but thought it 'impossible'. It was the
kind of challenge Scot liked. So after returning to
Limassol to do the groundwork and look into the
feasibility of the scheme, he returned to Tel Aviv with
some good news for his new friends. They were sceptical,
but persuaded after Scot said he'd take half the financial
risk on the first two shipments. God knows what he would
have done if the whole exercise had gone wrong. He'd
have been bankrupted. But it hadn't. Even today, it was
one of the best continuing money earners he had. Once a
week a container loaded with produce, including eggs and
frozen chickens – packed without any indication of their

origin – was flown from Tel Aviv to Amsterdam's Schiphol airport. There, the container was transferred to an aircraft bound for Tehran. It had taken surprisingly little effort to ensure the Certificates of Origin were changed in Europe, and that the Air Waybills and other documents carried to Tehran showed no hint the cargo had begun its journey in Israel. Scot always suspected Iranian officials knew the origin of the produce. After all, the Israeli plane and the Iranian airliner, which flew the second leg of the journey, often parked side by side in Amsterdam. But it would be discourteous to allow some slip-up in documentation to flout the source of the cargo.

Suddenly there was a long screech of car tyres from the street below. Scot screwed his eyes tight. The screech seemed to go on endlessly before a heavy crashing thump. In his mind, a car skidded on a wet road and rolled over and over before ending up on its side against a pylon. After recovering his senses, he rushed to the balcony and looked down. A woman was lying on the footpath. People were rushing towards her. A male driver standing beside a dented car was leaning, collapsed against the car's roof, and holding his head in despair. Scot's mind strayed back to Australia.

The cold came suddenly to Melbourne, and there was even snow on Mount Dandenong to the east of the city. It was the first winter Scot and Lisa had spent together in Scot's home city. It was his birthplace anyway, if not really his home. He'd spent much of the past eighteen years overseas, so didn't really know whether to call Melbourne and Australia home just yet. It was going to be their home. Things had moved quickly since they'd met, left Cyprus, and settled in Melbourne. They hadn't had a chance to decide upon buying a house. So for the time being at least, they were renting a flat in Parkville, just north of the city's CBD. Surrounded by Victorian-era terrace houses with balconies decorated with cast-iron latticework, the flat was spacious with two bedrooms, a large lounge and dining area, and a separate study or office, which they both shared. There was central heating and a big fireplace in the lounge area. They were still gathering furniture, but they'd stamped their own style on the place with their knick-knacks gathered – together and separately – in the Middle East and beyond.

Their arrival home caused something of a flurry at the city's Tullamarine airport, as their romance had been quick and their marriage sudden. So Scot hadn't got around to sending his family any photographs of the ceremony at St John's in Nicosia. And he'd neglected to tell friends and family that Lisa was black. It was something Lisa had thought might be important. 'I'm English, yes, born and brought up in Leeds, but they'll assume I'm white,' she'd told him repeatedly in her northern English. But he'd forgotten, mainly because he didn't see her as black or white, but just as 'Lisa' his friend, lover, and now wife. When getting a visa from the Australian High Commission in Nicosia, she'd looked closely at the country's promotional posters and remarked 'Everyone's white! Thought you said the White Australia Policy was a thing of the past.' Scot pointed to a man playing a didgeridoo, but it failed to convince Lisa. 'I rather think you ought to tell them.' And maybe he should have. Because at the airport, his small family welcoming group looked somewhat surprised. Not judgemental, just surprised. In fact, Scot had become a bit sensitive as they cleared customs and went out into the arrival hall. He'd held Lisa's arm, despite the fact it was difficult to steer the luggage trolley, just to make sure his family knew that the woman was Lisa.

Lisa was surprised at the mixture of races of people living in Melbourne. There were a lot of Asians around Parkville – many of them studying at Melbourne University, where Scot had studied economics before going into journalism. They often ate at the Vietnamese restaurants in Victoria Street, or Chinese in the city. And Lisa came home from her first visit to the supermarket in nearby Carlton, and remarked: 'There are more Moslem women in scarves in that shop than in the whole of Arabia!' A bit of an exaggeration, he thought.

'They're just more noticeable,' Scot offered.

As well as leaving Cyprus, they'd both decided to make a clean break with the past. So Scot decided to give up newspapers. Instead, he tutored at the university, part-time, worked on the idea for a book, and then joined a meat exporting company that appreciated his Middle East experience. Lisa got a good job with a stockbroker in the city.

They bought a Ford Festiva, which was big enough for just the two of them, and travelled a lot to the country and the beaches south of Mornington on Port Phillip Bay.

'And I thought the beaches were good on Cyprus. But this is something else – so much sand. Imagine what the Germans would think!'

Although they were busy and didn't miss Cyprus, they often talked about it, recalled places and events. The German tourists were remembered often because they were up early each day to reserve their beach beds beside the sea. They were determined not to miss a minute of sun, and turned a lobster red during their two weeks on the island.

It wasn't just their shared experiences, and their easy talk that was so attractive to Scot. Lisa was tall, about his height. With her high cheekbones, soft skin and silky hair, she was extremely sensuous. Scot could tell other men thought that also. He wasn't jealous, but proud. 'You don't need a suntan,' Scot said as he unbuttoned Lisa's blue silk shirt and unhooked her bra. They kissed ravishingly, and fell on to the bed in a controlled sort of way. The rhythm slowly became faster, and the breathing louder. And they both sighed noisily with relief, ignoring the phone as they lay, satisfied. She fondled his hair. 'Home. It's funny to feel at home so far from home.'

Life went on happily, Lisa finding her work more stimulating than Scot expected. Realising her expertise, her company sought her advice on developments in the Middle East, which might affect the markets – particularly the oil market. In fact, her work became more satisfying than his, so he took up an idea of an old friend. He took some work as a consultant for a group of global risk managers. He was not all that confident about the advice he gave, but they liked it. And that was what mattered. It introduced him to a wider group of people, including some import-export traders. Things were going swimmingly.

A verbal bombshell can be welcome, even if it's a surprise. Such was the case one late winter weekend when they'd been in Melbourne about three months. 'I'm having a baby,' she told him. They hugged gently.

Scot extended the lease for another twelve months to ensure they wouldn't have the upheaval of moving in the first few months after the baby was born. The second bedroom was painted ready for the baby. 'I didn't think you could be so useful,' Lisa jibed.

One Saturday, Scot was invited by some old journalist mates to a football game at the Docklands Stadium. He hadn't been to the new Melbourne stadium. But despite his interest in seeing the new ground, he was reluctant to go. Lisa persuaded him, as she wanted to see an old friend from London, who lived in the foothills of the Dandenong ranges. 'She's very lonely since John abandoned her. The cad's run off with someone in his office.' So they agreed to go their separate ways. 'Anyway you'll enjoy the football. And I couldn't stand it.'

The flat was really chilly when Scot arrived home just after dusk. It had started raining about four o'clock. He felt a bit mellow after lunch at the ground, a few drinks at half time, and a couple more after the game. Not drunk, but mellow. He turned on the heating and grabbed some logs from the pile outside, and lit the fire. Then he put in the oven some pre-prepared fresh lasagne they'd bought at Donnini's in Carlton's Lygon Street that morning.

The telephone rang.

'Scot Wallace.'

'Constable Hegarty here, Mr Wallace. Carlton police.'

'Yes?' His heart pounded.

'First, you are Mr Scot Wallace, husband of Lisa Wallace?'

'Yes ...'

'I'm sorry Mr Wallace, but I have some news, not good.'

Scot remained silent, listening.

'Your wife's been involved in a serious accident on the Eastern Freeway. She's been rushed to the Royal Melbourne Hospital.'

'She all right?'

'She's in a serious condition. I'm sorry.'

Scot thanked the constable, who sounded very young but efficient and put down the phone, dazed. He put the screen in front of the fire, grabbed his coat, and dashed out the door. The hospital was only about a kilometre away, so he ran up the street and along Royal Parade to the hospital's casualty entrance. Breathless, he managed to make himself clear to the nurse at the entrance, who pointed down a corridor to a curtained-off cubicle.

Scot introduced himself to a man in a white coat leaving the cubicle. The doctor gently put his arm on Scot's shoulder, and said: 'I'm sorry. She was dead on arrival. We tried to revive her, but no luck.'

Nothing made sense. Even the doctor's voice seemed blurred. A haze clouded the scene. Everything was silent, but trolleys were being moved, and nurses were talking on telephones. It was as if the audio had been muted.

A nurse came and asked if he'd like to see Lisa. He nodded before breaking open the curtains, to see her shattered face. Some blood remained on her face, but the worst had obviously been wiped off. She was lying on a clean white sheet. He hugged her. 'We're sorry, Mr Wallace ... It was a very bad accident, we're told,' the nurse said.

Scot nodded thanks to the nurses and the doctor, who'd broken the news. They offered to call someone for him, but he shook his head. He didn't say a word, and didn't cry. Everything was a blur; nothing registered. He wandered out into Royal Parade, carrying his coat. It was raining heavily now. But that didn't matter.

Oblivious to everything except the wet asphalt of the footpath, he walked up the tree lined road. His body felt weak so he placed his feet firmly on the ground one after the other in an unconscious bid to drive energy back into his body. People passed him on the footpath but they looked out of focus, detached from his world. He walked straight into the front bar of Naughton's Hotel and ordered a double Scotch. The bar – adorned with oars used in inter-collegiate rowing – was crowded with students and football followers noisily dissecting every move of the day's game. It was never his scene, and certainly not tonight. So he tossed off his drink and left.

The smell of overcooked lasagne struck Scot as he opened the door to the flat. After switching off the oven, he slumped into a chair, thinking about his life, which had changed so suddenly forever. He wept for himself as much as for Lisa and the baby he'd never see. To be honest, he cried more for himself. He was the one who had to live with the loss. The flat was so empty, and always would be. The next few days were going to be tortuous – ringing Lisa's parents, talking to the police, and arranging the funeral.

Those immediate tasks, albeit difficult, at least kept him going. So did his work. But as the days became weeks, the loneliness of returning to an empty flat each night increased his loss. The double bed felt empty, and he dared just occasionally to enter the repainted bedroom readied for a baby that would never arrive. Lisa had called it 'the nursery', but it was cold now, and empty, and would never hear any rhymes. The flat was not a home anymore. Friends did their best, but Melbourne didn't feel like home either. He'd spent too much time away from the city of his childhood, adolescence, and education. Most of his old friends had families now, their own lives to lead. He didn't have the energy to rediscover the city. Not alone, anyway.

At work one day, a colleague mentioned the firm needed a roving representative and salesman based in the Middle East. 'That's your old hunting ground, isn't it?' Although the retainer wouldn't be enough to live on, it would be a start. Scot resolved then and there to return to Cyprus. With the help of his contacts, he would start a small business and work alone. People would say he was running away from reality. They were probably right, but he didn't care. Because reality, he decided, wasn't to his liking. As well as business, he'd search for meaning.

6

The telephone ended the daydream. Scot looked down from his Limassol balcony to see the seriously injured woman being loaded into an ambulance. Police were taking all kinds of measurements, and talking to the driver. Scot then answered the phone ringing in the flat. 'Lionel London here.' It had been several years, but the pukka English voice threw Scot's mind back to the dinner at Episkopi. 'We're right here in Limassol and Lilly and I just must see you. For old times' sake of course, but we wish to pick your brains.'

Scot looked at his watch and was surprised to see it was 8.30 p.m. 'It's short notice, but I'm going around to the Club Downtown for a bite to eat. Alexander Belfort-Smith owns it.'

'He's the cause of our problem. He got our daughter Debbie a job with an NGO and now she's missing. We've telephoned him, written to him, but he just won't respond. So I'd prefer somewhere else, perhaps tomorrow?'

Scot arranged to meet the Londons at the Apollo Café the next day. 'Look forward to seeing you. It's been a long time.' The news about Debbie London reinforced his decision to see Alex this evening. Although he'd never met Debbie London, he remembered her photograph. After the brush-off Alex had given him in Kakopetria he almost relished the chance of passing on the news that Lionel London blamed him for Debbie's disappearance. He now had quite an agenda for the evening. First he wanted thanks for delivering the book to Baghdad. Also, just who were those Americans?

'Good break in the mountains?' Scot tried out a gentle opening query as Alexander joined him.

Alexander shrugged. 'Like most business in pleasant surroundings ... a change.'

Scot thought his trip to meet Ahmad Kareem could also have been described as a change! 'Rick and Brad are pleasant people.'

'Yes,' Alex said firmly, indicating any elaboration was off the agenda.

'Adnan's dead.'

Alexander nodded, a tinge of sadness – or was it inevitability? – creeping across his face.

'But I met his father.'

'Well, thanks for taking the book. It was an awful imposition. And too late.' He hesitated then as if the clockwork of the mind was sorting the information. 'You said you met his father ... Archaeologist isn't he?'

'Archaeologist by training, but more a bureaucrat these days.'

'Iraq. What a place to be a bureaucrat.'

Scot didn't respond, expecting something more. But the Englishman merely gazed into the distance.

'Did you know Adnan – the son – well?'

Alexander tightened his lips, and looked at Scot as if making an effort to concentrate. 'Know him well? Yes, quite well. He was an artist. Quite good too. Met him in Paris about ten years ago.'

'His illness ... how'd you know about that?'

Alexander eyeballed Scot, appearing to sincerely answer the question. 'Don't know exactly how I heard the news,' he said vaguely.

Scot didn't pursue the matter. However, it occurred to him Alexander would remember how he first heard the news and also how he got updates. Otherwise, why be so determined to send a book to Baghdad?

Scot was about to mention Debbie London's disappearance when a heavily built and avuncular-looking man from a nearby table, who'd been sharing a bottle of Johnny Walker, appeared behind Alex, and put his hand gently on the restaurateur's shoulder. 'I recommend the Club Downtown to all my friends. Excellent, Alex.' Although the words – drawn out and exaggerated – were aimed at Alex, the customer's eyes were directed towards Scot.

Alex noticed that too. 'Let me introduce you, Scot … Mustafa Rasool.'

Scot stood up. 'Scot Wallace.'

Mustafa Rasool extracted a business card from his button-down shirt pocket. It read: 'Mustafa Rasool Trade Consultant'.

'A trade consultant, but what sort of business?'

'Shady.' Mustafa Rasool chortled, slapping Alex on the back gently. 'I believe you live here in Limassol, Mr Wallace?'

'Not five hundred metres away, on the esplanade.'

'Wonderful. I myself divide my time between Aleppo and Limassol.'

'Scot's in business also.'

'Well, we must catch up. And thank you, Alex, for a wonderful evening. I think I've impressed my friends.'

As he broke away, Scot handed him a business card, which looked very ordinary compared with Mustafa Rasool's gold embossed card. Scot waited until the customer was out of earshot. 'Syrian, then?'

Alex nodded. 'With a bit of Kurdish blood, so he claims.'

'Lionel and Lilly London … Remember them?'

'Absolutely, but I haven't seen them for ages.'

'I had a call from Lionel tonight. Their daughter's missing, northern Iraq I think. They say you got her a job with an NGO.'

Alexander organised brandy, which was delivered by Dimitri, before responding. 'Debbie, yes ... Has been for some time. But I didn't get her a job whatever Lionel might say. I steered her in the right direction that's all.'

'She evidently hasn't been heard of for weeks.'

Without any indication of surprise, Alexander shook his head ruefully and said: 'Dangerous part of the world.'

Scot noticed a man walk through the restaurant with a guitar. Then drums arrived. Soon the bar was brimming with younger trendy Cypriots – many of whom, Scot guessed, worked at the other restaurants and hotels around town. Alexander and Dimitri had made this the place to be seen. There were a number of tourists as well, mainly women looking for a good time. White and blue jeans predominated. The music started. Laser lights caught the dance floor flashing in time with the throbbing music. After listening for a while and finishing the brandy, Scot decided it was time to leave.

As he walked home around midnight, Scot thought about Alexander's reaction to the disappearance of Debbie London. Dangerous part of the world, it might be. But people just don't go missing. And to dismiss Debbie's disappearance in such a matter of fact way seemed odd. Scot remembered Lilly's words from all those years ago. After mentioning Alex had taken Debbie to a regimental dinner at Episkopi, Lilly had said something about being worried Debbie might end up 'being married to the army as well'. Well that wasn't to be, and now Alex appeared to have washed his hands of her altogether.

'Is that what he said!' Then Lilly London added: 'Well, Debbie wouldn't be in that dangerous part of the world if it wasn't for Major Belfort-Smith retired.'

'Alex was a reasonable chap once,' Lionel added. 'Now he won't help at all.'

'And we know he knows people who could help, don't we Lionel?'

Lilly's comment was clearly designed to sow thoughts in Scot's mind, and it succeeded. He thought of Alex's two American friends. 'You mean he still has contacts in intelligence?'

Lionel responded. 'What is it they say about spooks? They never retire!'

Situated amidst shops and office buildings, the open-air Apollo Café was a favourite haunt on hot days. Vines and flowering pots divided the tables. There were pieces of stone columns and other relics of archaeological sites. The courtyard provided an escape from the bustle right within the centre of Limassol. 'If she's been missing a matter of weeks, it's surprising there hasn't been anything in the newspapers or on BBC World,' Scot said.

'Conspiracy of silence,' Lionel responded.

'That's where we thought you could help,' Lilly said. 'Ask a few questions of the British High Commission.'

Scot explained he'd given up journalism for trade. 'But that doesn't stop me asking questions.'

'Please do,' Lilly begged. 'We've asked our local member of parliament, written to the Foreign Secretary, but all to no avail. We're at our wits' end.'

7

Without warning, the equivalent of US$200,000 was deposited in the account Scot had opened for Ahmad Kareem. It had been wired by a boutique British bank, not one of the well-known main-street institutions. The account now held the initial deposit of US$5,000 plus the new deposit. Scot heard Mr Kareem's voice ringing in his ears. *Just a small account.* He wondered whether to check with the bank personally? Perhaps it was a mistake? No, he'd forget about it for twenty-four hours in the hope there would be a debit entry for the same amount indicating an error.

The telephone dashed that hope. Scot answered to hear a female voice – speaking stilted English with a European, maybe Italian accent – talking to someone, who punctuated his speech with the occasional Arabic word. The female voice was clear, whereas the other voice – apparently male – had a slight echo as if speaking into a cheap cordless phone. The female voice then asked: 'Can I speak to Scot Wallace … Mr Scot Wallace?'

'Speaking.'

'Mr Scot Wallace?' The woman was insistent.

'Yes, it is Scot Wallace speaking.' He enunciated every syllable carefully.

The woman dropped off the line, and the man spoke. 'Mr Wallace?'

'Yes, it's Scot Wallace.'

'It's Ahmad Kareem here. Nice day on Cyprus?'

'It has been,' Scot said deliberately. 'The weather's fine and hot, and the sea blue.'

'Thank you for your message. We are very pleased.'
Scot didn't respond.
'You still there Mr Wallace?'
'Yes.'
'We are sending a message so I telephoned to confirm that we are the sender. Okay? It is correct to follow its instructions. Okay? We didn't want you to worry that it wasn't from us.'
Scot said reluctantly: 'I understand'.
'You recognise my voice?'
'Yes, I do.'
The line then went dead.

Since the meeting in Baghdad, Scot had wondered how he'd get instructions. It was all becoming a bit too sinister, but he was relieved at least that Kareem had shown some discretion. Neither Baghdad nor Iraq had been mentioned. And the bank account had been raised only obliquely. He wondered what route the call had taken. Judging by the woman's voice and Kareem's email address, it had been patched through Italy.

It was several days before Ahmad Kareem's instructions came. They arrived – not by email or fax – but by ordinary mail. There was no return address on the envelope, and the only clues to its origin were the Italian stamps. Inside was a single sheet of thermal fax paper. After ordering coffee at a pavement café near the post office, Scot looked for identification marks of any fax machine. There were none. Therefore, apart from the stamps, there was no indication of the letter's origin. And the stamps were misleading for anyone but Scot, as the message was from Baghdad. Scot was certain.

'Very much pleased to hear when we spoke by telephone today that the weather is good on Cyprus,' the letter began. It was dated four days earlier – the day of the telephone call from Kareem. The only other indication of the sender was 'Ahmad K.' at the bottom of the message.

'Friend of the Iraqi people, Mr Mustafa Rasool – businessman in Aleppo – is undertaking some research into aspects of the Ilisu Dam the Turkish authorities constructing on the Tigris River and of much importance to us,' Ahmad K. wrote. 'Very much pleased if you could give him a quarter of the recent deposit in cash personally in Aleppo.' The note went on to detail Mustafa Rasool's address in Aleppo, and the date the 'recent deposit' was made.

Bloody cheek! Ahmad Kareem presumed he could drop everything, and dash off to Aleppo. And why was he being involved anyway? Surely this payment – if the reason for the expenditure was correct – was quite legitimate? Why couldn't Iraqi officials in Damascus carry out the task?

Kareem's note added as a post script: 'Of course, your expenses will be paid, together with a small commission, of say, up to five percent of the amounts deposited in the account. Also, you may be interested that Mr Sadeq Ramadi, of our trade department, has a new business opportunity, which you may find quite lucrative. I am led to believe you are closely acquainted with Mr Ramadi. He will contact you separately on this matter. We appreciate your assistance so far.'

With a firmness of step brought on by fermenting irritation, Scot walked back to his apartment. There were two things he needed to check. The first was simple enough. Scot found the computer printout he'd made of the account at the Aphrodite Bank. The date of the deposit in Kareem's note corresponded with the date the equivalent of US$200,000 had been deposited. The second thing worth checking was just an outside chance. He fumbled through business cards collected over the past few months. The gold embossed card he was looking for

stood out from the others of more restrained design.
'Mustafa Rasool Trade Consultant'. He checked the
address against the address in Kareem's instructions. It
was the same. The Syrian he'd met at Club Downtown
with Alex was the man he was requested to pay. Some
coincidence! 'Syrian with some Kurdish blood,' Scot
recalled Alex saying.

Scot fumed all morning over Mr Kareem's
instructions. The second part of Kareem's letter didn't do
much to reduce his irritation. A commission of up to five
percent of the amounts deposited could mean nothing, half
a percent, or five percent. Also, what was Sadeq Ramadi's
new business opportunity? Did Ramadi know his name
was being invoked? And finally 'we appreciate your
assistance so far'. As it came after Ramadi's name had
been mentioned, it could be read to imply that unless
Kareem's instructions were followed, all Scot's business
with Iraq would be cancelled.

Scot looked at his Iraq file with the idea of quitting the
market altogether. Then he could kiss Ahmad Kareem
goodbye – forever. But the more he looked at his trading –
mainly in Australian-made canned fruit and cheese – and
thought about how the deals had come about, he decided
he was reluctant to pull out. It had been Sadeq Ramadi in
the first place who'd suggested the business and Scot was
reluctant to let him down. He thought back to that first
week he'd spent in Baghdad. It had been an exploratory
trip and – as he knew now – an extraordinarily naïve idea.
He went to Iraq cold, with no contacts, and nothing to sell.
He'd sensed the absurdity of the trip as soon as he settled
into his Baghdad hotel. In the lobby, there was what
seemed like a platoon of carpetbagger salesmen. Just
about all of them looked suspicious, and most had beady
eyes which followed his every move.

At breakfast the day before he'd been due to leave Baghdad, Scot sat at a table next to a couple of dark-suited businessmen – one apparently Bulgarian and the other Italian. Their common language was English, embellished and punctuated with lavish hand gestures.

'Sadeq Ramadi crazy,' said the Italian.

'He says he can't understand a word I'm said,' said the Bulgarian. 'And I speak English perfectly good.'

'Crazy … How old think?

'Too much years Sadeq Ramadi,' responded the Bulgarian.

That episode was what Scot always described – when anyone bothered to listen – as First Time Lucky in doing business against the odds.

It was worth a try, so Scot jotted down phonetically 'Sadeq Ramadi' on his paper serviette. He left the coffee shop, collected his briefcase from his room, and hurried to the Trade Department – for the third time in a week. At the scratched and dirty reception counter in the dingy entrance hall, a verbal brawl was under way. Behind the counter, a man dressed in a blue shirt tucked without any care into crumpled black trousers was facing six or seven foreign businessmen. Beneath his white *keffiyeh*, a kindly ageing Iraqi faced – with a benign smile – the foreign onslaught of shouting and fists thumping the counter.

'Excuse me, sir,' Scot remembered he'd said politely and firmly, just loud enough to be heard by the Iraqi. He caught the eye of the Iraqi.

The old man with a two-day growth called Scot to the counter to the side of the foreign vultures. He'd asked: 'Appointment?'

'Mr Sadeq Ramadi.'

'Passport?'

The old Iraqi then stepped back to a telephone on a desk behind. A greeting in Arabic was all that Scot recognised. Then he heard his name being mentioned and the words *'men Australie'*. From Australia, Scot understood. The Iraqi returned to face him, and said: 'You are most welcome.'

That was Second Time Lucky!

Following directions given by the ageing official, Scot found himself outside an office from which shouting was emerging. He realised he was on a roll and had a chance of being Third Time Lucky. Two ashen-faced men in tired dark suits were being dispatched with no uncertainty. 'Mr Wallace from Australia, I think?'

Scot remembered uttering 'Sir', shaking Mr Ramadi's hand lightly, and quickly handing over his business card. Fortunately, Mr Ramadi retrieved one of his own from his shirt pocket and an exchange took place. It was fortunate because Scot had no idea of the correct spelling or position of Mr Ramadi. Scot glanced down at the card and barely had a chance to digest Mr Ramadi's senior position when the Iraqi said: 'I hope you deal in Australian canned fruit and vegetables.'

'Yes, of course,' Scot had lied. 'Very good quality too.'

The most curious part of that whole episode, Scot recalled, was that the most difficult part had been persuading an Australian manufacturer to supply the goods. Every obstacle the companies could think of was touted as a reason for not going ahead. Things had changed now, but it had taken time.

Since that first encounter, Scot had come to like and trust Sadeq Ramadi. As he considered scrapping his trading with Iraq – and his relationship with Ahmad Kareem – he realised he couldn't. It would be like giving a free kick to those foreign salesmen – the Bulgarians, the Italians and all the others.

The recollections of his early deals in Iraq had a cathartic affect on Scot's anger towards Ahmad Kareem. Maybe something good would come from following his instructions. Maybe it would lead to the mentioned opportunity? And maybe he'd even receive a full five percent commission on all deposits made into the bank account? Anyway, he'd always wanted to make contact with the management of the Aleppo Pharmaceutical Company. Medicine was big business! The more he thought about it, the more he liked the idea of Kareem paying expenses for the Aleppo trip.

Then, a cloud of sober reflection threw a shadow over his mood. He didn't want to become further entwined in Kareem's agenda. If nothing more, it just added complications. And why was a foreigner being asked to make the payment? But as he thought of reasons against going to Aleppo, Scot's pendulum of moods threw up arguments for making the trip. The Ilisu Dam was a real issue for Iraq. To be built by the Turkish government the Ilisu and other dams would control fifty per cent of the downstream flow of the Tigris River into Syria and Iraq. It would flood the archeologically rich medieval town of Hasankeyf – an historic jewel of Kurdish culture. The Baghdad regime was bitterly opposed to the Ilisu and other dams being proposed by Turkey for the Tigris and the Euphrates. Water was being predicted as a catalyst for war in the region. Mustafa Rasool of Aleppo was of Syrian and Kurdish blood, so perhaps it was logical he should be involved in doing research for the Iraqis.

To hell with the risks! He would make the Aleppo trip. Scot dialled the country code for Syria and the area code for Aleppo, then added the digits from Mustafa Rasool's card. After negotiating his way through a receptionist, a meeting was arranged in Aleppo at noon the following Tuesday.

'We shall have lunch – a typical Aleppo *mezze* – after our meeting,' the Syrian said. 'Looking most forward to seeing you. And remember me to my friend Alexander.'

Scot emailed Kareem's Italian address telling the Iraqi of his plans. He added: 'I have found a villa near the mountain village of Kakopetria, which may be suitable for you – if you are really serious about buying a house.' He described the house, surrounded by its orchard and pine trees. 'There is an agent in Limassol, who is handling the sale.'

Then he focused on the possible commission on the bank account, and the mooted new business opportunity in Iraq. Both were very vague and uncertain, but at least he'd get a free lunch in Aleppo.

8

A brass plate marked a shabby wooden doorway on Baron
Street, Aleppo. In Arabic, English and French, it read:
'Mustafa Rasool, Trade Consultant, Third Floor'.
Climbing the narrow stairs amidst a fetid smell of
yesterday's cooked vegetables, Scot couldn't help
comparing the drab ambience of the building to the
prosperous – if overdone – image created by Mustafa
Rasool's gold-embossed business card. After knocking
lightly on the office door, he entered.

'My friend,' said Mustafa Rasool, gripping Scot's hand
firmly. The greeting was carried out with such apparent
sincerity it crossed the Australian's mind that perhaps the
trade consultant didn't get many visitors. 'My friend, I
trust you had a good trip.'

Scot nodded with a half-smile as he looked around the
modest corporate headquarters. There were two rooms,
both painted stark white contrasting dramatically with the
drabness of the dimly lit staircase. A large black and white
photograph of Mustafa Rasool shaking the hand of the
Syrian president dominated the first room, which included
a couple of leather-covered club chairs and a desk for a
receptionist. The club chairs had an unused appearance
raising the suspicion it would be rare for any visitor to
have to wait for trade advice.

'Straight down to business, my friend,' said the
avuncular consultant as he led the way to his office. The
two windows with half-lowered white Roman blinds
provided a good view of the Baron Hotel. 'You know this
hotel? It is, as much as the *souk* and the Grand Mosque,

part of Aleppo history. The king of Syria greeted crowds
from the hotel's balcony before the people kicked him out.
So the meddling English, they move him to Baghdad to
become King of Iraq. Maybe that's why the Iraqis got rid
of the monarchy in the end. They didn't want used kings.'
Mustafa Rasool guffawed with a laugh that rapidly
degenerated into a heavy smoker's cough. His face turned
red, and he slapped his chest several times quelling the
splutter. 'Too many laughs, they bad for me.' Undaunted
he added, 'Another king stayed there too ... Australia's
flyer Kingsford-Smith on one of those air races.
Remember?'

'Before my time,' Scot noted, looking across to the
hotel, which had opened during the dying years of
Ottoman rule over Syria. 'But I knew he stayed there,
yes.' The Baron Hotel – with its pointed arch windows,
cantilevered balconies, and terrace accessed from the bar
and dining room – had seen a lot of history.

Mustafa Rasool shook his head slowly. 'Yes Syria has
too much history. Too much remembering. One lifetime is
too short for the learning of all the history of this country.
So lunch? You must be hungry!'

'Before we go, maybe, I should give you –' Scot
fumbled into his leather briefcase.

'The money?'

'More discreet than in a restaurant.'

'Whatever you wish. But my friends at the restaurant
are used to seeing me receiving much money.' It was
clearly an ostentation Mustafa Rasool didn't mind
observed.

Scot placed the American dollar bills – sealed in
hundreds – on the desk. 'Bank fresh, but you should count
it.'

Mustafa Rasool looked bored just thinking of the effort
of counting $50,000 in hundred dollar bills. So instead, he

randomly selected a bundle and shuffled it like a croupier, then checked that a $100 note topped all the bundles. 'Receipt?'

'Thank you.'

The Syrian retrieved a pro forma receipt book out of his desk and began writing. 'For what shall I say?'

'Maybe Ilisu Dam project?'

Mustafa Rasool gave a look of bafflement, then said vaguely: 'Very clever idea.' Handing the receipt to Scot, he placed the cash in the bottom draw of the desk – except for one bundle of $100 bills. That was stuffed into the back pocket of his trousers. 'Well, now lunch maybe?'

'It'll be safe? The money?'

'As houses,' the Syrian said.

The phone rang. '*Marhaba ... Na'am.*' Scot could hear the caller rattling on in Arabic as Mustafa nodded, occasionally adding '*Na'am*'. '*Na'am*' or '*Yes*', Scot understood, but judging by Rasool's frowns and other facial contortions, he was not pleased – or at least puzzled – by what he was hearing. Then the Syrian exclaimed in English to the caller, as if clarifying what was being said, 'US dollars?' There was further nodding and then he said '*Qubros, Larnaca, na'am.*' He put down the telephone, shaking his head as if expressing frustration, and expelled a long sigh. After a minute or so of silence, and more shaking of the head, he faced Scot directly and said: 'So now lunch!'

As soon as they stepped out on to the Baron Street pavement, Mustafa Rasool began talking like a government tour guide. 'Oldest continuously inhabited city in the world.'

'Thought Damascus was?'

'Also,' the Syrian said. 'Just fancy, one country having the two oldest inhabited cities in the world.'

'Quite amazing,' said Scot, feeling there was little he could add to such an arguable claim.

'For me as a trade consultant, Aleppo is more exhilarating than Damascus. Start of the great Silk Road. So we are great traders. And there are many different people here who have wandered along the Silk Road selling this and that,' he said quaintly. 'Then they made money in our *souks* and decided they couldn't be bothered walking home. That's why you see so many different people: Kurds, Armenians, Turks, Persians, Azerbaijanis, Arabs, and some Jews. Aleppo is a melting pot,' he added, grabbing Scot's arm and steering him down a narrow lane. 'Tourists never find this restaurant. It's my favourite, my second home.'

A stone step flanked either side by Roman column capitals marked the freshly painted green door, which led into the restaurant. A waiter greeted Mustafa Rasool as an old friend and the greeting was lavishly acknowledged with a kiss to the waiter's cheeks, first the right and then the left. 'They know me here,' the Syrian said with some understatement.

The restaurant was as surprising as it was stunning. It had a domed roof and the tables – covered with starched white linen tablecloths – were set out around a stone fountain which played an elegant spray up towards the dome. About a third of the tables were occupied, mainly with well-dressed businessmen. To the side and near the back of the restaurant a couple of young men were playing backgammon and drinking beer. Mustafa Rasool headed straight towards a large table in the corner of the restaurant. Clearly, it was his regular table. They sat, and almost instantaneously a bottle of Johnny Walker Black Label and an ice bucket arrived. 'You drink whisky!' It was a statement rather than a question, and Scot nodded.

'Service very good here,' the Syrian said, as the first dishes of the promised *mezze* arrived.

'Are you coming to Limassol again soon?'

'Near future, I don't think so. I'm very, very busy.' After a hesitation, he added: 'Too much on my plate as you say in English.'

'The Ilisu dam project must be taking a lot of time.'

Mustafa Rasool again looked puzzled before catching hold of the thread of what Scot was alluding to. 'The Turkish dam, yes it takes much time.' After dipping bread into the bowl of *hummus*, and taking a healthy swig of whisky, he added: 'I was very surprised this morning. I had a telephone call from our friend Alexander.' After taking a more modest sip from his glass, he added: 'Alexander has a big problem. I just don't know if I can solve it for him. He has a friend who is missing somewhere in Kurdistan. A girl friend,' he made a point of giving Scot a knowing look.

Scot was surprised, wondering whether the Londons were wrong about Alexander's inaction. 'I think I know of the woman,' he said, thinking of Debbie London. 'I know her parents.'

'Rich?'

'Her father was an officer in the British Army, so I guess they're comfortable, but not rich.'

Mustafa Rasool looked a touch disappointed. 'Not for me, of course, but the Kurds may want money. Buckets of it! I've said to Alexander I will talk to some people, but the Kurds can be very difficult as they argue with each other as much as with Turkey and the Iranians. You never know who to deal with and whether the people you're dealing with are the right people. Very confusing … Too much confusion!'

The Syrian then fell silent, his eyes looking blankly over the other diners, apparently at nothing in particular. A couple of times his lips tightened as if holding words back. Then he rubbed a finger of his left hand along his lips slowly backwards and forwards. His eyes drifted upwards, and hovered there before shifting to eyeball Scot. 'This girl friend of Alexander … Political?'

'Never met her personally. She's said to be very clever, and she's very good looking. I know that from a photograph I've seen. But political in what way? She works for an NGO, so I guess she's committed to helping people.'

'But which people?' Mustafa Rasool's eyes drilled into Scot's like lasers seeking to extract the truth.

'Poor people, I suppose.'

The Syrian's lips released a noisy puff of cynicism, before being lubricated by more whisky. 'My friend, I've made some enquiries already for Alexander. And it seems she may have been up to no good. No good at all! Maybe, even, she is an agent of British imperialism. A contact tells me she is too interested in Kurdish business dealings, and asking this and that about where the guns, etcetera, etcetera come from. Not minding her own business. And about drugs, but I don't think she's a drug addict?'

'I doubt it,' Scot said, surprised.

'So why you think she asks my friends, contacts, about drugs?'

Scot shrugged, indicating he didn't have a clue. 'Have you asked Alexander?'

'Maybe I will, and maybe I won't. Because it makes me think why is Alexander Belfort-Smith so concerned about this person?'

'I think he helped her get a job and feels some responsibility.'

Mustafa Rasool nodded slowly, his mind working overtime as if assembling a jigsaw puzzle. 'So who am I helping? A man who runs a restaurant in Limassol, or someone else? I have to think carefully because I can't betray my business friends. Trust is everything around here. People come to me because they know they can trust Mustafa Rasool. They don't go to a lawyer and get a contract. Our contracts are written on trust, not paper.'

'But betray? You said "betray". You think your contacts have something to hide? Drugs?'

Mustafa Rasool just stared at Scot as if stocktaking the Australian's credibility. Or naïveté!

The Black Label was loosening Scot's tongue as he sought the wider picture. 'Maybe I shouldn't mention it, but Alexander said he thought you had some Kurdish blood.' He then added, as if diluting the personal nature of the statement: 'Of course, you're Syrian and Arab mainly.'

Mustafa Rasool ticked off fingers of his right hand one by one. 'I'm a Halabi – the Arabic word for Aleppo or Halab – number one. I'm Syrian number two. And I'm Arab number four. And my grandmother was Kurdish number five.'

Scot noted to himself that number three had been drowned in the Black Label. Grilled quail arrived as a main course, and the waiter took it upon himself to top up the glasses. 'You eat well in Aleppo!'

'Because my grandmother was Kurdish, it makes me very useful for business. I know many of the Kurdish leaders and that is very handy to many people.' The Syrian suddenly broke off his boasting, and he indicated towards a table on the other side of the fountain, his eyes sparkling. 'See, they're Iranians I am sure. They love the whisky. Once out of sight of the *mullahs*, they all drink whisky. Much better than the home-made vodka they drink in Tehran or wherever. Traders probably!'

Mustafa Rasool got up from the table and walked towards the Iranians and introduced himself. Scot couldn't hear the talking, but noticed the Syrian draw a number of business cards out of his shirt pocket and leave them in a fan display on the Iranian's table. He then returned to Scot commenting, 'Very nice people. From Tehran, as I thought. Surely they need some help!'

Scot felt mellowness verging on drowsiness descending, brought on by the whisky and the relief at having handed over the money. After sharing a *mezze* of ten hors d'oeuvres and the quail, he'd eaten more than enough, but accepted when Mustafa Rasool suggested crème caramel and coffee.

'We'll stick with whisky, okay? Or would you like a Cognac? I find it doesn't suit me to mix drinks.'

Scot nodded reluctantly against better judgement. And more whisky was splashed into his glass. 'So you must know Ahmad Kareem in Baghdad quite well?'

'For many, many years,' the Syrian said. 'He's also got some Kurdish blood somewhere in the family tree. Before many generations, I think, but it's there.'

Scot looked surprised.

'No, not unusual, the people of the Middle East have many ingredients … Crusader, Hittite, Kurdish, etcetera, etcetera, all in one big cake. Course, Ahmad Kareem doesn't talk about his Kurdish ancestors in Baghdad too loudly, but I know.'

'Do you do a lot of work for Iraq?'

'From time to time I'm most useful to them,' Mustafa Rasool said. 'Have you enjoyed this lunch, and the whisky?'

'Very much,' Scot said quietly with a distinct premonition something was about to be requested. There was no such thing as a free lunch.

'You know, ever since I met you with Alexander in his restaurant, I have known you are a man I can trust. Some people you can judge, just like that,' the Syrian said heightening Scot's wariness. 'I suddenly remember there is someone in Larnaca that I need to pay some money to. Maybe you could come back to my office and I will give you the dollars, and you could take them. It's only a little way from Larnaca airport.'

Scot nodded vaguely.

'Thank you,' Mustafa Rasool said. 'I wouldn't ask, but it's very urgent. Thank you.' Before the deal could come undone, the Syrian semaphored the waiter by holding up his left hand and writing an imaginary bill with his right. The bill arrived and Mustafa Rasool stood up, retrieved the bundle of $100 dollar bills from his trouser pocket, and settled the account.

Back in his office, the Syrian got straight down to business. 'Now, this is the address in Larnaca,' he said, writing details on a scrap of paper. 'And this is her name. Be sure to give it to her personally. Ana's very beautiful, with blond hair.' He rolled his eyes, and his lips mimicked a noisy kiss. 'You'll like her, I'm so certain.'

'She works for you?'

'She works too hard.' His eyes glazed as he appeared to search for an explanation. 'On the Big Dam project. That's it. The one you mentioned?'

'The Ilisu.'

'That very one.' After reaching into the bottom desk drawer, he counted out two hundred from the bundles of notes Scot had carried from Limassol.

'That's $20,000!'

'Yes, you count correctly. As I said, I could tell I could trust you right from the first time we met.'

Scot protested his reluctance, but Mustafa Rasool defused the protest by quickly looking at his watch and saying, 'I must rush to work on Alexander's missing girl friend. Tell Alexander, I'm working hard as hard on the situation. And I won't ever tell him you liked my restaurant better than his.'

After checking in at Damascus airport for the flight to Larnaca, Scot went straight to the bar and ordered a large beer. Sitting with a bowl of nuts for company, he pondered what he'd got himself into this time. There were serious penalties for carrying large amounts of cash through airports and customs posts in this part of the world. But he'd got through the Damascus checkpoint without the money being discovered, and at Larnaca his baggage and briefcase had never been inspected. He'd have to be unlucky this time.

And, anyway, this wasn't what was dominating his mind. More, the depressing thought that he was being used in some Machiavellian cum Levantine plot about which he didn't have a clue. Ignorance may be bliss in some cases, but certainly not this one. If he had felt annoyed by Kareem in the past, he felt distinctly used now. That was a depressing state of mind in which to be placed. At least annoyance was a reaction personally generated. It had its own kind of satisfaction. The feeling of being used, however, was something of someone else's doing. It amounted to loss of control. And Scot didn't like that a bit. He rued the day he'd ever agreed to open a bank account for Kareem. But then, he hadn't had any choice.

Lisa would have thought he was mad. He knew that. She was so controlled and sensible. That's why she had been useful to the United Nations. He could see her eyes, her high cheekbones and silky hair. They should never have gone to Australia. Then all would be different. She'd never have been on that freeway. The accident would never have happened. They'd thought they'd have a new start together. But why? They'd been happy together on Cyprus. They'd have been happy anywhere. Scot felt tired, exhausted even. And very alone.

He wandered to the bar and ordered another beer, more for the couple of words he'd have with another human being rather than the drink. He sought any encounter that would take his mind off Lisa, break the destructive train of thought. It worked. He thought of the $20,000 in the briefcase he was tightly clutching. Why was he carrying it back to Cyprus? Had Mustafa's mystery phone call before lunch been all about this money? Certainly, 'Cyprus' and 'Larnaca' had been mentioned, and 'US dollars'. Had Kareem given the orders? His encounters with Kareem and Mustafa Rasool had their funny sides. What on earth were they up to? What a way to run a country's Interior Ministry. Even without sanctions, half the country would be likely to starve to death with these kinds of antics. The crowds he saw on television rallying in support of the president, maybe they were really shouting: 'Death to America, give Scot Wallace another twenty grand!'

And who was this woman in Larnaca who deserved $20,000 for work on a project Mustafa Rasool had clearly heard little about. Scot had first thought she must have been a prostitute, who was owed for past favours. But she would have had to do a lot of screwing to deserve that many bucks. And she'd be unlikely to agree to put it on a slate. Unless she was mad. And she may well be. After all, she'd become embroiled somehow with a Mafia of sorts spanning Baghdad and Aleppo. Anyone who did that was not quite normal. Scot knew that.

At least, he'd made some contacts with the Aleppo Pharmaceutical Company. They were normal people! Spotless white coats, down to earth, frank about the realities of the difficulties of their business. Maybe they'd swing some business Scot's way some day.

The public address system was announcing something in Arabic. Scot picked up the word 'Qubros', tossed off his beer and began heading for the departure gate. 'Cyprus

Airways flight bound for Larnaca is boarding now,' the
official repeated in English. 'All passengers please
proceed immediately to boarding gate five.' Scot was glad
to be going home.

9

Passport stamped, Scot headed for the nothing-to-declare green exit channel at Larnaca airport. Clutching the briefcase stuffed with the dollars, he looked straight ahead nonchalantly. Hailing a taxi outside the terminal, he said: 'Limassol, but Larnaca town for five or ten minutes first.' He showed the driver the mystery woman's address, and the driver exhaled a puff of annoyance.

The address was a block of flats with small balconies overlooking Larnaca Bay. They looked like holiday flats, which had been taken over by permanent residents. On one balcony, a woman, perhaps a Sri Lankan guest worker, was belting the dust out of a rug draped across the veranda rail. As dust wafted around, some to the ground, some to other balconies, the woman had an uncaring look of distain. There was a board with ten bell buttons, some had names, some were blank. There was one marked 'A.Z.' Scot pushed it, and heard a bell ringing somewhere above, perhaps on the first floor. He stepped back towards the road, but could see no activity. He returned to the bell and pressed it for longer. There was still no answer from the speaker beside the bell buttons. After a third try, he pushed several of the other buttons. Finally, a woman responded and agreed to come down to the locked security door. Dressed in black, the woman had a friendly look. She said she had a telephone number for the mystery woman in her flat. She disappeared, and after a couple of minutes returned with the number written in big numerals on a folded tissue. Scot thanked the woman effusively.

As the taxi jostled its way through traffic and out of the town, Scot thought it hardly surprising Rasool's mystery woman wasn't home. Why would she be? She probably wouldn't have known that a total stranger was about to call and deliver US$20,000 in cash. Now he had her phone number, she might even collect the money herself in Limassol. Scot knew he'd hot foot along the coast day or night for twenty grand.

It was dusk when the taxi arrived at Scot's apartment block. Rasool and Kareem's demands continued to rankle and the smallest things made home appealing.

'Good evening, Scot,' Nikos said as Scot entered the building. Despite all the shortcomings of the part time concierge cum manager, Nikos's voice was reassuring. It signalled no demand. Nikos didn't treat people like mules that could be used for anything and everything. Mule? Yes, that's what Scot felt like. It was surprising Rasool and Kareem didn't tether his legs when he wasn't needed. It had probably occurred to them. Most other donkeys in the Arab world had two legs tied together when between jobs.

Once in his flat, he checked his computer. There was an email from Ahmad Kareem.

> *I am very interested in the villa you have discovered so promptly. I believe you should interview the agent on the matter. In view of your reluctance to make a decision on my behalf, I shall suggest you contact an acquaintance of mine, a very reliable businessman named Boris Bragonov, who has very good taste and could be helpful to you in making a decision. He is well accustomed to acquiring property on Cyprus for Russian and other foreigners.*

Kareem gave a phone number for Bragonov. He added he'd transferred money for a deposit, in case it was needed, and mentioned he'd posted a legal document, which would facilitate the purchase of the villa.

As it was too late to visit a bank, Scot slid the briefcase under his bed. He would deal with that matter in the morning. It hadn't taken long to decide what to do with the money for safe keeping. He'd decided against depositing it back in the Aphrodite Bank account. He'd had enough trouble persuading the manager to give it to him in American dollars in the first place. Just the thought of having the manager looking curious – as if Scot had somehow over budgeted by $20,000 – provided the impetus for another option. He'd place it in a safe deposit box at his regular bank. It would be totally confidential and available any time during office hours.

Later, at Club Downtown, Alexander Belfort-Smith sipped his brandy as he talked about Debbie London. Every few minutes, his train of thought was broken by Dimitri's arrival at the table. The Englishman put his arm across the Cypriot's back, pulling his body closer. Scot had never seen them so affectionate. Alex wasn't drunk, but mellow certainly. 'I've got to go to Aleppo.'

'You have to go, I know,' Dimitri said as he gathered the used plates and cutlery in front of Scot. He left the wine glass and the half full bottle of Cyprus wine.

Scot was in a quandary. He wanted Alex's opinion of Mustafa Rasool, but didn't want to discuss his own business dealings with the Syrian. He just wasn't certain about Alexander, especially after what Rasool had told him over lunch. But the subject came up anyway.

'I've been on the telephone to Mustafa Rasool, and he says you've been in Aleppo.'

'I had to go to see people at the Aleppo Pharmaceutical Company, so thought I may as well say hello to Mustafa Rasool.' He added a reminder to obscure the real reason he'd met the Syrian. 'I met him here at Club Downtown. You introduced us.'

Alex nodded.

Seeking to shift the emphasis from his own dealings with Rasool, Scot asked the obvious. 'You seeing him in Aleppo?'

'Yes, I'm trying to find out what's happened to Debbie London, and he's got quite good contacts.'

'But she's missing in northern Iraq – the Kurdish area – isn't she?'

'Well, that's where she was working, I think,' Alex said. 'But anyway, Mustafa has good contacts in all the Kurdish areas, except perhaps the areas close to the Iranian border. It's none of my business really, but I feel a bit responsible for her. I tossed up the idea of her working for an NGO. She seemed to want an adventure.'

'What's she doing there?'

'Advising local communities on business and economic plans, I gather. She has a degree from the London School of Economics, so she could be quite useful.'

It seemed quite plausible, and Scot wondered whether Rasool's contacts may have got the wrong end of the stick. She may have been seeking answers necessary for meaningful business plans. Perhaps, Debbie London had been a bit too enthusiastic about her job, and that had led to misunderstanding.

'I don't entirely trust Mustafa Rasool,' Alex added. 'He has some dubious business contacts, but he could be helpful. It's a question of the devil you know. At least I know what I'm letting myself in for. That's the good thing about running a restaurant like this, in the hub of a good and dubious business area like Limassol. You meet people and they often get a bit shickered and talk more openly than they should.'

Scot wondered if he'd be considered one of Mustafa Rasool's 'dubious business contacts' if Alex knew about the US$20,000. He guessed he would.

'Nice woman Debbie,' Alex went on. 'I shouldn't have given her any encouragement at all.'

'You only mentioned the idea,' Scot said, deliberately ignoring the Londons' opinion Alex had actually helped her get the job.

'Well, to be honest it was a bit more than that. I pointed her in the right direction, introduced her to a couple of people in London. I didn't think the whole deal would ever go so pear-shaped.'

'Don't blame yourself. By all accounts, she's intelligent enough to have known the dangers in that sort of job.'

Alex nodded as if thanking Scot for the reassurance, even if he knew otherwise.

Dimitri came to the table again, having served a nearby couple. There was more touching. Scot guessed it would go unnoticed by anyone unaware of Alexander's background. It was little more than footballers get up to in the full view of big crowds. The Cypriot left, almost swaggering, as quickly as he'd arrived.

Alexander shook his head slowly, side to side. 'Don't know what I'd do without Dimitri,' said Alex with a frankness Scot had not encountered before. 'My life changed when we met. You could never know what it was like – in the army and after the discharge. I won't bore you, but the discharge was actually a great relief. I could suddenly live however I wanted. And your story – despite my initial anger – was a great help. I didn't have to tell anyone. Two million people had read it in black and white.

It must be one of the biggest *outings* in the history of mankind.'

They both laughed – Scot with considerable relief. The Australian wondered why Alexander, usually totally controlled almost to the point of annoyance, was letting his hair down this evening. It was partly the brandy talking, sure. But why was he drinking the brandy?

Alexander may be relieved to be out of the army now, but some bitterness lingered. 'You know, by any guesstimate hundreds, maybe thousands of gay troops fought for the Allies during the Second World War, and at the same time, Hitler was sending homosexual Germans to the concentration camps. Still, it took us Brits more than fifty years to get rid of the ban in the armed forces. It's bloody crazy. A bastion of democracy, we may well be, but we're capable of so much injustice. Like many Western nations, we're first rate at judging other countries' frailties and human rights abuses, but not our own. And it wasn't even that we said "this is wrong, we must lift this ban". No, it took the European Court of Human Rights to make us. Embarrassment was worse for us than injustice!'

Scot was lost for words. So he nodded sagely, and sipped at his wine. The live band had started, and the late crowd was arriving, gathering at the bar and taking the empty tables around the dance floor. 'What happened to the chaplain involved in your discharge?'

'Chaplain? Left the army, I think. Puzzling thing, though … I don't know if he was to blame or not. Something the investigators said in London, indicated they were acting on a letter sent by a fellow officer.'

'The chaplain would be a fellow officer, surely?'

'Yes, of course, but from what they said it seemed a regular officer – if I can put it that way – was responsible. But it doesn't matter much now!' Alexander screwed his lips together, and – despite his protestation of 'relief' –

was clearly still emotionally fragile about the grim episode. Especially when drinking brandy. 'Course, ban or no ban, homophobia will continue,' Alex went on. 'Like racism, you can't ban thoughts. And in the army, where you train young men to the peak of fitness, add the power of the gun, and train people to fight, things bubble over from time to time. Too much testosterone!'

Scot didn't know where to take the discussion. After a suitable pause, he said good night. 'Great talking, but early start tomorrow.'

'Hope I haven't bored you.'

'Quite the opposite.'

As he walked back to his apartment, Scot made a mental note of his plans for the morning. He'd place the money in a safe deposit box, then ring the developer or agent for the villa in Kakopetria. He rather hoped it had already been sold. It would save a lot of trouble.

Finally, he'd make contact with the Russian businessman Kareem had recommended.

10

Boris Bragonov rose from the chair behind his large wooden desk, and reached across and shook Scot's hand firmly and for some time. 'So you acquired my name from Ahmad Kareem?'

'Yes, he thought you could help me decide if a villa was suitable for him. It's in the mountains, very near Kakopetria.'

'I could certainly be of assistance, but it may well transpire that it would be better for Mr Kareem to be looking for property in the hills above Limassol. It would be more convenient to night life, and beaches.'

Bragonov spoke with a heavy inflection, and the hint of an American accent, which was probably the result of watching Hollywood films.

The Russian and Cyprus flags were hanging from lacquered poles behind the desk. Between them were two framed photographs, one of former Russian President Boris Yeltsin, and the other of the current President of Cyprus. 'There is no picture of the current Russian President,' Scot observed.

Bragonov merely threw his head back and flared a nostril with distain.

Much of the Russian's life story was depicted in photographs displayed around the room. Bragonov was photographed being presented with a scroll by a man in an academic gown, another pressing very heavy weights in a gym, another standing by an oil rig, and yet another with a small group of men in combat uniforms, with semiautomatics slung over their shoulders and skolling small glasses of spirit.

'In Chechnya 1995 … we'd had a very good day on the streets,' the Russian said. 'We made a lot of progress against the terrorists.'

Pointing to the picture of Bragonov standing by the rig, Scot said: 'So you worked in the oil industry?'

'It was my life.'

On the desk there was a picture of a youngish blond woman in a bikini on a beach. 'My girryell.'

'Your girryell?'

'My girryellfriend at Governor's Beach.'

'Oh, your girlfriend … She's very beautiful.' Scot felt a tinge of embarrassment at having missed the pronunciation, but some of Bragonov's speech made him feel he'd somehow wandered on to the rehearsal stage of a Russian revival of *Guys and Dolls.* And, as he looked at the Chechnya picture again, he realised he wasn't with a Salvation Army character.

Scot explained to the Russian what Kareem wanted: something isolated in the mountains with four bedrooms, two with their own bathrooms, and a swimming pool.

'The developer is meeting us at the house,' Bragonov confirmed. 'Let's go, we'll take my car.'

On the street outside the office, the Russian activated his keys and the lights flashed on a late model black Toyota Land Cruiser, with heavily tinted windows. 'The sun is too bright here,' Bragonov said, explaining the windows.

After winding out of Limassol, they reached the main mountain road and Bragonov hit the button on the CD player. Heavy disco music came from the stereo speakers.

It ruled out any conversation, and that suited Scot. It gave him time to speculate about the Russian. The distain shown for the current Russian leadership, and the continued admiration for Yeltsin, inevitably led to the idea that Bragonov had been a beneficiary – either directly or indirectly – of Yeltsin's massive privatisation of Russian industry – including much of the oil industry. The Russian appeared about forty, but could have been older. He was muscularly fit, and wore an expensive lightweight suit, which had a subtle sheen to its fabric. He had a full crop of black hair groomed with gel.

The heavy incline of the mountain road, and the frequent curves, were no impediment to speed. Bragonov ignored the speed-limit signs and they reached the villa in just under an hour.

A late model silver Mercedes coupé had its nose into the drive leading to the house, and two older dented cars were parked beside the road. 'He's showing some others the house,' Scot said.

'Cousins.'

Scot looked at the Russian quizzically.

'They all do it, these Cyprus developers. They get their cousins and others along so real buyers think there's a lot of interest. It's stupid because everyone knows they're relatives.'

The developer was showing the people to the door, and gestured to Scot and Bragonov to enter. 'You're right on time, and I'm sure you'll be impressed.' He was neatly dressed in cotton slacks and a striped short-sleeved shirt, and clutched a mobile, which almost immediately rang.

'Excuse me one minute.'

'Another trick,' Bragonov said. 'Probably one of the people who've just left.'

The developer spoke in English into his phone. 'Yes, I'm at that property right now. Yes, there's a great deal of interest.' Then he went silent as he listened. 'Well, I really have to get back to Limassol, but if you promise you'll be here within an hour, then I'll wait.' He closed the phone and looked towards Scot and the Russian. 'Sorry about that.'

They looked around inside before heading for the veranda. 'It's a pity there's no furniture. It's difficult to judge the size of the rooms,' Bragonov said. 'Empty, it gives a feeling of coldness. I'm shivering just looking.'

'But the rooms *are* a good size, and the view of the mountain is dramatic,' Scot said.

The Russian glared at Scot. 'Rooms, well, yes and no … And I'd prefer a sea view.'

'Oh, I have plenty of other properties with sea views,' the developer said.

'I'm sure you do,' Bragonov said. 'The market is flooded.'

The developer said it would be simple to install a swimming pool at the edge of the granite-paved veranda. 'I've spoken to the builder, and he said it would be simple. The pool could be ready in three months.'

'And what is the price?' Bragonov asked.

The developer quoted an amount.

The Russian expressed incredulousness by way of slow deliberate laughing. 'Well, I think my time has been wasted.'

The developer asked how much he believed the property was worth.

'Well, at a guess, I'd say about half what you quoted.'

'I've obviously been wasting my time too,' the developer said firmly before turning to Scot. 'You like the house, though, I can tell that.'

Scot nodded half-heartedly. 'There wouldn't be any problem with the title deed to the property? The deed would be handed over at the time of purchase?'

Scot was alluding to a problem faced by thousands of Cypriots and foreigners – particularly British – who'd bought property on Cyprus, handed over the payment, but had failed to get the title deeds. They'd been lodged with banks by builders and developers as collateral for a loan to do further developments.

'The deed to this property is safely locked away in my office safe,' the developer said.

It was the Russian's turn. 'In the unlikely event our client, our acquaintance, decided the property was suitable and the negotiated price satisfactory, the deed would have to be handed over at the time payment was made.'

The developer nodded.

'Otherwise the consequences could be severe.' Then, rather menacingly, Bragonov added: 'Any developer who failed to hand over the deeds to me wouldn't have a life worth living ... But I'm sure you're honest – or honest enough.'

Scot changed the subject, and addressed the developer. 'I'll email my impressions to Baghdad today, and get a response. Then I may contact you.'

'Well, don't delay too much. There's a lot of interest,' the developer said, shaking Scot's hand. He failed to even farewell Bragonov.

As they drove back to Limassol, Boris Bragonov said: 'It could be suitable for Kareem. It seems to be rather well built, and it does have a pleasant view.'

With dusk descending, there was a heavy knock on Scot's apartment door. It was Dimitri.

'I've had a call from Mustafa Rasool in Aleppo ... Alexander's missing.'

'What? Missing? Tell me slowly what's happened. Slow down, Dimitri.'

'He arrived yesterday, okay? Even rang me last night to see how I was managing. He'd seen Rasool, and was due to go to see him again this morning, and have lunch. But Mustafa Rasool says he never arrived.'

'Where's he staying?'

'The Baron Hotel.'

'Just across the road from Rasool's office, so he'd hardly get lost.'

'Can you help? Maybe you could ring Rasool. Alex told me you saw him just the other day, and that I should speak to you if he got out of touch ... I'm so busy at the restaurant. It's the worse time of day for us at Club Downtown, preparing dinner.'

Scot looked at his watch. It was 6.30 p.m. 'It may have to wait until the morning. I don't have his home number.'

Dimitri handed Scot a piece of paper torn out of a notepad. 'This is it.'

Scot looked at the number. 'Okay, I'll try and reach him. Have you tried the hotel?'

'No.'

'Look, I'll see what I can find out, and call you ... No, I'll call around for a drink. But don't worry too much. These things happen.'

Dimitri looked far from convinced as he opened the door to leave. 'You will let me know if you hear anything?'

Scot nodded.

Dimitri forced a smile and left.

Scot took a beer to the balcony. The familiar scene of tourists plying the footpaths and boats coming back into shore was reassuring. The scene further lessened the slight concern he had for Alex. People changed plans, missed appointments. He went over what Dimitri had said. 'I should speak to you if he got out of touch ...' Did Alex expect to get out of touch, go missing?

Scot hurried to the telephone, and dialled the Baron Hotel and asked to speak to Alexander Belfort-Smith.

'Not present in the hotel,' the receptionist said immediately. So quickly in fact, it was as if she didn't need to check. She'd tried before.

'Could you connect me to his room.' Scot spoke slowly, clearly, to avoid misunderstanding.

'If you wish, but Mr Belfort-Smith is not present. I know for certain.'

The phone rang unanswered.

So Scot tried Rasool's home number. The phone rang and rang and he was about to give up. Then finally it answered. *'Na'am?'*

'Na'am ... Ana Scot *men Qubros,'* said Scot exercising his extremely limited Arabic.

'Aaah, Scot, my friend ... I think we'll speak English.'

Scot got straight down to business. 'There's some problem with Alexander, it seems?'

'It is not good news. He's missing.'

'I just rang the hotel and he's not there.'

'I know that. I've been across at the Baron more than three times, but there's no sight or sound of him.'

'But you saw him yesterday?'

'He came to my office after he'd checked in at the hotel. He was returning to my office at 11.30 this morning. I was going to take him to the restaurant we went to, but he didn't arrive.'

'Maybe he changed his plans?'

'Without telling me? No, I don't think so. Because ... because, the third time I visit the hotel, I asked if we could look in his room. I know the manager, of course, and he was most helpful.'

'And?'

'And his bags were in the room, but Alexander wasn't. The bed didn't look as if it had been slept in at all.'

Scot fell silent, thinking.

'Still on the line Scot?'

'Yes, I'm just wondering what could have happened. You have very good contacts, do they know anything?' Scot deliberately flattered the Syrian in a bid to coax his maximum cooperation.

'So far I've not been able to discover anything. But two people are helping me, and they are asking other people, and say they'll ring me back with or without any concrete information.'

'When do you think they'll do that?'

'Maybe anytime, tonight or in the morning.'

'Police?'

'My friend is the Chief of Police in Aleppo. He's investigating, but for him a lot of people go missing so I'm not too hopeful. It's not like a murder with blood and guns or like a car accident with a smashed car and bodies. It's difficult for him to investigate because there is no evidence.'

'Yes, I understand what you're saying, but someone must have seen him after he left you.'

'I know, I know, and the police chief knows that too. Believe me it's a big worry because we haven't found anyone who saw him. Like you say in English, it seems he disappeared into thin air.'

Scot hesitated before going on, acutely aware Syrian security authorities could be listening, bugging the line. Scot guessed Rasool could be on the *mukhabarat*'s internal security list. 'Remember our conversation at the restaurant? About what your friends said about the English girl?

'I remember,' Rasool said discreetly, cautiously.

'Do you think your friends would know something?'

'I've been thinking about that too and I have made the arrangements. Understand?'

'I understand,' Scot said.

'You must be patient. Things take time. Maybe I'll have better news in the morning, *inshallah*.'

'Yes, God willing.'

Scot thanked the Syrian, and was about to hang up when the inevitable question came. 'So you went to Larnaca and visited my friend?'

'It's all under control,' said Scot vaguely as he put the phone down.

Scot wandered back to his beer on the balcony. He would gather his thoughts before going to see Dimitri. What would he tell him? If anything, what he'd learnt from Rasool reinforced Dimitri's concern. Scot didn't want to be alarmist, but his hopes that there would be some perfectly rational explanation seemed to be fading. Rapidly. Piecing together Alexander's advice to Dimitri if 'out of touch' plus his thirst for brandy – and his frankness – the night before he left, Scot wondered if the Englishman had experienced some kind of premonition, or knew danger was looming. He'd certainly been squaring the books with Scot. Even the newspaper story – the rocky beginning of their relationship – had been 'a great help'. That was a big change from Alexander's attitude the first time they'd met face to face outside the unfinished Club Downtown.

And Scot had another thought about the people who'd told Rasool that Debbie London had been too inquisitive about guns and drugs. Had Rasool told them Alexander was going to Aleppo? If they'd thought Debbie may have been an 'agent of British imperialism', they could have thought Alexander was too.

Scot realised it wouldn't be too surprising. After all, a similar idea had crossed his mind when he'd met Alexander in Kakopetria by chance with the two Americans. Hopefully, Rasool hadn't passed on

Alexander's plans. Then, perhaps, one line of enquiry could be eliminated.

He finished his beer, stubbed out his cigarette, and headed around to Club Downtown. Dimitri met him at the door and asked immediately: 'Any news? Good news I hope!'

'I spoke to Mustafa Rasool and he's looking into matters very carefully. We're hopeful,' said Scot, not wanting to further alarm the Cypriot. After being seated at his usual table, Scot spoke about Rasool having involved the police, and asking his contacts to help. But he didn't mention Alex hadn't appeared to have slept at the hotel last night.

'Well, thank you,' Dimitri said. 'At least you're a friend of Mustafa Rasool. I've met him, but he'll do everything he can for you. I'm sure.'

Scot wondered, and nodded the touch of a smile.

Stumbling to the balcony for a hit of nicotine early the next morning, Scot got an ominous warning. Not far out to sea, a pirate ship was proudly flying a skull and crossbones ensign. He'd seen the boat along the coast at the port of Paphos, but never off Limassol before. The symbolism of its presence was more real than its purpose. For the ship had no hostile intentions other than persuading children to hijack their parents into paying for a day cruise. It focused Scot on Alexander's disappearance.

The phone rang. Thinking it was too early for any news from Aleppo, he stubbed his cigarette out slowly, and ambled back inside to the phone.

'Good morning, Scot. Didn't wake you I hope?' It was Mustafa Rasool.

'No, no, any news?'

'A development, yes. My close friend the Chief of Police has just telephoned. They have spoken to a man who thinks he saw a foreign man being – what you say? – pushed into a car the night before last.'

'Where?'

'In Baron Street, maybe about two hundred metres from the hotel.'

'You mean pushed against his will?'

'Against his will of course, otherwise the police wouldn't be interested. The police chief wouldn't have telephoned me!' Rasool hesitated before adding: 'Scot, it's very grim news ... It must have been Alexander.'

'Your friend the police chief thinks the witness is reliable?'

'Of course.'

Scot asked Rasool whether he'd any leads from other contacts. It was too early, the Syrian replied.

'I've got to go to Nicosia today, so I'll call you later. Thanks for ringing.'

Scot wandered back to the balcony. Analysing Rasool's information, he wondered about its importance. By foreign, what did the witness mean? There were so many tourists and traders in Aleppo, it didn't mean much. He assumed the witness meant European, but even that didn't mean Alexander. And what was Rasool's relationship with the police chief? He thought of his own experience in Aleppo and of the $20,000 in the safe deposit box, and guessed the worst. The police chief could be a 'very good friend' because he turned a blind eye when it suited. And what did he get in return? If he got a regular stipend from Rasool, he'd be sure to come up with information when Rasool reported a missing person. If this was correct, then the witness may not even exist, or be a toady interviewed in such circumstances.

Scot accepted he was being a touch cynical, but he'd avoided a fine for running a red light in Damascus once by giving a policeman just one cigarette. Friendliness, it had been, rather than bribery. But others could interpret it as more sinister – a symptom of police corruption.

He decided against passing on Rasool's news to Dimitri. It would alarm him.

After showering, he decided to pick up a newspaper from a shop along the road, and have coffee and a croissant at a table on the pavement. A short story of just a couple of paragraphs on the world news pages of *The Times* reported that American and British aircraft had been in action again against Iraqi defence installations in the north of the country. The item sparked more speculation about the claim Debbie may have been a spy. For many Kurds their saviour – their survival even – had been American and British enforcement of a no-fly zone in northern Iraq for more than ten years following the 1991 Gulf War. If it hadn't been for 'American and British imperialism' the Kurds would never have had their own administration over a large chunk of northern Iraq. Scot thought that if he were a Kurd, he might even welcome an agent of British imperialism. But the Kurds still depended upon Iraq for trade – mainly the business of trucking oil through their region to world markets. And Iraq certainly wasn't a friend of 'British imperialism'. The Brits and the Americans could easily get in the way of arms and drug deals. Rasool would be the only person to know the identity of his contacts – and he'd be unlikely to share the information.

Every thought about Mustafa Rasool sparked another. He must try and ring the woman in Larnaca, before driving to Nicosia. He had another cigarette and finished the coffee, before heading up to the apartment. The woman's phone just rang and rang. Perhaps he should

have invested the money! The morning sun was very hot
and the car uncomfortable before the air conditioning took
over. He wound along the narrow streets away from the
sea, before entering the motorway to Nicosia. Looking at
his watch, he knew he was in plenty of time for his
meeting at CYTA – the Cyprus Telecommunications
Authority – in their building quite near the old Ledra
Palace Hotel on the Green Line dividing the city. He
wanted a second telephone line, and thought it would be
best to go and see an old friend at the authority's
headquarters. As that meeting should last little more than
half an hour, he tossed up whether to head straight back to
Limassol, or talk to a contact at the British High
Commission about Alex's disappearance.

After the meeting at CYTA, he called the High
Commission on his mobile. His contact, Matthew York,
was out so he rang Sophie, his wife, who said Matthew
had had to go to the 'other' side – the Turkish occupied
area – of the island, and wouldn't be back until around 4
p.m. 'But we'd love to see you … Are you staying the
night?' The welcoming tone of her voice, plus the solitary
nature of his life in Limassol, prompted Scot to say 'yes'.
He would stay at the Nicosia Grand on Makarios Avenue.

After showering for dinner, Scot rang Aleppo, but
there was no news. So, he telephoned Dimitri on the off
chance Alex had telephoned, but he hadn't. The voice on
the other end was really down. So Scot said hopefully: 'I
have spoken to Mustafa Rasool twice today, and he's
chasing things that end. I'm also having dinner with a
senior man from the British High Commission tonight.
The Brits have real clout in Syria, and top contacts. So
look after yourself and hang in there.'

Dimitri mumbled 'thanks'.

As he drove to the Aegean restaurant, Scot wondered whether he'd been right not to tell Dimitri about the police witness. If he were Dimitri he'd be furious if he learnt the whole truth hadn't been passed on. He vowed to fill the Cypriot in fully once he got back to Limassol.

Evening traffic slowed Scot's approach to the ancient moat, and he turned right into the street skirting the old city. Nicosia's Venetian walls looked magnificent, the floodlights giving them a warm orange tinge. He entered the walls at the Famagusta Gate, and searched for the road to the restaurant. Taking a wrong turn, the car was halted by a barricade close to the city's dividing line. Not twenty metres away and just the other side of a narrow lane, Turkish soldiers could be patrolling. Eeriness pervaded the dimly lit and sparsely inhabited area. It was around 8.45 before he found the restaurant.

Through the heavy doors, most of the candlelit tables in the courtyard were taken. Amidst the crowd, Scot found Matthew and Sophie York, their fair hair standing out, the candlelight giving them a casual youthfulness.

'Good to see you,' he greeted them.

There was a bottle of Cyprus white wine on the table, and Matthew filled a glass for Scot.

'This is lovely, seeing you,' said Sophie.

'How's life in Limassol?'

Scot hadn't intended to broach the subject of Alexander's disappearance until later, but Matthew's question provided an opportunity.

'Well great, but something rather disturbing has happened. You know Alexander Belfort-Smith don't you?'

Although the *outing* had predated their arrival at the High Commission, they knew the story inside out especially as he'd returned to the island and opened a restaurant.

'As a matter of fact, we ate at Club Downtown maybe six weeks ago,' said Matthew.

'The music was great,' Sophie noted.

'Well, it seems he's gone missing in Aleppo.'

Scot's bombshell dumbfounded Matthew and Sophie. Scot filled them in on all the details – including the story of the 'alleged' police witness – but was vague about his source. The British High Commission didn't need to know that the self-confessed shifty businessman Mustafa Rasool, with dubious links to Baghdad, was an associate of Scot Wallace.

'It sounds extremely serious. I'll pass this on to the High Commissioner first thing. Although – as you say – there may be some perfectly rational explanation, we'll see if the embassy in Damascus knows anything, and London of course.'

Sophie had been silent, just digesting Scot's account of the disappearance. Then she spoke, albeit cautiously. 'You don't think he may have latched on to a boyfriend?'

The idea had initially occurred to Scot, but he'd discounted it on the basis it depended upon a simplistic stereotype of gays.

It was Matthew, however, who gently rebuked his wife. 'Typical explanation of a red-blooded hetero woman!' Scot could see Sophie reacted well to the description. 'You think that because Alexander is gay, he arrives in Aleppo randy as hell, driven to suss out a local gay meeting place, and disappears for a few days with a totally new boyfriend!'

'Well, heterosexual men do it all the time with new women!'

Both Scot and Matthew accepted her counter bid to a point, but Matthew mustered a comeback. 'They don't usually disappear for a few days!'

It was about midnight before they finished their coffees, split the bill, and wandered towards their cars.

'I'll ring when I hear something from Damascus or London,' Matthew said as they parted.

As Scot drove back towards the hotel, he envied Matthew and his 'red-blooded hetero woman'. He was destined to end up alone in a double bed.

11

After a breakfast of poached eggs and bacon, Scot settled back on the hotel balcony chair and looked beyond the hotel swimming pool and across the city. Sipping coffee, he looked towards the Turkish flag – assembled from hundreds of rocks – on the distant hills. It was a constant reminder to Greek Cypriots that the Turkish army occupied a third of their island.

After the dinner with Matthew and Sophie York, he'd slept longer than planned, but – looking at his watch – still had time to go to the supermarket near the walled city before checking out. The store had imported delicacies he could never find in Limassol.

The supermarket was almost empty, and Scot gathered his food and a cask of French red wine in a plastic basket and headed to the checkout. He stood behind a man of Arab appearance with a box of spirits. He was wearing a straw hat. As some bottles were gin and others whisky of different brands, the check-out attendant had to lift each bottle out of the box and scan them individually. Finally, the man paid with a Visa card.

'Thank you Mr Belfort-Smith,' the attendant said as the customer hurriedly left the store. Scot looked down to see the credit card slip still being processed by the cashier. The signature was clear: 'A. Belfort-Smith'.

Scot quickly paid and rushed out. But he was too late. The man was already in a car speeding down the street.

Just after 11.45 a.m. as Scot approached the hotel reception to settle his account, he saw the dark-haired man from the supermarket entering the lobby through the revolving door. There was no straw hat, but it was the same man. To avoid being noticed, Scot glanced along the corridor towards the newspaper shop where a cluster of men in red, yellow and blue racing suits were greeting each other. It must have been the annual Cyprus car rally.

His eyes drifted back to the lobby, where the man from the supermarket had greeted a blond woman of around thirty wearing black leather jeans and sporting a blue T-shirt. Scot dialled the British High Commission on his mobile, but Matthew was out, and the receptionist didn't know when he'd be back. There wasn't even a vague resemblance between Alexander, and this apparent imposter. The woman looked a lover rather than an acquaintance, and was dressed for appearance and air conditioning rather than the 35C degree heat outside.

Scot spoke softly to the hotel manager behind reception. 'Do you know that man?'

The hotel manager followed the line of Scot's pointing finger. 'With the woman … Yes, Mr Wallace, like you he's a good client of ours … From Syria, I believe.'

'Really?'

The manager looked at Scot with a slightly cocked head and quizzical look as if expecting more.

Scot lowered his voice further. 'This might sound silly, but I think I just saw him using a stolen credit card … a card belonging to a friend of mine.'

'I don't think so, Mr Wallace. Mr Hussein is an important businessman, I believe.'

Scot looked away wondering how much further he could take the matter. He'd been obsessed with Alexander's disappearance for days now, perhaps too obsessed. There was a touch of irony about the situation. Except to total strangers, Mr Hussein couldn't pass himself off as Alexander Belfort-Smith. For not only would he have had to change his appearance, but his sexual orientation too. Scot followed the couple to the bar, and settled at a discreet distance at a table overlooking the swimming pool.

A waiter arrived and Scot ordered a beer. 'How is sir this morning? Nice day for a swim.'

Scot nodded without thinking, then, as an afterthought, pointed to the man and woman. 'Do you know if that man's name is Belfort-Smith? Think I've seen him some-where.'

With a smile creeping across his face, the waiter replied: 'Doesn't look very Belfort-Smith to me.'

'You don't know him then?'

'Never seen him before.'

So the man was known to the hotel, but clearly not that well. As Scot focused on the pair, he'd a feeling he'd seen the woman before, somewhere. She was strikingly and sensually attractive. And Scot was lonely. So he wondered if his feeling of recognition was a trick of the mind and nothing more than wishful thinking.

The Nicosia Grand in the sun-drenched Cypriot capital was one of Scot's favourite hotels. Although he lived just a little over an hour's drive away, he took the excuse to stay whenever in Nicosia on business. The hotel was a centre of hubbub in the divided city. It was not that he'd ever picked up much gossip at the hotel, but rather it was where politicians and spies from around the Levant were said to gather. There was an air of mystique. It was a reputation the management seemed to have no interest in discounting. It was good for business, even if the reputation was exaggerated. In the old days – before Turkey's 1974 invasion of northern Cyprus – the Ledra Palace Hotel would have been the place to meet and be seen. But that hotel was right on the green line dividing the Greek and Turkish sides of the city and occupied by the United Nations. So in the rush of post-war development on the Greek side of the city, the Nicosia Grand had won the race to be the centre of lavish social life – and intrigue.

Scot left his beer and walked briskly to the concierge. He asked if he could page 'Alexander Belfort-Smith'.

'Give me a couple of minutes, Mr Wallace.'

Scot returned to his table hurriedly, and sipped at his beer and nibbled nuts as he glanced across the bar to the couple. The man had his arm wrapped around the woman's lower back and his thumb tucked into her leathers just below her belly button. Her lips were leaning out to him, and Scot – feeling something of a voyeur – wondered why they didn't go off and just do it. Why wait for lunch?

The answer came soon enough. Another man, of Arab appearance, neatly dressed in a lightweight grey suit and tie matching the bright blue of the woman's T-shirt joined them. The men talked intensely and the one named Hussein released his arm from the woman's waist. After a couple of minutes or so, both men slapped each other's hands elaborately. The woman gave both men a look of puzzled admiration. Some deal or stroke of intrigue appeared to have been concluded.

A young man dressed in a porter's uniform, walked into the bar carrying a blackboard chalked 'Alexander Belfort-Smith'. He rang a small bell drawing attention to his board. The woman and two men at the bar looked towards the blackboard, the woman and the man who'd joined them, glanced away. But the focus of Scot's attention appeared to do a double take as he looked at the name before rejoining the others in conversation. Scot drew no concrete conclusions, but it was enough to demand some action. Paying the waiter, he returned to reception, where by now another manager was on duty.

'I think a man at the bar has used a stolen credit card. Call the police.'

'At the bar he used the card?'

'No, at a supermarket. I'm almost certain.'

'You told the supermarket?'

'No, I was in a rush to follow him and he sped off.'

'The car number?'

'It went so fast I couldn't get it.'

'But you're certain, Mr Wallace, it's the same man?'

'Almost certain.'

The manager looked at Scot in bemused disbelief. 'The police are very busy people. I think they may want you to be completely certain.'

Scot nodded, and turned away towards the entrance. The two men and the woman from the bar were leaving the hotel and getting into a taxi. 'That's the man, he's leaving.' The taxi pulled away.

The manager looked at Scot patiently, as if testing all his rehearsed skills in customer relations. 'I think it's too late to call the police, sir.' Then he returned to the tried and proven script. 'But we certainly hope to see you again, Mr Wallace.'

Scot headed for the car park. It was time to return to Limassol. He retrieved some change from his pocket as a tip as a porter loaded the bags into the car boot. As he steered the car out into Makarios Avenue and towards Limassol, he thought the woman in leathers was possibly Russian for the only English she'd uttered had been fluent, but accented. As his mind drifted to Alexander, he suddenly recalled where he'd seen her before. It hadn't been wishful thinking after all. It was at The Mill Hotel in the mountains. He remembered it clearly now. He'd been sitting at the next balcony table, when she'd doused her lunch companion with a glass of water. The companion had stormed off. Alexander had been in the same village at the same time with the two mysterious Americans.

Back in Limassol, Scot mulled over events in Nicosia. Events were happening so fast, it was time to tell Dimitri about the police witness. On his way to the Club Downtown, he called at the post office where a large manila envelope with Italian stamps was waiting. It contained a brief letter from Kareem and a power of attorney document.

I authorise you and Mr Boris Bragonov to pay a deposit on the purchase of the villa you have identified as suitable for me near the Cyprus village of Kakopetria. You will have already received money sufficient for the deposit. At your convenience you are authorised to complete the purchase. I thank you for discovering the house, and I am sure I shall enjoy staying in it when the time comes.

The attached legal document appointed 'Mr Scot Wallace, Australian, of Limassol, and Mr Boris Bragonov, citizen of Russia, of Limassol, as Power of Attorney, both jointly and severally, to act on my behalf for a period of one year'. There were two sheets to the document. The original was in Arabic, and there was a copy in English. Both were witnessed by two people and both sheets were stamped with the round blue stamp of the 'Ministry of the Interior Baghdad'. Scot wondered about the legality of such a document in Cyprus as he walked on to the Club Downtown to brief Dimitri.

The Cypriot listened intently, sadly. With elbows on the restaurant table, fisted hands supported his olive-skinned cheeks. Finally he spoke.

'But we don't know for certain that it was Alexander being "pushed" into the car.'

'No,' said Scot.

'And as you said, the police witness may not be totally reliable.'

Scot nodded slowly, emphasising his own doubts about the evidence.

'Maybe Alex is being cunning,' the Cypriot spoke wishfully. 'Maybe, just maybe, he thought he could find this Debbie London without Mustafa Rasool's help. Maybe he thought Rasool's friends were not going to lead him to the woman.' He gained enthusiasm as he talked. 'He's very fit, and alert, and he knows all sorts of things and tricks because of his army training.' His eyes appeared to sparkle and his mind ticked over. He was on the verge of being positively hopeful.

Scot overrode his own fears for Alex in a bid to be supportive. The Cypriot's hopes – although unlikely – were not out of the question. He had his own doubts about Rasool.

'We'll just have to be patient,' he said.

'Yes, we'll just have to be patient, of course, but I think I am right. Alex is very good at looking after himself.'

Scot thought about the incident at the Nicosia Grand earlier in the day. 'Presumably, Alexander is carrying his credit cards?'

'He just has Visa … I guess he will have it with him. Why?'

'Just wondering.'

'He always carries a lot of cash too. Mainly English pounds.'

'A lot?'

'Maybe a thousand pounds or more. I tell him he carries too much.'

Scot shrugged, thinking that was a drop in the ocean compared with his own recent experience. The music was starting, and Dimitri looked towards the tables by the dance floor.

'Back soon,' he said.

Scot was surprised he hadn't heard from Matthew. It wasn't that he expected the High Commission to have any news just yet, but thought there'd be a call saying he'd passed on the news about Alexander's disappearance. He caught Dimitri's eye and said he was going, but would keep in touch.

Once home, he rang Matthew but there was no answer. Then, drawing a deep breath, Scot dialled Rasool's mystery woman in Larnaca. With little hope he hung on as the phone rang.

Suddenly, a woman's voice said: 'Yes, can I help you?'

12

She appeared demure – almost vulnerable – and nothing like she'd looked at the Nicosia Grand or after she'd thrown a glass of water at The Mill Hotel. But she was the same woman. Scot was sure of that.

She stood at the door of her Larnaca flat in a chic cotton dress and sandals. Dumbfounded, Scot looked without speaking for several seconds, his mind whirring over and over. Then he asked: 'Ana?' The name was almost muted, a consequence of his mouth only just catching up with his surprise at seeing her.

Tilting her head as if cocking an ear, her blond hair falling over her left shoulder, she replied: 'Ana? Yes.' With her left hand, she invited entry and, only as an afterthought checking, 'Mr Wallace, I think?'

'Yes,' said Scot entering the living room, which had a small balcony overlooking the sea. 'I am glad to catch you … I have tried many times,' he added enunciating deliberately.

It clearly wasn't enough. 'Catch me?' she asked with a furrowed brow.

'I mean I have been trying to contact you many times.'

She nodded comprehension, but just enough to underline the point that word selection should be a priority.

'Coffee?'

'Thank you.'

She turned towards the kitchenette, her suntanned legs disappearing behind the bar across the back of the room. But the glimpse, along with her chic girlish sensuality was sufficient to put on hold Scot's well-rehearsed plan to hand over the money as quickly as possible and leave. Breaking the spell of magnetism that glued his eyes, Scot deliberately turned, his briefcase still dangling on his left hand, and shuffled towards the window overlooking the sea.

'You like my view of the seashore?'

'I like it,' Scot said. 'My own apartment in Limassol overlooks the sea ... It also has a view of the seashore.'

'Really and truly?'

Scot echoed the quaintness. 'Really and truly.' Enjoying the encounter, he rebuked himself for having resented the chore of collecting the $20,000 from the safe deposit box. And the cursed obscenities directed at Rasool and Kareem, which had punctuated his drive from Limassol. Things had turned out quite differently, and he was becoming quite grateful to his Aleppo and Baghdad contacts. It was no hassle at all!

Ana indicated towards a chair as she placed the coffee on the square wooden table. Scot helped himself to sugar and stirred the mug before sitting. There was an ashtray holding a spent butt on the table, so he asked: 'Do you mind if I smoke?'

'No, because I do.'

Tapping the briefcase, Scot said: 'Mr Rasool in Aleppo asked me to give you this money.'

'I am sorry to have caused you inconvenience.'

'No inconvenience,' he uttered unnecessarily, fleetingly wondering whether she ever felt she was an inconvenience. 'It's good to put a name to your face.'

'A name to my face?'

'I was sitting at a table next to you at The Mill in Kakopetria and I saw you in the Nicosia Grand.'

Without a word, she looked at him questioningly as if he was something of a voyeur.

'No, it was by chance … You had a problem with a lunch companion.'

'I see, I remember. I thought I'd seen your face also.' Then, either polishing her English, or flirting, she added: 'It's good to put a name to your face.'

'Well, down to business,' Scot said, releasing the catches on the briefcase.

'You carry much money.'

'Not always … It's your money.'

She smiled gently, gratefully.

Scot took the notes from the briefcase and counted the bundles. 'There are ten one-hundred dollar notes in each bundle, and twenty bundles.'

'Where should I keep this money?'

'Somewhere safe … In your bank?'

'I use a bank, but it is occurring to me I shouldn't put so much money in the bank.'

'Cyprus banks are very safe.'

'I know they are… But I am in Cyprus on a tourist visa and I am fearful it may lead to questions.'

'Friends? Maybe friends could look after the money for you?'

'I have friends of course, but maybe it would be difficult for them also.'

Scot held back from suggesting any further solution. Although this was an extension of the task set by Rasool and Kareem, he felt no irritation. Sensuality was soothing. 'Listen,' he said, looking at his watch, then pointing towards the restaurants on the beachfront. 'Maybe you would like a sandwich or something while you think about what to do?'

'I would like that.' She fetched a hessian bag – of a kind used to carry belongings to the beach – from the bar of the kitchenette and stuffed in the dollar bills. She then placed a newspaper on top, and said 'Ready!' in a determined sort of way.

As they walked out of the building towards the long row of restaurants on the wide-paved promenade, Scot asked, 'Which restaurant?'

Without talking, she led the way past the first couple to the first restaurant that had a spare table right beside the palm-tree-lined road dividing the promenade from the beach. 'We shall sit here if you wish.'

'Jellyfish.' He spoke without thinking, perhaps prompted by the tingling feeling emanating from his lower body – a sensation he'd not experienced for a long time.

'What! You like to eat jellyfish?'

'No, it's a saying … If you wish jellyfish.'

She looked at him with genuine puzzlement.

'Fish and jellyfish rhyme, so people – mainly children – some times say "if you wish jellyfish".'

A waiter arrived, fleetingly giving Scot some relief. But only fleetingly. 'We have no jellyfish today, but very good spaghetti or calamari or toasted sandwiches.'

'Maybe a drink first,' Scot said looking initially at the waiter, then towards Ana.

'What are you having?' she asked.

'A beer for me, and you?'

'Same.'

'Carlsberg or Keo?'

'Carlsberg,' Scot said to the waiter.

Looking towards the sea, but thinking of how he'd come to meet Ana, he decided against any questions that might douse the excitement he was feeling. 'Do you eat at these restaurants a lot?'

'From time to time … I like them very much.'

Despite the heat of the sun, a light sea breeze and a sandy coloured awning made the restaurant very comfortable, relaxing. A young boy trying to harness the faltering breeze ran along the beach towing a red kite. When he stopped running, however, the kite plummeted to the sand.

'There must be more wind for a kite,' Ana observed as the waiter returned with a beer and a large bowl of peanuts.

'Have you been in Cyprus long?'

'Three months, but I have been out of the country twice during that time.'

'For your work for Mustafa Rasool?'

'Not only for Mustafa Rasool.'

Avoiding what might appear interrogation, Scot changed the subject. 'What would you like to eat?' He clutched the menu, and leant towards Ana so she could see. As she looked at the menu, she placed a hand gently on Scot's thigh, but he couldn't decide the motive. He assumed the gesture was merely to provide support as she lent. But, at the very least, it indicated she was not physically averse to her new acquaintance! They decided on toasted cheese and tomato sandwiches, and Scot drew the waiter's attention.

'Do you swim in Limassol?' Ana asked.

'Occasionally in a hotel pool, but for the sea I drive beyond Latchi,' he replied.

'I swim here in the early morning just before the sun rises. The sky just above the sea is a brilliant red which turns pink as the sun comes up. I like to swim naked,' she said catching Scot with a wry smile. 'However, here there are too many people later. In the early morning, I share the sea with just one or two old fishing boats, but the fishermen can't see me clearly. I think the water is more clean after the night.'

Scot registered the preference, but didn't comment.

As they ate, Scot cautiously questioned Ana about her background. She was not, as he'd first thought, from Russia, but Serbia.

'As a child we lived in a village in the countryside, but later in Belgrade. I studied political science at Belgrade University.'

'So how did you end up in Cyprus?'

'I like the sun and the sea.'

'Yes, but there are plenty of places in the world with sun and sea.'

'Plenty … But Mr Mustafa Rasool told me how beautiful and free it was on Cyprus.'

'So you have known Mustafa Rasool for some time?' Scot asked the question in a vague sort of way to disguise his intense interest in the answer.

'For some time, yes, but less than one year.'

That was as much as Ana let slip about Rasool. This didn't fuss Scot as he had a feeling he'd see more of Ana. And it wasn't long before the likelihood of that became more certain.

'Do you think you could help me look after the money?'

'Help spend it?'

'No, I'm thinking you maybe have a bank account?'

'Yes.'

'If you could look after half of the money – ten thousand dollars – it would be very helpful.'

The suggestion didn't irritate. It would give Scot an excuse to build a relationship within his lonely world. Nevertheless, he couldn't suppress a laugh about how Rasool and now his 'agent' always wanted to hand back money.

'What's funny? Are you planning to rob me?'

'Of course not. Just, not everyone is so trusting on their first meeting with me.'

She lent over and kissed him on the cheek, and her sparkling eyes locked into his. 'I know you're a good man. I know I can trust you. You didn't forget to bring me the money. Mr Mustafa Rasool must trust you also.'

'Okay.'

After settling the bill, they walked back to her apartment. Having agreed to look after her money, he felt he could ask another question. 'I saw you at the Nicosia Grand yesterday.'

'Maybe.'

'With two men ... in the bar.'

'They are friends of friends. They had just arrived in Cyprus.'

'From where?'

'Syria.'

'Have you known them long?'

'First time I meet them.'

'One said his name was Belfort-Smith, I think.'

She looked at Scot firmly. 'No, not one of them is called Belfort-Smith. They are Syrian, or maybe one is Kurdish, or Iraqi.'

Reaching the apartment building, she reached for the key inside the hessian bag. 'What are their names?'

'Hussein and ... I find it difficult to remember the other's name, but it wasn't anything like Belfort or Smith. I have Hussein's name on a scrap of paper.'

She showed Scot the scrap of paper, and he stared at Hussein's full name closely in a bid to remember it. 'They live in Syria, you say?'

'I think near Aleppo.'

Scot kissed her on the forehead, mainly as a means of thanking her. She returned the kiss, and put an arm across his lower back. She then said slowly: 'It's good to put a name to your face.'

The small talk continued for a while, then Ana led the way to the bedroom and pulled down the blind. Putting her hand gently behind his head, she pulled their lips together, and flipped off her sandals. Furiously they undressed, and fell towards the bed. Their bodies came together. It was as if they'd reinvented satisfaction.

It was late afternoon by the time Scot arrived home to his apartment in Limassol, and the thoughts about Ana that dominated the hour's drive still obsessed him. The light was flashing on the answering machine, so he pressed the play button to learn that CYTA wouldn't be able to install a new telephone line until next week. The delay might have annoyed him in the past, but not today. Nothing could annoy him today! The sea view had always cheered up his down moments, but it looked even better today. His life of loneliness had turned a corner. And even if there were setbacks in the future, Scot felt he'd rediscovered energy and enthusiasm.

He acknowledged, but recklessly dismissed, how little he knew about Ana, and about how quickly their relationship had developed. It would continue for a time at least. He held a $10,000 deposit on that. And he was even thinking more kindly than he'd ever felt about the ogres in his life named Kareem and Rasool. It crossed his mind he'd like to tell them how much he enjoyed doing business with them, but only fleetingly. On the one hand, they might think he was crazy. Or, they easily could have anticipated the development and merely take it as an indication that Scot Wallace was ready for more Machiavellian tasks.

He went over and over the encounter with Ana. Immediate infatuation leading quickly to bed was something that happened in films, but not to real people.

Maybe film writers had it right all along? It was not as if he had made the running, even though he'd been instantly infatuated by her girlish sensuality and suntanned legs. But he hadn't been the one to talk of swimming naked. And it had been Ana who'd made the first physical contact by placing a hand on his thigh. She had kissed him first! He'd just responded! He felt good about that.

Scot thought about how little he knew about Ana, and what she was really doing on Cyprus. Such was his infatuation, it didn't worry him. But that didn't stop him wondering. He knew she was from Belgrade, and had studied political science. But how a political science graduate from Belgrade University had come in contact with a self-confessed shady businessman in Aleppo, he didn't have a clue. And did she know Rasool had Iraqi connections? Maybe, maybe not. The other odd thing was that although Rasool was paying her quite generously, there was no evidence of any work equipment in her apartment. There was no computer, not even a filing cabinet. It was often said the mark of an efficient executive was a tidy desk, but the bareness of Ana's flat took this philosophy to an impossible extreme. He recalled her saying she'd left Cyprus twice since first arriving, but hadn't mentioned where she'd gone. Maybe home to Belgrade? Or maybe she'd just left the country in order to gain an extension to her tourist visa. Because of his feeling towards her, and the rejuvenation she'd inspired in his lonely life, he refused to believe she was a prostitute. Anyway, who's ever heard of a hooker getting a guy she hardly knew to mind ten grand?

The fact she confirmed she'd been the woman Scot had seen at the Nicosia Grand provided more intrigue. In this jigsaw puzzle, he was certainly missing a few pieces – more like half the board! Maybe the men she'd been with were – as she'd said – just friends of friends. Perhaps she'd welcomed them for a friend who was busy that day. But the body language between Ana and at least one of them – the man named Hussein – indicated a more established relationship. She was certainly making him feel at home. Scot recalled her reaction to his suggestion that one of the men was called 'Belfort-Smith'. Her immediate denial had a ring of sincerity and honesty. But she didn't instantly remember their names, and instead had to refer to a piece of paper. Even then, she only had one name.

Scot looked towards his desk. Its untidiness indicated he'd never be judged efficient. Most businessmen, though, didn't deal with the likes of Mustafa Rasool, Kareem and Ana. Their overseas trips weren't to Aleppo and Baghdad, but rather to the sanity of places like London and New York. Their friends and colleagues rarely went missing in places like Aleppo. And if they did, they'd delegate the task of finding them to the head honcho of Human Resources. Scot felt glad he worked alone, even if his desk remained untidy.

The phone rang. 'Scot? It's Richard Jordan … Remember we met in Kakopetria with Alexander Belfort-Smith?'

'Sure I remember you. You're well I hope.'

'I'm well myself, but somewhat concerned about Alexander. I arrived on Cyprus today and staying in Limassol.'

'Yes, it's a real worry.'

'Look Scot, I'm going around to Alex's restaurant to see his partner in about an hour. I'm wondering whether I could tempt you with dinner around 8.30 p.m., and we could exchange notes. By that time I should have had a chance to talk to his partner. His name's Dimitri, isn't it?'

'Yes, Dimitri, that's right. And yes, I'll meet you.'

Scot put down the phone, intrigued the Associate Cultural Attaché at the US Embassy in Athens was on Alexander's trail. He remembered speculating in Kakopetria about Alex and the two Americans. Rick Jordan's phone call underlined his suspicion all three were involved with some kind of intelligence work. Furthermore, Rasool's comments about Debbie London's questions raising suspicions with some of his nameless contacts took his thoughts further along this track. Certainly, Alexander seemed to feel a level of responsibility for Debbie well beyond the accountability a career adviser might feel.

There was a heavy knock on the apartment's front door. It startled Scot, as most visitors rang from the front desk before being admitted to the building. Opening the door, Scot's apprehension increased as he saw the visitor – a motorcycle rider clad in full black leathers and a crash helmet. The helmet's visor was open, and he asked, 'Scot Wallace?'

'Yes,' Scot said hesitantly.

The motorcyclist then removed his helmet and explained he was a courier with a letter from the British High Commission in Nicosia.

Scot breathed a sigh of relief, and with a trembling hand signed the courier's receipt book. 'Thanks very much,' he said as the courier replaced his helmet and returned to the lift.

Closing the door and, with increasing paranoia, he attached the security chain – something he usually neglected. From his desk he retrieved a Sheffield stainless steel letter opener – a gift from Lisa – and removed it from its blue leather sheath. Apart from 'Mr Scot Wallace' and his Limassol address, the white envelope had no other identifying marks. There was no British crest, which usually marked the back of letters from the High

Commission. Inside, however, there was a handwritten note from Matthew on High Commission notepaper:

Dear Scot,
Sorry not to have got back to you sooner. But you can be reassured that we have alerted the embassy in Damascus, and London, about Alexander Belfort-Smith's situation. As yet, we've had no significant feedback, but you can be certain things are being followed up fully and strenuous investigations are in train. As an old friend of ours – and Alex – I've attached a cutting you may be interested in. I beg you to treat it with the utmost discretion, and please never tell anyone you got it from me. Also, I stress the point I have no idea about the accuracy of the information in the cutting. As we have a courier going to Limassol today, I thought I would get it delivered directly to you. Sophie and I really enjoyed seeing you over dinner the other night. Hope you're well, and we must catch up again soon.
Best regards,
Matthew York

The photocopy of the cutting was from a newsletter calling itself *Beirut Underground*. Under a bold tag line 'EXCLUSIVE', the lead article was headed: 'Spies in our midst'.

The first paragraph of the story proclaimed: 'The *Beirut Underground* has secured a confidential list of Intelligence Agents – mainly from European countries and the United States – who operate in Beirut, Syria and the Middle East generally.'

With considerable pomposity, it went on:

This newsletter considers disclosure of the material contained in the following list to be in the public interest. With so many parties and factors threatening the future of Lebanon and the reconstruction and rejuvenation of Beirut in particular, we feel failure to publish the material would be a severe dereliction of duty.

We do not claim the material to be a comprehensive list of agents operating in the area. For obvious reasons, we cannot disclose the source of the material but are confident about its accuracy.

Underneath, there was a list of about thirty names headed: 'The Spy Nest'. They were not in alphabetical order. Some names were identified with the name of an agency, but others were printed without identification. Scot scanned the list, noting a couple of people he had met at various embassy functions. Near the bottom of the list, he noted 'Alexander Belfort-Smith: UK & US Agencies'. He double-checked the list and found no mention of Debbie London. That was something at least.

The masthead of *Beirut Underground* gave no clue to the identity of the publishers. There was no claim on the one page sent by Matthew York that the journal was produced by one of Lebanon's diverse political factions. The only contact information was a post-office box in West Beirut, and the number of a Beirut fax machine. Full identity of the publishers could be on another page of the publication. But that didn't matter much anyway. The point was the list – whether accurate or not – was in the public domain. The circulation – big or small – hardly mattered. Because, if the British diplomatic service had a copy, it could be assumed it would have been seen by

every newspaper editor in Beirut and by the key figures in
every political faction in the city – and probably beyond.
Also, it would be certain that the intelligence agencies of
Lebanon, Syria, Jordan, and Israel had a copy – and
Ankara and Baghdad too.

Scot studied the masthead again. Publication date was
given. It was about six weeks prior to Alexander's trip to
Aleppo. So, there'd been plenty of time for the list to
reach key political players and dubious power brokers in
the area by the time Alexander had checked in at Larnaca
airport en route to Aleppo.

The information didn't help at all with the task of
locating Alexander. In fact it complicated matters as it
strengthened the case – first alluded to by Rasool – that
Alex's disappearance was political rather than a random
abduction and robbery. Matthew had done a favour by
providing the cutting, and Scot assumed he'd not faxed it
to avoid being accused by some small mind within the
High Commission of spreading gossip detrimental to
British interests. Scot scanned Matthew's letter again, and
underlined in his mind the words 'I stress the point I have
no idea about the accuracy of the information'. That was
probably true. Matthew would almost certainly know the
identity of the intelligence officials within the High
Commission itself, but not the names of those operating
outside in clandestine networks.

Scot thought back to his days in journalism. It could be
ten years or so ago, but he remembered another similar list
being published by a small newsletter in Beirut. He
recollected it clearly because he had a friend, who'd been
named in the list. Over a drink, he'd raised the matter with
the friend, who had flatly denied he was a spy and added –
either sincerely or exercising extremely professional
acting skills – 'I just don't know how they came upon my
name'.

This latest list of about thirty names was clearly not exhaustive, and *Beirut Underground* acknowledged that. European countries, including Britain, plus the United States could have many times that number of agents operating in the turbulent area centred on Beirut and Damascus. As well as collecting political intelligence, they'd be involved in surveillance of drug and arms smuggling, money laundering, and chemical and other weapons development. An interesting thing about the list was it didn't include even one name that appeared to be of Arabic or general Middle Eastern heritage. Nor were there any names that appeared to be of Russian or even East European origin. That led to Scot speculating about the source of the list. But it was a mind game hardly worth pursuing.

However, the fact Alexander's name was listed did fascinate Scot. Whoever his spymasters were – if indeed he had controllers – would have assumed that Alexander had a fairly good cover as joint proprietor of the Club Downtown. The thought jolted Scot's memory, and he quickly checked his watch. There were just fifteen minutes before his rendezvous with Rick Jordan.

13

Jordan was alone drinking beer at Scot's usual corner table at Club Downtown. 'Call me Rick, please … You did in Kakopetria and all my friends do. It's only my business card that calls me Richard X. Jordan.'

Dimitri soon emerged from the kitchen area, and greeted Scot with a sullen smile. He handed out menus. 'Drink?'

Scot looked at Rick's beer glass. 'Make it two more beers, thanks Dimitri … You've met Rick Jordan, haven't you? He's a good friend of Alex's'

Dimitri nodded, and Rick said, 'Sure, we've had a good talk, haven't we, Dimitri?'

'Yes, we've talked already.' Dimitri had lost his optimism. The idea that Alexander knew all sorts of tricks and was very good about looking after himself seemed to have disappeared from the Cypriot's psyche. Had Jordan been too intrusive and demanding and knocked the wind out of Dimitri's sails? Or was it that no news was bad news?

'Must say I'm looking forward to eating,' Jordan said. 'Left Athens early, and just had a sandwich on the plane.'

Scot thought of his lunch on the beachside at Larnaca. It seemed a long time ago. 'Feeling a bit the same way.'

Dimitri arrived with the beer, and took their dinner orders. Then they both took a sip, and echoed 'Cheers'.

'Is there some American cultural event on in Cyprus?' Scot asked wryly. 'Or you here just because of Alex's disappearance?'

'Alex is an old friend. Thought the least I could do was come and see if there was some way I could help.'

'Dimitri helpful?'

'Yes and no. I don't know if he knows any more than me.'

A lot less, Scot guessed, thinking of the curious meeting in Kakopetria plus the copy of the cutting from *Beirut Underground* in his shirt pocket. 'Of course there maybe some perfectly rational explanation. Or, he could have been the victim of a random tourist assault and robbery. It does happen, you know.'

Rick took a while to reply. He eyeballed Scot as if assessing whether he was going to get anything of value and honesty, or just how frank he could be with a lone trader with dubious Middle East connections. 'You may be right, there could be a perfectly rational explanation.' Then, after a few seconds of silence, he said, 'But I do wonder. Sure, tourists get robbed everywhere in the world, but they rarely disappear from the face of the earth.'

'I was just putting a hopeful spin—'

'Sure, it would be nice if he just turned up safe and well.'

'So what's your thinking?'

Rick drew a deep breath, and exhaled slowly. He seemed to be assessing how much he could, or should, disclose. 'Maybe, he's been mistaken for someone else. There are plenty of dubious characters and factions operating in Syria and Lebanon, and particularly around the Turkish border with Syria. And they're not too damned diligent about research. In fact some of them border on the careless.'

Avoiding the key facts – or what passed for facts – plus his own assessment that Alex's disappearance was probably intelligence related, Scot said, 'So you think he may have been mistaken for a businessman involved in some trading feud. Or a spy?'

The word 'spy' triggered Rick's eyebrows to lift abruptly. 'Maybe the former ... the business scenario.'

Dimitri arrived with the orders, and Scot ordered a bottle of Cyprus red wine.

They fell silent as they finished their beers, and began eating. Scot guessed the conversation would warm up a little as the dinner progressed. They would have to disclose more to each other for the meeting to be any value. 'You have a family in Athens?'

'Wife, but our kids are studying in the States.'

'You must miss them.'

'We do, of course, but it gives us some more freedom. It takes us back to the days when we were just married.'

'It's time to visit Xanadu maybe?' After the small talk, Scot cut to the chase. 'When did you and Alexander first meet?'

'Well, I'm not sure what year it was but it was in Washington.'

'One of Alex's army colleagues told me he'd worked in some kind of British-American intelligence liaison role when in the US.'

'Not sure what his exact role was, but he was certainly still a serving officer.'

'And you? What was your job at that time?'

'Same as today – the fringes of the State Department.'

'Cultural affairs as now?'

Rick caught Scot's eyes before replying calmly. 'A bit of that, but I was something of a Jack of All Trades ... maybe more correctly a dog's body.'

They were getting somewhere, but slowly. Scot topped up the wine glasses.

'Gather from Dimitri you were in Aleppo recently and have been in touch with this mysterious Mustafa Rasool? What do you make of him?'

Scot thought carefully before replying. 'Well, he's an avuncular style of man, who describes himself jokingly as a "shady trade consultant". I've been to his office opposite the Baron Hotel. It's neat and spick and span, but there's no evidence of what kind of work he carries out and there were no other clients when I visited.'

'So you're a client of his?' Rick's interjection was immediate.

'No, I just had a bit of time to kill in Aleppo so thought I'd call,' Scot lied. 'I'd met him here at this restaurant. It was Alex in fact who introduced us. And in my business, I'm always looking for trading opportunities and building contacts.'

'So Alex knew him quite well?'

'Just as a client of the restaurant, I think. But he certainly saw him in Aleppo the day before he went missing. In fact it was Mustafa Rasool who raised the alarm when Alex failed to turn up for lunch the next day.'

'Yeah, Dimitri said that too. And I've been giving some thought to the fact it was Rasool who raised the alarm. Logically, that rules him out of the frame. He'd hardly play a role in Alexander's abduction and then immediately raise the alarm. Unless—'

'What?'

'It's a long shot and highly unlikely, but I guess there's a chance he could have thought that by immediately raising the alarm, he wouldn't be considered a suspect.'

Scot agreed it was a possibility. 'But I've talked to Rasool a few times on the phone, and get the impression he's doing his best to help. He seems sincerely concerned about Alex.'

Rick nodded. 'Dimitri said something quite confusing about a woman contact of Alex's who's gone missing. What's that about?'

Scot went over the Debbie London saga and Alex's role in getting her a job with an NGO. Then, thinking it might flush out more information from Rick, told the American how at least one of Rasool's contacts had thought she might have been an 'Agent of British Imperialism'.

'Shit! And is she?'

'I wouldn't have a clue.' There was silence again, and Scot noted Rick's eyes staring into the distance as if seriously concentrating. He could almost hear the American's brain ticking over. Scot thought carefully before raising the stakes. He unbuttoned the breast pocket of his shirt, and removed the copy he'd made in his fax machine of the *Beirut Underground* cutting. 'Have you seen this? It was published about six weeks ago.'

Rick reached for his glasses and studied the cutting carefully. Scot couldn't be certain, but the vigilant way he was studying it indicated the American hadn't seen it before.

'Who faxed it to you?'

Scot thought quickly. 'Well, on my way back from Aleppo, I called on an old journalist friend in Damascus and he gave it to me. It was not faxed, my mate copied it in a fax machine.'

Rick seemed to accept the explanation.

'Have you seen it before,' Scot asked, eager to recapture the initiative?

'No ... no one has shown this to me,' said Rick, apparently sincerely. 'But it sure raises the stakes on the whole situation. It looks very serious indeed, even if it's a load of bullshit. There are enough people in Syria and Lebanon – and Turkey for that matter – who'd believe it.'

Scot raised the bar a level higher. 'Is Alex a spy? After all, as I told you, I was once told he'd been involved in intelligence liaison in Washington.'

The American looked Scot straight in the eyes. His cheeks carried a wry smile. 'I don't know, and even if I did, I couldn't tell you.'

'You're like the captain of an American warship unable to confirm or deny whether there are nuclear weapons aboard.'

Rick coughed a half-laugh, but didn't say anything more on the matter. In fact, he broke the cycle of discussion by dividing the remaining wine between the two glasses.

Scot noticed Dimitri approaching and alerted Rick, who turned over the piece of paper. He put his glasses on the blank sheet.

'That was a really great meal, Dimitri,' Rick said. 'You certainly seem to be managing the restaurant okay during Alex's absence.'

'Thanks and I am coping okay.'

Dimitri's cheeks were sagging and for a moment it looked as if he were going to burst into tears. But he recovered, and addressed Scot. 'So have you heard any news? Or do I have to continue to be patient.'

'Well, I heard from my friend at the British High Commission today. And he says the government in London, and the British Embassy in Damascus are working hard on the matter. I think he used the words "strenuous investigations are in train". So we can hope.'

'I'm most certainly hoping. Coffee?'

Scot and Rick nodded yes, and Dimitri left with the plates.

Once Dimitri was out of earshot, Rick said: 'Nice guy, and I understand the difficult position he's in, but there's just one thing I wish he'd agree to help me with.'

'And what's that?'

'Well, I'd like to see Alex's computer ... I don't really want to read his email, just to whom recent emails have been sent. And maybe have a look at what sites have been visited recently. And maybe, his address book.'

Scot thought carefully before answering. He had continued doubts about the American's real job. If Alexander was really involved in intelligence, then he assumed any communication to do with that role would be encrypted somehow, but he couldn't be certain. And the meeting between Alexander and the two Americans in Kakopetria was far from cast-iron proof they were on the same side. 'I can understand his reluctance. Ask Dimitri again, but I don't want to get involved. I'm just a friend, not a professional colleague of Alex's.'

For the first time, Rick turned somewhat cool. 'Shit Scot, every lead is worth pursuing. If I were missing, I'd hope my friends would turn over every God damned stone in an effort to find me.' His word 'friends' was punctuated with a sarcastic explosion of air from his lips.

Scot left a moment of silence before responding in a tone of controlled anger. 'Look, Rick, I want to help, but despite what your business card says, I frankly have never heard of the title "Associate Cultural Attaché". Maybe I've read too many spy novels, but it sounds to me like another word for spy. And in view of the fact it's such a cliché, I wonder if the CIA or other American agencies still use it. Sounds more like something the Russians, or the Libyans, or even the Iraqis would use. The point is who do you work for?'

Rick just stared at Scot, cool as a cucumber. His face didn't get flushed. There was no visible sign that Scot's intemperate words had even penetrated the American's crocodile skin. He just let the staring and the silence continue a little longer, then uttered just two words. 'Quite finished?'

Well, thought Scot, his coolness and lack of reaction indicated that Rick either *was* a spy, or indeed as he claimed, an Associate Cultural Attaché and well used to dealing with stroppy and temperamental artists, musicians, and actors.

Dimitri arrived with the coffee and two balloon glasses. 'The brandy's on the house.'

They both said thanks, as much for breaking the ice as the brandy. After the Cypriot left the table, Rick and Scot engaged in some small talk, before returning to the core issue. Fairly certain Rick and Alex were indeed professional colleagues, Scot said: 'There is something I should mention to you ...'

'And what's that?'

Scot recounted the scene from the Nicosia Grand Hotel. 'I'm not a hundred per cent certain he was passing himself off as A. Belfort-Smith, but I'm pretty sure.'

'Well, that sounds like a lead worth following. Why didn't you tell me earlier?' Rick spoke as he got up from the table and drew a mobile phone from his pocket. 'Excuse me a few minutes, making a call.' He walked halfway towards the front door of the restaurant, then turned back to the table. 'Now Scot, think carefully, have you any idea what the man's name was?'

Scot thought of the name Ana had shown him on a scrap of paper. But what if they really were Ana's friends, or friends of friends? He'd no reason to doubt her and didn't want to betray his new love quite so soon. On the other hand, Alex was a friend, Dimitri was distraught, and Ana was involved with Mustafa Rasool, who seemed to be trying to help with the disappearance.

'Well, I have the name of one man.' He drew a scrap of paper from his wallet.

'How'd you get this name?'

'The man at reception. He said the one named Hussein – the one I think I saw signing the Visa card – was a regular customer of the hotel.'

'You're a gem,' said Rick, patting Scot on the shoulder as he headed out of the restaurant.

After a minute or so, Scot turned to look towards the road, which was quiet now. Rick was standing in the middle of the street animatedly talking into his mobile.

It was about five minutes or so before the American returned. 'Sorry about that. Urgent call.'

'I've been thinking while you were on the phone. Maybe there's something else I should tell you.'

'Go on.'

Scot recounted Alex's demeanour the last time he had seen him. He mentioned the brandy Alex was drinking, and his somewhat emotional state. Also, the affection he was demonstrating towards Dimitri. 'We were sitting right at this table. It was only later that I wondered whether he'd had a premonition that something could go awfully wrong on the trip to Aleppo.'

'You're certainly a slow starter, but you do eventually come up with the goods.' The American thought deeply for a while, nodding just fractionally backwards and forwards. 'Well, I suppose he could have seen that cutting from *Beirut Underground*, or at least have known about it. But I asked Dimitri what kind of mood Alex was in before he left for Aleppo, and he said "Normal".'

'Well, there's quite a bit of stress in running a restaurant. Especially, this one. I gather it doesn't close until two or three in the morning. Maybe Dimitri didn't notice anything unusual.'

'Maybe'.

The music was getting under way, and the late crowd was arriving.

'I'd seen these younger people arriving, and wondered how late the place stays open. You could be right, they'd both be exhausted by closing time.'

'How long are you staying?'

'I assume you mean on Cyprus rather than here. I'm not one for dancing into the early hours ... I'll be here on Cyprus for at least a couple of days. I want to go up and talk to our embassy guys in Nicosia tomorrow, but plan to be back in Limassol tomorrow night. I like the hotel overlooking the sea.'

He signalled Dimitri for the bill, and Scot got his wallet from his shirt pocket. 'No, I'll pay. You've been a great help,' the American insisted. 'Can I keep this newsletter cutting?'

Scot nodded. 'I've got another copy.'

They left the restaurant and stood for a moment on the roadside. Rick had the last word. 'I'll keep you in touch. And just one other thing, I don't work for the Russians, the Iraqis, nor the Libyans.'

14

Scot woke early the next morning, his mind churning over his discussion with Rick Jordan. Although relaxed about having mentioned Alexander's demeanour before leaving for Aleppo, he wondered if he'd done the right thing disclosing the name of the man he'd seen with Ana at the Nicosia Grand. He took his radio to the balcony, and tuned in to the BBC World Service.

It was just before 7 a.m., but tourists were already pacing the footpaths below, enjoying the early morning heat before heading for the beach. Some stopped at the café tables for coffee and breakfast, others walked as if for no reason other than to make the most of their Mediterranean holiday. A young woman power-walker overtook most of the others, clearly determined that fitness as well as leisure and the beach were to be part of her break in the sun.

'BBC World Service,' declared the radio just after the beeps marked the hour. The news reported that the US President had told the UN General Assembly to confront the 'grave and gathering danger' of Iraq, or stand aside while Washington acted alone.

Scot's thoughts were closer to home. He thought more about the two men, one of whose name he'd given to Rick. He tried to persuade himself that if the hounds from the American Embassy and local police managed to track them down, they'd probably get a good hearing. If they had nothing to hide, they'd have nothing to fear. Or would they?

Would it be too early to phone Ana? He looked at his watch, and although it was only 7.20 a.m. decided to ring. She might be difficult to catch later in the day. She sounded glad to hear Scot's voice, but a touch tense.

'Why not come to Limassol for lunch? There are good restaurants near here,' he said.

'Not lunch because I have to work today and that may take until two o'clock in the afternoon.'

'Forget work today.'

'I can't forget about work today, but I could come to Limassol for dinner. I could get there maybe by five o'clock?'

'That'd be great,' said Scot, giving her the address of his apartment and, for added guidance, describing the landmarks nearby. 'But how will you get here?'

'Taxi ... I use them all the time. I'm rich remember?' Her demeanour was lightening just a little.

Putting down the phone, Scot felt rejuvenated for the second day running. Since Lisa's death, he'd felt lonely, but never really sorry for himself. Or that's what he was telling himself now. He returned to the balcony where the radio was still talking, now about the overnight money markets in Europe. He listened to the exchange rates, and then just let the radio ramble on in the background as he prepared for a meeting with Boris Bragonov at the villa developer's office. They were paying a deposit on Kareem's mountain hideaway.

Bragonov pulled up outside the office in his black Land Cruiser right on time.

'There're a couple of things we have to get straight with the developer from the start,' the Russian said in lieu of a greeting. 'First the pool must be finished by the payment date, and the title deed must be handed over right then. Okay? Don't give an inch. These bastard developers say one thing and do nothing. Don't give him the idea we can be played with.'

They were led into a small conference room, with windows overlooking a large car park. There were framed posters of developments under way, and another highlighting – in point form – the dangers of buying property in the Turkish-occupied north of the island. A young woman offered tea or Nescafé. Shortly after drinks arrived, the smiling developer entered.

'Well, you've certainly come just in time,' he said. 'Three buyers telephoned me last night, the last at eleven-thirty p.m. They all wanted to buy the Kakopetria villa. Amazing the interest in that property. I had to tell them all, one after the other, I had a verbal agreement with you two, which I couldn't break.' And he added rhetorically, rather foolishly: 'Can you believe that?'

'No,' Bragonov replied.

The developer was less than happy with Kareem's power of attorney document, which was not unexpected. 'But I have a way around this, so as not to disappoint you by cancelling the sale.'

'Yes?' Bragonov's eyes bore into the developer.

'I am thinking I shall take the deposit today, a little bit more than normal because of the risk I'm facing, and temporarily put the property in three names – Ahmad Kareem, Scot Wallace and Boris Bragonov. This will be a temporary measure.'

Scot and Bragonov swapped glances, verging on glares.

'I have with me a Cyprus power of attorney document my lawyer has prepared,' the developer went on. 'Once you have Mr Kareem's signature upon the document, with witnesses, the final sale documents can be prepared transferring the property to Ahmad Kareem.'

'But—'

Bragonov lifted his right hand and halted Scot's sentence.

The developer went on: 'Otherwise, it might transpire Mr Kareem will find himself on Cyprus earlier than expected, and in which case he can sign the documents in person.'

'What about the pool?' Bragonov asked.

'Nearly completed.'

'Deeds?'

The developer looked at the Russian with a confident smile. 'All in train.'

'Meaning?'

'The deed will be handed over on the day the contract is exchanged and final payment made.'

Bragonov scribbled an imaginary signature on the palm of his left hand, and directed Scot: 'Cheque.'

Reluctantly, Scot wrote a cheque for the deposit, and they all shook hands.

Back in the Land Cruiser, Scot asked: 'How are we going to get Kareem's signature on this new power of attorney document?'

'I will. Today if you like. We do it all the time.' He then guffawed. 'It's my business, and I am very good at it.'

Scot didn't ask anymore. He didn't want to know.

By 4 p.m. Scot was impatiently waiting for the last hour to pass before he'd see Ana. The sun was burning the balcony, so he made himself some tea and kept himself busy at the desk cutting relevant business stories out of a pile of newspapers and filing them in an unmethodical and disorganised way. He then checked the yellow in tray on his desk marked 'URGENT ACTION' and was able to dump more than half the pile, which was at least six months old. The files, sheets of paper, newspaper cuttings and scribbled notes stuffed into the waste bin no longer seemed to fit the in tray's description.

Just after five o'clock the security phone from Nikos's desk rang. Shortly afterwards, there was a gentle knock on the door, and he greeted his new friend with a kiss on both cheeks. She smiled affectionately, but looked exhausted.

'You found the flat without any trouble, obviously?'

'No trouble at all but I'm very glad to be here ... with you!'

'You work too hard.'

'My work is not too hard, but it's difficult. But let's forget about that. Let's not talk about my work. Distract me ... Tell me news about Limassol.'

'I don't think I mentioned my friend Alexander Belfort-Smith who's gone missing in Aleppo?'

'No, the only time that you ever mentioned the name Belfort-Smith was when you thought one of the men in Nicosia was named Belfort-Smith.'

Scot noticed they were no longer her friends, or friends of friends, but just 'the men'. Significant? He recounted Alexander's story. She seemed genuinely concerned, and listened carefully to every word. 'You should get Mustafa Rasool to help. He knows everyone in Aleppo. He's very kind, he could help.'

Scot explained Rasool was on the trail. 'How did you first meet Mustafa?'

She hesitated for a while, before looking straight at Scot. 'My father was killed during the NATO – American – bombing of Belgrade. He was not a target I am sure because a shoe repairer is not a big political threat to the power of NATO. Unless they thought they could destroy Milosevic if all the people in Belgrade had broken shoes,' she said. 'He was on the wrong pavement at the wrong time when a bomb struck a building near to him.'

Scot frowned sympathy. 'Awful.'

'Awful, yes,' she said. 'So awful that after the funeral I decided I was going to leave Belgrade for a while and see the world, or a little bit of it. But I didn't want to go to European countries because they'd sent the bomb, so I travelled towards the Middle East, through Bulgaria and Turkey to Syria ... where, with very good chance I met Mustafa Rasool. I was standing outside the Hotel Baron and thinking about whether or not I had enough money to go inside and have a coffee in the beautiful place. I think it has much history, and Mr Rasool has told me so.'

Scot nodded, remembering Rasool saying Syria had too much history for anyone to remember.

'As I had been travelling all night in a bus I think I looked tired and very poor. Mr Rasool was unloading big boxes of cigarettes out of a taxi, and he asked me if I would like a job helping him to carry them to his office. He said he'd pay me money, or pay me with cigarettes. Although I thought this very suspicious, I was short of money and agreed. I said I wanted money for my work and a carton of cigarettes. He agreed with me that that was a very good arrangement.'

'I didn't know he traded in cigarettes?'

'Well he must, because the next day when I went to his office all the boxes had gone again.'

'Still listening,' said Scot as he went to the balcony door and slid it open a little. 'It's cooling down, why don't we sit out here and have a drink and you can tell me more? Beer?'

'Would it be rude to ask if you have any gin?'

'Sure,' he said heading off to the kitchen. Returning with a beer, gin, a bottle of tonic, some ice, two glasses and some biscuits, he found Ana already sitting on the balcony lighting a cigarette. 'You can pour your own gin and tonic,' he said, pouring his beer.

He noticed she poured more gin than he'd have offered.

'Maybe you find my story very boring,' she said.

He shook his head. 'It's really fascinating.'

'Well – what you say? – one thing led to another. His girl who answered the phone had to leave to return to her village because her father had died, and he thought maybe I would like to do the job. It was okay, but very difficult for me as I speak very little Arabic and most of the people only spoke Arabic. Some spoke English, but not many. But by this time, he was thinking that I was trustworthy, so he said there were other things I could help him with.'

'What sort of things?'

'Small things, all kinds of things.'

'Mustafa Rasool works with some people in Iraq doesn't he?' It was a tactical question designed to learn exact information about Rasool's work for Iraq.

'Maybe and maybe not.'

A dead end, but it led to insights into Ana's thinking.

'For more than ten years the British and the Americans bombed Iraq, just like they did to my country. Those bombs kill ordinary people like my father. They're like the bullies in a schoolyard.' She poured herself another heavy gin and tonic and lit another cigarette.

'Do you think you'll return to Belgrade soon?'

'You want me to leave?' She looked puzzled.

He shook his head.

'Good, because I am staying. I acquire more money here. And I like Cyprus. Even if I went back to Belgrade, it's too difficult to get a good job. Many people there want to go to other countries for work.'

The sun was setting, and they both fell silent, looking out to sea. He wondered what Ana was thinking, while he pondered the inevitable consequence of violence and war. Losers became embittered, even if they enjoyed the stability that followed, and victors' feelings were so often bittersweet. He guessed Ana might always have been a radical idealist, always taking sides against big powers. Balkan history was full of feuds fuelling feuds, and occupations making martyrs. The daughter of a shoe repairer could easily have grown up with an inclination to take the side of the underdog. In a sense he envied her firm commitment, for his life was now based upon money rather than ideals. 'It is time to think of going out to dinner. Do you like fish?'

She said yes, and within half an hour, they'd left the apartment and were walking towards a fish restaurant near the original port of Limassol. She took his arm, more he sensed to signal that she was spoken for rather than out of affection, although he hoped there was a little bit of that too. Over dinner he asked if she needed more of her money, but she didn't. However, the mention of money did lead to a question.

'Do you make a lot of money in your business?'

He forgave her cheeky impertinence. 'Enough!'

'You love asking questions, Scot, but don't like giving answers. It's true, isn't it?'

Responding with a shrug, he reached across the small table and took her hand. They'd finished dinner, and the music would have begun at the Club Downtown. Against his better judgement, he asked: 'Like to skip coffee here, and go dancing?'

'I was tired, but now I'm not. So maybe dancing would be good,' she said in a formal sort of way, which made him imagine a matriarch in a Serbian village. Although he'd never met one, he guessed such a woman would be full of efficiency and straight talk, and have no time for affection unless for family planning. But he already knew

Ana wasn't like that – at least as far as affection was concerned.

It was close to eleven o'clock by the time they reached the Club Downtown, Scot having explained its connection to his missing friend, and Dimitri's sensitive state.

'I understand!'

Dimitri welcomed them, looking surprised to see Scot with a girl friend. He led the way to the usual table, but Ana wanted to be nearer to the dance floor and music.

'You have more attractive company than last night,' whispered Dimitri, alluding to Rick Jordan. 'I'll bring coffee.'

Before the coffee arrived, Ana had drawn Scot on to the dance floor, amidst the laser lights flashing in time with the throbbing music. They danced close amidst a throng of suntanned bodies clad mainly in blue jeans and T-shirts. The music was loud, which made it impossible to talk. Fortuitous, in a way, because neither was in mood for questions and answers – there had been a surfeit of them all evening. It was body language that counted now. And their bodies were talking.

They broke for coffee and Dimitri told Ana it had been the first time Scot had taken any interest in the music. With the music still dominating, she didn't bother to utter a word. Instead, she smiled broadly at Dimitri, then at Scot, and nodded, as if to say 'that's good'. They then went back under the laser beams, and rocked on.

It was around 2 a.m. by the time they reached Scot's apartment. 'It's too late to catch a taxi to Larnaca,' said Scot.

'No, never too late in Cyprus. But maybe I'll stay?'

'Of course, love you to.' They kissed.

He was woken in the pitch black of early morning by whimpering, Ana whimpering. He lay there thinking until the whimpering turned to a loud choking sound, as if she was trying to shout. It went on – and on.

In the morning, once they were out of bed, and drinking coffee on the balcony, Scot said: 'You were dreaming in the night, remember?'

'Just occasionally I dream, after I've been working too hard.'

As Ana's taxi pulled away from the kerb outside the apartment building, Scot wandered towards the newspaper stand thirty metres or so along the esplanade. As he got closer he noticed the screaming headline of the *Cyprus Daily*: 'ARAB SHOT DEAD IN HOTEL'. After buying the paper, Scot sat at a pavement table at the small restaurant next door, and read in astonishment.

> *Police are investigating the murder of an Arab tourist found dead in his bed in the Nicosia Grand Hotel. The naked body was discovered lying in blood-soaked sheets by a maid, who entered the room for cleaning.*
>
> *The man, who police confirmed was from Syria, had been murdered by a single shot to the heart by a small calibre weapon. No weapon has been discovered.*
>
> *Police believe the dead man was preparing for sex at the time. A condom had been removed from its package, but remained curled and unused beside the body.*
>
> *Hotel workers have been unable to help police as no visitor was observed entering the dead man's*

room. Police investigations have been hampered further because the security camera on the floor of the room has been faulty for two days.

Police recovered the dead man's Syrian passport, and other personal papers and belongings. A police spokesman said investigators were puzzled as the personal belongings included a Visa card bearing the name 'A. Belfort-Smith'.

The dead man entered Cyprus on a tourist visa issued at Larnaca Airport, the police said. He had flown to the island on Cyprus Airways from Damascus.

The passport photograph of the dead man was reproduced next to the newspaper story. Scot's recognition was immediate. It was the same 'Hussein' he'd observed using Alexander's credit card in the Nicosia supermarket. It was the face of the man he'd seen meeting Ana in the hotel's lobby just an hour later. The name was the same as the one on Ana's slip of paper.

Scot ordered a long black coffee as his mind spun with myriad thoughts. He held no sympathy for the dead man, as somehow he'd obviously got hold of Alex's credit card, and probably had something to do with Alex's abduction. The card could belong to a totally different 'A. Belfort-Smith'. That thought registered in Scot's head, but was immediately discounted. He kicked himself for not pursuing his hunch about the man. If nothing more, it could have saved a life. He'd tried to ring Matthew York, but not hard enough! That may have led to the British High Commission solving the mystery of Alexander's disappearance. But now the trail was cold again, stone dead.

15

Scot's thoughts turned angrily to Richard Xanadu Jordan, so-called Associate Cultural Attaché at the American Embassy in Athens. Scot went over and over his dinner with Jordan. He couldn't forgive himself for handing over the dead man's name. And there was a lingering question. Would the body of the second man be found?

Rick Jordan – and his associates – were behind this murder. Scot was convinced of that. But why would American spooks – if that's what they were – want to kill the only link to Alexander's disappearance? Unless they'd already got what they wanted? Maybe they had, and soon there'd be some good news about Alex. Everything could get back to normal. Scot's first thought had been to ring Rick Jordan at his hotel and give him a blast. Maybe that wasn't the best tactic. First, he'd listen to the American's story.

Scot sat at his desk, lighting a cigarette, then phoned Rick Jordan's hotel. 'Jordan,' said a sullen voice.

'Rick, it's Scot Wallace here,' he said with as much amiability as he could muster. 'I've just seen the *Cyprus Daily*.'

'I've seen it. Knew about it late yesterday. Our guys heard about it by chance. One of them was drinking at the hotel.'

'Our guys?'

'Embassy people.' Jordan spoke gruffly.

'So the police didn't tell you?'

'For God's sake, the dead man's a Syrian national. Why would they tell the American Embassy?'

The question was rhetoric, but Scot answered anyway. 'Because I gave you the dead man's name. I assumed you'd try and trace him through the Cypriot authorities, the police.'

'We have our own ways of operating, Scot,' Jordan said a little more warmly.

'So you spoke to him before he was killed?'

Rick Jordan fell silent, except for breathing heavily and slowly into the mouthpiece. The American's time was being wasted. That was the message.

But Scot – former journalist turned trader – wasn't going to be put off. 'So you spoke to him or didn't?'

There was more deep breathing.

'Tell me yes or no, whether or not you've let the only lead we had on Alexander die, or I'll—'

'Or you'll what, Scot?'

'Go to the police, say, I thought I saw the dead man using the credit card, and passed on the information to you – an American Cultural Attaché.' Having stressed sarcastically the word 'cultural', he then added: 'Sorry, I mean Associate Cultural Attaché.'

'I wouldn't do that.'

'Why? The police are asking for leads.'

'Why? Because you might just end up in the frame, mightn't you?'

'Don't be so bloody ridiculous.'

'Ridiculous? I'm sure the police would wonder why you didn't report the credit card incident. You had your suspicions the dead man was linked to your friend's disappearance. They might just see that as motivation for murder.'

'Yeah, and they might be interested that I passed on my suspicions to the hotel, and the name of the dead man to you and therefore the American Embassy. And within a matter of hours, he was dead.'

'I wouldn't do that, Scot. Calm down, pop a Valium or have a few heavy Scotches.'

Scot seethed with anger.

'Anyway, I'm expecting a call, so I'll leave you to calm down.' The American cut the line.

Scot paced the room recalling the American's every word. Trying to halt his anxious walking, he stared out at the sea as a distraction. But it didn't work this time. Then he remembered Rick Jordan had referred to 'your friend's disappearance'. He didn't say 'Alexander's disappearance', or 'our friend's disappearance'. Had Rick Jordan and his colleagues washed their hands of Alexander? Had they closed the Englishman's file? Pursuing this line of thought, Scot felt he may be responsible for that too. He'd shown Jordan the cutting from *Beirut Underground*. In fact, the American had taken the copy of the cutting, and presumably passed it on to his colleagues. If the *Beirut Underground* was correct, Alexander's cover had been blown. Maybe he wasn't any use to the Americans, or anyone, anymore? Maybe it was better if the Englishman was never found – or found dead? No such thing as a free lunch, it's said. Nor a free dinner, it seemed. Scot remembered Jordan insisting on picking up the bill. The result of that free dinner? One man murdered, and Alex most probably abandoned.

He looked at his watch, then tried Ana's phone number. It didn't answer. After waiting another fifteen minutes, Scot tried again.

'Hello,' said Ana softly, as if scared, upset or both.

'Ana, I have got some awful news. In today's *Cyprus Daily*—'

'I know ... I bought a copy just near my apartment. As soon as I left the taxi. That man was very nice, although I only met him one time.' She burst into tears.

Scot tried to calm her down with some small talk, but it didn't work.

'And they say such awful things in the newspaper. His wife will be so upset if she reads the newspaper.'

'He had a wife?'

'He told me that … In Syria his wife was, he said. And the police talk about sex and condoms.' More tears flood the phone line.

Scot spoke gently. 'I think you should go to the police. They'd like to hear whatever you can tell them.'

'My friends are going to the police,' Ana said. 'He was their friend. Remember I said he was just a friend of friends?'

'Yes, I remember.' Maybe it was better, Scot reasoned. Ana was an attractive woman, and the police would probably insist on taking DNA samples, and trying to match them with body fluids or perspiration found on the murdered man's bed or body. Why should Ana go through that ordeal? 'It's better that your friends go to the police.'

'I feel so sad and lonely suddenly. To think I was so happy last night.'

'Would you like to come and stay here a couple of days. It would give you a chance to get over the shock.'

'Could I?'

'Of course, I'd love you to. I'm lonely here by myself. I'll drive to Larnaca and pick you up. What time?'

'You are too kind, Scot, but I will catch a taxi like yesterday. Most certainly, I will catch a taxi and get to your flat about two o'clock this afternoon. Okay?'

Scot put down the phone, and walked to the balcony window. The sea view was doing its trick again. Or was it that Ana was coming to stay? After the shock of the murder, and his telephone conversation with Rick Jordan, Ana would distract him from lingering guilt. He would be too busy for introspection. They wouldn't go out for dinner. He'd cook fish. They would eat on the balcony catching the evening breeze.

Thoughts shifted to Dimitri. He'd better ring to alert him to the discovery of a credit card bearing Alex's name. Even if the Cypriot hadn't seen the newspaper, lunchtime customers would mention it. Regulars inhabited the Club Downtown at lunchtime. They were mainly businessmen who would have read the newspapers. Looking at his watch, he was surprised it was just 11a.m. He'd have time to walk around and tell Dimitri personally. He could be very upset. They'd be preparing lunch, and it would be some time before lunch guests arrived. Scot would buy some fish for dinner on his way back.

Another waiter was setting tables for lunch. 'Is Dimitri here?' Scot asked. The waiter pointed towards the kitchen. Scot pushed the door open just a little, and saw Dimitri loading goods into a refrigerator. 'Dimitri, sorry to disturb you?'

'You have some news?' The Cypriot had a quizzical look on his face – bordering on the hopeful – as he walked towards Scot.

'Come and sit down. There's something to tell you. Have you read the newspapers today?'

'No, I don't get up until around ten o'clock because we have late nights, and I came here to the restaurant straight from my home. Why?'

Scot chose his words carefully while recounting the story, and finished by saying, 'It's not even certain it's Alexander's credit card. It could belong to another A. Belfort-Smith.'

'Scot,' said Dimitri. 'Don't treat me as if I'm a boy. I'm Alexander's business partner, I now manage this restaurant single handed, and I'm Alex's lover. I'm a man, Scot. I can face facts.'

'I'm sorry, Dimitri … Yes, I think it's probably Alex's card.'

'So do I. Alex goes missing in Syria, and a Syrian is found murdered in a Nicosia hotel with a card carrying the name A. Belfort-Smith. Of course, it's his card, and I can probably prove it.' Getting up from the table, Dimitri walked to the cash register and opened the drawer. 'After using the card, Alex usually leaves the receipts in an envelope for safety. He always keeps them until his Visa bill arrives.' He returned to the table and opened the envelope. 'This is the card number.'

The card number had not been published. Dimitri would have to ring the police in Nicosia and check the number on the card found at the murder scene. 'But there is a downside to this Dimitri … Alex's disappearance will probably be published in newspapers and become public knowledge.'

Dimitri scoffed. 'Everyone knows Alex is missing in Syria. Do you think the customers don't ask where he is? They know he's missing. You just can't keep secrets like that in Cyprus no matter how much you try. Cyprus is the biggest village in the world.'

Now Scot felt he was being treated like a boy.

'I'll ring the police shortly,' Dimitri said. 'Then we'll be one hundred per cent certain. Also, because I am being helpful to them, they may know who this dead Syrian met since arriving on Cyprus. That could help us find out more information about Alex. We could pass any information on to Mustafa Rasool and the British High Commission.' He then hesitated, a frown developing on his brow. 'The High Commission hasn't been any help so far, has it?'

Scot shook his head. 'They're trying, we know that.'

'Alex is a British citizen. They should do more than try. And he went missing when trying to find a British woman. That's their job! He shouldn't have had to go looking at all.'

'There's a lot we don't know, Dimitri.'

'There's even more they don't know. That's what I think.'

'The discovery of the credit card may spur them into action. If it's his – and you're right it probably is – it proves Alex was the victim of foul play.'

'I never had any doubts at all about that.' The Cypriot spoke angrily. 'What did you think? There was a chance he was running away from me?'

Scot shook his head and got up to leave. 'I'll let you get back to work. I need to do a few things. Maybe you could ring and tell me what the police say?'

Dimitri nodded as Scot left the restaurant and wandered along the pavement busy with lunchtime shoppers. After buying four small red mullet, he walked in a dream back to his apartment. Dimitri was probably right. The police would almost certainly be checking on people the dead man met since arriving. He hoped this wouldn't embroil Ana in the investigations. Her friends could do the talking.

'Hi Scot,' Nikos said from behind the reception desk. Scot responded with a smile, and headed straight for the lifts. The telephone was ringing as he entered the apartment.

'Scot, it's Mustafa Rasool in Aleppo.'

So much had happened he hadn't given Mustafa a thought, but said: 'I was about to ring you. There's been a development.'

'Yes, I believe I know what you are going to say. The newspapers here are full of it. A Syrian national has been shot dead in Nicosia, and a credit card belonging to Alex has been found.'

'Yes, it's sad for the man, and a puzzle about the card,' Scot said.

'Sympathy for that man? I feel none. My friend the Chief of Police says the dead man was well known to the police, and for the wrong reasons. He says he had many enemies, and was like a paper target waiting for a bullet.'

'Do you think it provides some clue to what happened to Alex?'

'Maybe it does. I am working on the matter.' Mustafa hesitated a few seconds before changing the subject. 'I am ringing you in the hope you may be able to drive to Larnaca as a matter of urgency. I have been trying to ring the woman you have met. You remember?'

'Of course.'

'Her telephone is ringing and ringing and ringing, but she doesn't answer. I need to speak urgently to her.'

Scot thought before answering. He didn't want to give a hint to Rasool that he was infatuated with Ana, and the feeling appeared to be mutual. 'Actually, she is coming to my apartment about two this afternoon. She has some business to carry out in Limassol, I gather. But I don't think she would have left Larnaca yet.'

'Well, the telephone is not answering. No matter. It's good she is visiting you. Could she ring me urgently when she arrives?'

'I'll pass on the message.'

'No, don't just pass on the message. Insist she rings me. I have some urgent work for her to do.'

Scot put the telephone down, but it rang again, almost immediately.

It was Dimitri to say the police had confirmed the credit card found with the dead man was Alexander's. 'They said I was very helpful and they would keep me informed of any developments. They are interviewing all the hotel staff in case someone remembers seeing the dead man with other people. Our police in Cyprus are very good. They'd tried ringing Alex and my home, but I'd left.'

As a courtesy, Scot rang Matthew York at the British High Commission, and passed on Dimitri's information. The diplomat appeared to already know, but thanked Scot effusively. Almost too effusively!

It was 2.15p.m. when the security phone rang. Scot unlocked the door, and waited for Ana by the lift. They kissed a long kiss as they entered the flat, and Scot closed the door and attached the security chain. She placed a large overnight case on the desk. 'How do you feel now, dear Ana?'

'With you, I feel much better.' She smiled weakly.

They drank weak tea, and sat talking small talk. It took a lot of effort, but he tried to avoid anything that would remind her of the murder. 'By the way, Mustafa Rasool has been trying to contact you. He wants you to ring him urgently. Something about some work he wants you to do.'

'Mustafa Rasool can wait a while. I'm relaxing, and he's probably having a siesta.'

'You enjoyed last night?'

'The best night I've spent on Cyprus. The dinner, the dancing, and waking up with you beside me. The music at that club of your friends is very good.'

'You like dancing?'

'With you, I do.'

After an hour or so, Scot reminded her about Rasool, but she said he could wait a little longer. He then ventured around the outskirts of the murder. 'Your friends must be very upset.'

'They are, although I don't know how well they knew the poor man. They said they were going to the police, but I don't know whether they can help.'

'Mustafa says the murder is in all the Syrian newspapers. He said the dead man was well known to the police.'

She frowned and asked: 'Well known?'

'Evidently, the Syrian police knew him as a criminal, or for being involved in bad things.' Scot deliberately tried to keep his English simple.

'So this man would have many enemies?'

'According to Mustafa, yes.'

'Well, maybe someone came from Syria to kill him.'

'Maybe. That would complicate matters for the police.'

After a few moments of silence, Ana stood up and said she'd better ring Rasool. 'Then I can relax and forget about him.'

'Well, don't agree to do too much work for him. You are too tired and upset.'

She smiled as if grateful for the sympathy, and walked to the desk. She retrieved a small book of phone numbers from the overnight bag and dialled Aleppo. 'Mustafa?'

Even though he was sitting at least two metres away, Scot could hear a loud babble coming down the phone line, but couldn't make out what the Syrian was saying. He picked up the odd word, so knew Mustafa was speaking English. All the talking was being done from Aleppo, Ana just responding occasionally with 'Yes' or 'Yes I understand'.

The conversation went on and on, so Scot carried the teapot and cups to the kitchen and washed them. He heard the handset being replaced on to the receiver, and a little later Ana was standing alongside.

'He wants me to go to Syria tomorrow and has booked a morning flight for me to Damascus. It connects with another plane to Aleppo.'

'You should have said you were too tired and upset.'

'Well, he doesn't know I met the murdered man.'

'You should have told him,' Scot said gently.

'After what you said about the police knowing the man was a criminal, I thought it better not to say that.'

'I'll ring him back and say you're sick and seeing a doctor.'

'You're a very kind man, Scot, but maybe it is better I travel and forget about the whole matter, and do some hard work for Mustafa.'

Scot reluctantly agreed to the logic. 'I'll miss you'.

'Maybe after a few days, you could come to Aleppo? You may find some information about your friend who is missing.'

The idea was attractive to Scot. 'I've got a few things to do over the next couple of days, but I'll definitely think about it. We could stay together in the Baron Hotel.'

She smiled at the idea before carrying her bag to the bedroom. She re-emerged with a surprising request. 'I feel I'd like to walk to a church. Is there one near here?'

He told her about the Metropolis Church about ten minutes walk away. 'I'll take you.'

'If you don't mind, I think I'd like to go alone.'

'It's a Cypriot church, of course.'

'The Cyprus church is related to the Serbian church. Anyway, the same God is in all of them.'

She insisted on going alone. 'While you're out, I can start preparing dinner. I thought we would eat here tonight. Is that okay?'

'Yes, I'd like that.'

It was coming up to 5 p.m. as Ana left. Scot grabbed the TV remote and turned on BBC World. The third item in the news headlines drew Scot's attention. 'Fears are held for a British national reported missing in Syria.' The item, when it came, told Scot no more than he knew. But there was something of interest. The report quoted a British Foreign Office official as saying the British government had been unaware of the man's disappearance until notified by the police in Cyprus today after the man's stolen credit card was found near the body of a man murdered in Nicosia. 'Investigations are under way, but the missing man's name has not been released,' the reporter said.

Scot switched off the TV and started peeling potatoes. Analysing the report, he reckoned the government's spin on Alex's disappearance, and the outright lie that the Foreign Office had only just learnt about it, more or less confirmed Alex was a spy – either for the British or the Americans. Just as the *Beirut Underground* had reported. That would be the reason they'd not released Alex's name too. Normally, they would release the name of a missing British national because the authorities would want all the help they could get. Maybe that was why there'd been no coverage of Debbie's disappearance too. Mustafa Rasool's contacts might be correct and she was a spy.

It was about 6 p.m. when Ana returned. 'I lit a candle for the murdered man. Maybe he was a criminal, but he was a human being.'

They hugged.

'I've made the salad and I'm baking potatoes. So we can eat on the balcony about eight? All I have to do is cook the fish when we're ready.'

She nodded, looking pleased with the idea. 'Would I have time to shower?'

'Of course,' said Scot as he walked to the cupboard near the bathroom and retrieved a towel.

He got drinks and the cutlery ready while Ana showered. She emerged after about thirty minutes having exchanged her short blue cotton dress for black jeans and the blue T-shirt she'd been wearing at the Nicosia Grand Hotel.

'Gin and tonic?' He carried a tray of drinks to the balcony. The sea breeze was blowing lightly. Boats were coming back into port, and ships lay at anchor.

'This view is too nice,' she said. 'I'm glad I'm sharing it with just one person – you.' As she ate dinner, she complimented him on his cooking. 'You're a very useful man, Scot,' she said leaning over the table and kissing him.

'I think I'll come to Aleppo in a couple of days. I'd get bored here alone.'

'Good,' she responded quickly as if nailing down the arrangement. 'I'll get Mustafa to book us a room at the Hotel Baron. He knows the manager. He'll get us the best room.'

Scot woke from a deep contented sleep. It was pitch black, and he could feel Ana's warmth alongside. It took a few seconds for the ringing of the telephone to register. Grabbing a dressing gown, he rushed to the desk and answered it.

'Hello,' he said quietly, still half asleep. He looked at the clock. It was just past 4 a.m.

'Sorry to disturb you, Scot, it's Dimitri. But my house has been broken into.'

'Sorry, but how can I help?' He spoke coolly – something he immediately regretted. Although a friend, and embroiled in Alexander's disappearance, he was not

Dimitri's keeper, or the police. Surely, there must be Cypriot friends and relations Dimitri could contact?

'Alex's personal papers have all been gone through, and a little telephone book of special Limassol numbers has been left on top of a pile of other papers. And the computer has been left on.'

The details of the break-in woke Scot completely with their personal resonance. 'Anything stolen?'

'Nothing obvious. The TV's here, the computer's here, the sound system. I can't be certain but I don't think so.'

'You know, the same thing happened to me some time back?'

'What did the police say?'

'For some reason, I didn't go to the police.'

'I'm going to ring the police because I know who did it.'

'Yes?'

'That American creep who was at the restaurant the other night. Mr Jordan – the one you had dinner with. He wanted to see Alex's computer remember?'

'I do, yes.'

'And I wouldn't let him, so he's come here by himself when he knew I'd be working. I know he's a friend of yours, but he's a real creep. My police friends will be very interested and put him in gaol. Maybe they'll want to question him about the murder?'

After Scot's hostile phone conversation with Jordan, he wasn't at all averse to the idea of the American being heavied by the police. For a split second, he wished he were still a journalist. It would be a great story to write up. But instead he cautioned Dimitri. 'What you're saying makes sense. Be careful about what you say, though. I'm not saying this because he's a friend of mine; he's definitely not a friend of mine. He's just an acquaintance. Actually, I met him with Alexander in Kakopetria.'

'Even so I'm going to tell the police everything I know. People like that can't just break into houses when the owner says they can't use the front door.'

'Yeah, tell the police, but that man may have diplomatic immunity, yet maybe he wouldn't in Cyprus as he's based in Athens. It may depend on whether he's accredited here in Cyprus.'

'Even better if he has this diplomatic thing you mentioned. Because the Cyprus Foreign Ministry may become involved and expel him in disgrace and demand an apology from the American Ambassador.'

Scot couldn't decide which fate he'd prefer for the Associate Cultural Attaché. Prison with petty criminals, drug smugglers and murderers, or the embarrassment of expulsion and an apology from the American Embassy. It was almost line ball. But prison did have an attraction. He could visit him – maybe take him a book or some cake. Something to cheer him up!

'Well, do what you feel's right, Dimitri. It's your country.' Scot noticed Ana enter the room and sit in a chair near the television. He blew a kiss, and she mouthed 'who?' but no word emerged. Putting his hand over the mouthpiece, he whispered to her 'Dimitri'.

'Is someone with you?'

'Yes, a friend's staying the night.'

'That woman you brought dancing? She's really nice, and makes you happy, Scot. And she's beautiful.'

There was no point denying it, but no need to confirm it either. 'Yes, she's beautiful,' he said for Ana's hearing as much as Dimitri.

Dimitri returned to the break-in. 'Maybe Mr Jordan's hotel saw him leave last night or return around two or three this morning.'

'If you're right and he's responsible, I think he'd have got someone else to do the dirty work – the actual break-in.'

'No, that American slob would do it himself.'

'How did they get in?'

'Must have used a key because there's no damage.'

'Right,' said Scot, thinking that task would probably be beyond the capability of some poor drug user looking for cash. 'Would you like to come and stay here? You must be a bit lonely.'

'No, I had to hire a new waiter. He's from Polis, and hasn't got anywhere to live yet, so he came home with me.'

'That's good. I'll ring or come and see you late this morning. See if there've been any developments.'

They hung up. And Scot wondered if there was more than kindness behind Dimitri providing the new waiter with a bed. After all, Alex had been missing for some time now. Then he bit his gossiping tongue. But with Ana in the room, love – or was it lust? – was on his mind! He offered tea, but she said she'd rather get back to bed for another hour or so. She had to rise early for the flight to Damascus. They lay close, Scot thinking as much about the break-in, as of Ana.

The alarm went at 6.30 a.m. Scot kissed Ana gently on the cheek and then wandered to the balcony. Once back from Larnaca, he'd consider ringing Rick Jordan to tell him he was 'in the frame' over an early morning break-in. Maybe he'd think better of it later, but it seemed a good idea right now.

'What are you thinking about?' Ana had stepped on to the balcony and had her arm around his waist.

'How I'll miss you.'

'Just for two or three nights, and then we'll be together in Aleppo.'

They kissed, and then she went back inside to shower.

After a quick coffee, they were on the road to Larnaca within an hour. Compared with dinner, she was dressed conservatively for the flight in a simple light green cotton dress – the hem of which fell below the knees. He'd never seen them covered up before – except in jeans. And she wore no make-up. But no matter how much she tried, she couldn't disguise her suntanned beauty.

'Would it be too much trouble to bring the rest of my money to me in Aleppo?'

'I thought about that in the night. Wondered if you'd like some of it, but you'd like it all?'

'I think so.'

'So you're planning to stay some time in Syria? I was hoping you'd be coming back to Cyprus with me. I want to take you to the mountains, and to Latchi. A friend owns a beautifully simple beachside restaurant beyond Latchi; I'd like to take you there.'

'I hope I come back soon, too. But Mustafa Rasool has many thoughts, and he pays me a lot of money. I have to wait and see. So it will be better if you bring the money.'

They fell silent for a while as the car sped along the motorway. 'You know the man you met with the man who was murdered? Were they close friends?'

'I only met him that one time. I don't know really. They knew each other obviously, as they both were very pleased about some business deal.'

'What was the deal?'

'I don't know because they spoke in Arabic when they discussed that.'

'So how do you know it was a business deal they were discussing?'

'Because amidst all the Arabic, they mentioned US dollars, and other things like Bank of Cyprus. They spoke Arabic mainly. Just when they were trying to seduce me, they spoke English. They looked me up and down and raped me with their eyes.'

He changed the subject. 'Sure you don't need to go to your apartment?'

'No, as I said, I have everything I need in the bag.'

'You travel light.'

'Better for customs in Damascus.'

They drove around the parched salt lake as they approached the airport. The lake was completely dry, but a mirage gave the impression of water on the far side near the Tékké of Umm Haram. The mosque – in a cluster of green trees – looked a sanctuary of serenity.

As they drove into the airport car park, Ana reached to her bag on the back seat and retrieved a dark green scarf, which she placed across her hair and tied beneath her chin. 'But I like your blond hair,' Scot protested.

'I'm flying to a Moslem country, remember?'

'They're not too strict in Syria—'

'No, but it makes things easier.'

He carried her overnight bag to the ticket counter, where Ana collected the ticket Rasool had organised. 'Good – first class.' She then filled in the immigration form, and placed it in her passport. 'Well, it's time to say goodbye.'

They hugged, and kissed as discreetly as is possible in a crowded departure hall. 'I'll see you in a few days. Be careful. And I'll miss you!'

Ana left, and gave a final wave as she headed towards the embarkation officials and out of sight.

It was a lonely road back to Limassol. Thoughts of Ana were dulled only by the thought of Richard Jordan being interviewed by the Cyprus police. They might take his fingerprints? Even take a mug shot, or better still a picture of him standing glum holding a number across his stomach – hopefully 007. A bit of wishful thinking, perhaps! The police would be polite, because of the suspect's relationship to the American Embassy. But reality didn't halt Scot's fantasy.

Back in the Limassol apartment, Scot rang Dimitri whose words indicated developments only dreamt about were turning to a nightmare for Rick Jordan.

'The police are very interested because it's Alexander Belfort-Smith's computer.' Dimitri was the happiest he'd been since Alex's disappearance. 'Because of the credit card found at the murder, they thought it was very suspicious and they are sending some very senior officers to Mr Jordan's hotel. They asked me if he seemed dangerous, because they thought they might take armed backup. They thanked me very, very much for my help. I think I did the correct thing, don't you?'

'Of course, Dimitri,' Scot said, imagining sirens and flashing lights surrounding the hotel and armed police officers cornering Richard Xanadu Jordan. 'I wish I could be at the hotel to see the action.'

Scot hung up and went to the kitchen for a mug of instant coffee. Returning, he noticed the story on page one of the *Cyprus Daily*: 'Woman link to murdered man.'

> *Cyprus police last night pleaded with a woman seen drinking with the man murdered in a Nicosia hotel to come forward and help with investigations.*

> *They stressed the woman was not a suspect in the murder, but may be able to help police identify people the dead man contacted during his brief stay in Cyprus.*

Several witnesses have told police they saw the woman and a second 'Arab looking' man in the hotel's bar shortly after the dead man arrived on the island.

Scot wasn't surprised, and was glad Ana had left the country. She had a perfectly good reason to meet the man, and wouldn't be able to help the police. She wouldn't know any more than her friends – or friends of friends – had already told them. Scot pondered the chronology of the murdered man's first day in Cyprus in view of the latest newspaper report. If Ana was right and he'd just arrived on Cyprus, he must have gone to the supermarket – and used Alex's credit card – straight from the airport, and then gone to the Nicosia Grand. Why was he in such a hurry to buy the spirits? Perhaps he knew Alex was still alive and could escape or be released, find his credit card stolen, and cancel it. Or, he knew Alex was dead and feared the body would be discovered quickly. Either explanation provided an incentive to use the card quickly. But the second was more plausible. Because anyone using the card could face charges much more serious than using a stolen credit card. The charge would be murder.

16

The immigration official pounded the rubber stamp heavily on the passport. It left a blue egg- shaped stamp partially covering the small red rectangular entry stamp. The new stamp noted departure from Larnaca Airport and the date.

'Hope you enjoyed your time on Cyprus,' the official said.

Entering the departure hall, Scot noticed Rick Jordan sitting sullenly at a table. At first glance the only company he had was a cup and saucer, but a closer look revealed a uniformed official standing behind, feigning a nonchalant look. He didn't take his eyes off the Associate Cultural Attaché, even momentarily.

'Hi Rick,' Scot said, as he drew out a chair at the small table, and put his cabin baggage on another. 'Leaving Cyprus so soon?'

Jordan glared. 'Didn't occur to you that someone might be sitting there?'

'No, your only company I've noticed is standing behind. I'll move, though, if you'd prefer.'

'No, Scot, stay. You'd never believe the humiliation I've suffered over the past couple of days. It's a change to see a face I know.'

Scot feigned ignorance looking forward to Rick's version. It turned out to be surprisingly similar to Dimitri's – police sirens, flashing lights, and hotel arrest – but it went further. 'They even doubted the authenticity of my diplomatic passport. Alleged it was forged. Of course the embassy guys set them right – in the end. Once they bothered to break off their swimming party and came to the police station.'

'What prompted all this?'

'That little gay friend of Alexander Belfort-Smith. Got it into his screwed-up little head that I'd broken into his house, switched on Alex's computer and accessed secure bank sites.'

'Surely the police didn't believe him? I mean, they wouldn't think an American diplomat – a Cultural Attaché – would do such a thing?'

Scot's rhetorical questions had the effect of turning the American's glowering demeanour into the hint of a smile. 'What I've always liked about you, Scot, is that almost everything's a joke. Goddamit, for allies you Australians always take the Mickey. In the rest of the world, our allies respect us, even if they don't like us.'

'In Cyprus?'

'Don't talk to me about Cyprus. I'm a bit jaundiced about this little country.'

'What does your ambassador say?'

'He didn't say anything to me. Didn't meet him this time. But don't talk to me about him either. Just the thought of that guy makes my blood boil.' He then detailed how the embassy thought it was best to leave the country for Athens as soon as possible, and fixed it with the police. 'That's why I have this goon behind. Just in case, I should do a runner somehow.'

'Well, I suppose it's possible a Cultural Attaché could be trained in all kinds of illusion.'

'There you go again!' He hesitated, mulling over his situation perhaps, then asked: 'Where you off to?'

'Damascus.'

'And Aleppo?'

'Maybe, I have a friend – a woman friend – staying up there and I might look her up.'

'Long way to go for a date.' He leered at Scot as if a woman might be the excuse, but that Richard Xanadu Jordan knew the real mission was the trail of Alexander. He then leant towards the Australian and whispered. 'Look, I'll give you a lead. It's totally confidential and forget where you heard it, but I reckon our guys in Nicosia are a bit slack so someone may as well follow it up. Even if they get around to it, the more the merrier.' He then went over details of the murder at the Nicosia Grand. 'On the first day, the security cameras at the hotel show that the dead man met a woman – in the lobby and then the bar – and another man. The woman's not that important, but that other man looks very, very like a Syrian who's mixed up in smuggling all kinds of things – hashish and other drugs around the Middle East, and luxury items to Iraq. He travels under a number of names, but this is your best bet.' The American drew a piece of paper out of his shirt pocket, and wrote down a name. He handed the paper to Scot.

'You think he carried out the murder?'

'No, murder's a bit out of his league. But he may know who did and he may know something about Alexander. This is just a guess, but the murder – with the victim ready for sex – has all the hallmarks of one of Iraq's women assassins we've all read about.'

'They're still using women?'

'Old habits die hard, don't they say.' Then a smile crept across Jordan's face.

Scot became alarmed. 'So the woman in the bar?'

'For god's sake, no. That's not the way they operate. I've never known for them to be seen in public. They operate much more discreetly. There's a major problem with my theory though. There doesn't appear to be any reason why the Iraqis would want that man dead.'

'Maybe not, but he must have had something to do with Alexander's disappearance, and maybe Debbie London's as well.'

Jordan spoke in a tone of confidentiality. 'Scot, I don't think Alexander was on that woman's trail at all. She was just a decoy.'

The public address system was announcing the final call for Damascus. 'Must run, thanks.'

'Just one final thing, Scot. If you should ever meet up with Alexander again, tell him to get a new boyfriend. The one he's got is an arsehole.'

As the Cyprus Airways jet taxied towards the runway, Scot kicked himself for not asking why Jordan thought Debbie London was just an excuse for Alexander's trip to Aleppo. The aircraft lined up for take-off, and began to roll as the Rolls-Royce engines flaunted their power.

The taxi pulled up opposite the Baron Hotel, and Scot tipped the driver. Collecting his baggage from the car boot, he stood on the pavement admiring the grand hotel. A weathered old man wearing a black and white *keffiyeh* on his head was polishing Mustafa Rasool's brass plate. '*Salaam*,' said the man, as Scot passed through the doorway, and up the stairs to the trade consultant's office.

'My friend Scot, welcome back to Aleppo.' Mustafa kissed his visitor on both cheeks. In the reception room adjoining Rasool's office about six boxes of Marlboro cartons were stacked in a corner next to the club chairs. There were another two boxes marked Johnny Walker Black Label. Mustafa saw the Australian glancing at the hoard and said by way of explanation 'Very good deal. I can never resist a bargain.'

Scot looked at the empty receptionist's desk and chair.

'I know who you were hoping to see sitting in that chair!' The Syrian spoke with a knowing smile creeping across his face. 'She's on an errand. I have used all my influence with my friend the manager to secure the best room in the Baron. Double bed with all amenities.'

'Kind of you, thanks.'

'Nothing is too much trouble for you, my friend.' He led the way into his office, where another box of cigarettes was on the desk. It was open, and several cartons had been removed and were on the desk. In turn these cartons had been emptied and individual packets strewn alongside. 'With business I am very careful I get what I pay for. You wouldn't realise the dishonesty of some people. So I check each carton holds the correct number of packets.'

'Do you check that each packet holds twenty fags?'

'You joke too much. I check the seals instead,' the Syrian said, throwing Scot a sample packet. 'A welcome gift.'

'Any news about Alexander?'

'As yet, we have no firm leads on the case.' Mustafa spoke as if mimicking television police dramas.

Scot asked if he could meet the police chief.

'That could be very difficult,' the Syrian said. 'It may or may not be possible. You have to understand, my friend, that he's very careful not to be seen with foreigners in case he's suspected of being corrupt. The Syrian police have to be wary about being accused of corruption. No corruption is tolerated.'

'I understand,' Scot said, thinking an honest cop would hardly associate with the likes of Mustafa Rasool.

'Maybe I could persuade him if I explain that you have an international reputation and are above suspicion of any kind. Let me work on the matter.'

'Very kind,' said Scot momentarily flattered.

'There is another problem, however. The police chief doesn't speak English.'

'With your excellent command of English and Arabic you could translate?'

'And French! Yes, I could translate for you. I am respected far and wide as a translator although I'm not formally trained in that noble profession.'

Scot suggested he'd carry his baggage over to the hotel and check in.

'I've got a man working downstairs who could carry your bags.'

Scot thought of the weathered old man polishing the brass plate, and said he could easily manage his own luggage. 'Will Ana be returning soon?'

'Within an hour, *inshallah*. I will bring her across and we can all have a drink.'

Scot preferred the idea of meeting Ana alone, but realised Mustafa would get his way one way or another.

The reception area of the Hotel Baron was empty. After ringing the bell on the counter, he looked around excited to be back within the faded charm of the hotel. An original poster advertising the Orient Express adorned a wall, and he took a look into the wood-panelled bar. From behind a man said: 'Sir, can I be of help?' The receptionist looked at Scot's passport closely. 'We have reserved the best room in the hotel for you. As a friend of Mustafa Rasool, we've given you Lawrence of Arabia's room. But I think you have a friend accompanying you?'

'Mr Rasool is bringing her shortly.'

After filling in a form, Scot was shown to the room by a young man who carried the bags. French doors led to a balcony bordered by iron lacework. The bed sagged a little and looked as if it had seen better days, but that was of little importance. The bathroom was fitted out with complicated French taps and original plumbing, including a bidet. Scot opened his small suitcase and hung his sports coat and slacks in the wardrobe. After the long drive from Damascus airport, he felt like showering, but decided Mustafa and Ana might arrive soon so he went downstairs to the foyer and rested in a leather armchair. The same young man who'd carried his bags passed by and Scot asked if he could have a beer.

The drink had just arrived when Ana and Mustafa appeared. Scot rose and kissed Ana.

'I crossed my fingers that you would keep your promise and come to Aleppo,' she said quaintly.

Mustafa sat, indicating to Ana that she should take the seat next to Scot. He beamed as if he'd organised a match made in heaven. 'I shall stay for just one or two drinks, and then I'll leave you two alone together.' He ordered a whisky for himself, a second beer for Scot, and tea for Ana. 'In the short time since you left my office, I have spoken to my police friend.'

Scot was surprised.

'After I told him of your international reputation, he agreed to come to my office at nine o'clock in the morning exactly.'

Scot thanked Mustafa profusely.

It was late afternoon, and after half an hour during which Mustafa talked effusively about the hotel and the historic sites of Aleppo, the Syrian said he must leave. 'I have some urgent work to complete.'

After taking Ana's baggage to the room, and kissing and embracing enthusiastically, they decided on a short walk around the streets near the hotel. By now it was getting dark, and shop windows were lit up displaying an array of goods from cheap trash to high fashion. As they walked back to the hotel, Scot noticed an old green Chevrolet parked outside Rasool's office. Mustafa and the weathered old man who'd polished the brass plate were loading cigarettes and whisky into the boot. As the operation was being carried out under the cover of near darkness, Scot decided not to disturb Mustafa for fear of appearing inquisitive.

'Where does he sell those?' he asked.

Ana shook her head as if it was a mystery to her.

They returned to their hotel room, and struggled with the gurgling plumbing, which eventually produced some warm water. After having a bath, Scot felt rejuvenated as he waited while Ana bathed. He stood on the balcony and noticed the light in Mustafa's office across the road was still on. The trade consultant was working late.

As Ana emerged from the bathroom, Scot handed over her $10,000. 'Thank you very much.'

'Where will you keep it?'

'Maybe they have a safe downstairs, otherwise I'll put it in Mustafa's safe.'

Ana detected a sly smile. 'What is so funny?'

'I was just thinking the money could have stayed safely with Rasool all along!'

Entering the dining room, Scot thought of the famous identities of the Middle East who'd supped there since the hotel opened in 1909. As well as Lawrence, the hotel had been a temporary home to Freya Stark, Agatha Christie and her archaeologist husband, and Kim Philby. They were shown to a table and Scot ordered a bottle of Lebanese wine. In the faded charm, Ana's face looked even more radiant than usual. After dinner, Scot suggested a nightcap in the wood panelled bar, but Ana – with eyes sparking – said she'd prefer to try the bed.

17

Scot woke early, recalling the name Rick Jordan had jotted down at Larnaca airport. So he rushed to Rasool's office to float an idea before the police chief arrived. Mustafa studied the name carefully, without indicating any recognition.

'Do you think I should raise this name with the police chief? The name's been given to me as a known smuggler, and as someone who might know about Alex's disappearance – and the murder in Nicosia.'

Rasool – having grimaced slightly at the word 'smuggler' – shook his head slowly as if the weight of the world hung on his decision. 'Well, my friend, there are arguments for and against,' the Syrian began unhelpfully. 'But on balance I believe it would be best not to worry the police chief at this stage. Instead, I shall make my own inquiries.'

On the dot of nine, the police chief arrived. The image he conveyed wasn't what Scot expected. Being a 'friend' of Rasool's, Scot had conjured up the image of an overweight officer in a somewhat crumpled uniform. In short, the caricature of a policeman nearing the end of his career, and not averse to decision-making based on low-level corruption. Instead, the man who'd arrived was a trim officer – perhaps in his early forties – in a well-pressed uniform. He looked a man focused on climbing the career ladder, and destined for an illustrious future. Scot felt reassured and surprised, wondering whether Mustafa had hired a model to play police chief for a morning. Did Aleppo have its own central casting?

Mustafa looked proud of his ability to deliver such a high-level contact, who by now was closely studying the prominently displayed picture of the Syrian President and Rasool.

'The police chief is like a nephew to me,' said Rasool. 'His father and I have been friends since school days.'

The police chief smiled, which somewhat surprised Scot. For a man who Mustafa said spoke no English, the officer did a remarkable impersonation of someone who understood fully what his 'uncle' had said. A small point, thought Scot, especially as he was in no position to change the rules of the game.

The police chief spoke some Arabic. Mustafa translated. 'Welcome to Syria, and to historic Aleppo in particular.' The policeman then went on at some length, mentioning 'Alexander Belfort-Smith' several times. Although the officer talked for at least two minutes – with Mustafa nodding understanding and appreciation – the translation was clearly abbreviated. 'We appear to have come to a dead end in our investigations on Alexander Belfort-Smith's abduction.'

'So you do think he was abducted in Aleppo?'

The police chief rambled on again, punctuating his detailed explanation with head gestures to Mustafa, and in turn, Scot. Once the policeman stopped talking, the noble translator said: 'Yes'.

'Has the witness provided any more information?' The charade was repeated. Another long explanation by the police chief was reduced to 'yes and no'.

Scot was grateful to Mustafa, but annoyance was seething under the surface. Furthermore, he sensed the police chief was getting a little jaundiced at the game. So he decided to ignore Rasool's advice and show the policeman the name Rick Jordan had provided. The result was a surprise.

The police chief slapped Mustafa on the back, and spoke in clear English. 'This name is well known to the police. We have had him under investigation for several years. His family is also well known to my friend here, Mustafa.'

Rasool didn't show the slightest embarrassment. 'That's why I said not to worry the chief of police. I was planning to arrange a meeting this afternoon with this man, and then hopefully be able to pass on information to the police. His family is indeed known to me, but the rule of law must prevail.'

Scot thanked the police chief for his time. 'Just one thing, why did you pretend to speak no English?'

'It saves time. If foreigners knew I spoke English they'd be worrying me all of the time with petty investigations.'

Mustafa kissed the policeman on both cheeks, thanked him profusely and led him down the stairs to his waiting car.

Without apology, Rasool returned to the office. 'Very impressive, don't you think? He's the new breed of Syrian police officers, university trained mixed with on-the-ground experience. It's certainly reassuring for those of us carrying out legitimate businesses that enhance the country's image in the world.'

Scot was tired of the crap, but an explosion of fury would achieve nothing. 'So when do you think you'll speak to this other man?'

'I will try and contact him shortly.'

Scot wandered back to the hotel, where he found Ana sitting having coffee. He described the meeting he'd just had, and she laughed as if she'd experienced similar encounters. 'You're not going to Rasool's office today?'

'Mustafa said I could have the day off to enjoy with you.'

'Maybe he didn't want you to meet the police chief?'

'Why? No, he's a kind man and wants us to have a good time in Aleppo.'

Scot leant down and kissed her, then sat and ordered a coffee himself. 'It's exhausting dealing with Mustafa Rasool!' After coffee, they went to the *souk* and haggled with the shopkeepers selling oriental carpets, inlaid Damascene furniture, and elegant blown glass. After lunching at a small restaurant, they returned to the hotel where a message from Rasool was waiting.

Rushing across the road, and up the stairs of the trade consultant's office, Scot found the door between reception and Mustafa's room shut. From behind the closed door he could hear an argument raging. So loud were the voices, he felt it best to wait. The spat lasted close to ten minutes during which Scot picked up the name 'Alexander Belfort-Smith' several times, and 'Nicosia Grand' at least twice. The door suddenly opened, and the man Scot had seen with Ana and the man later murdered in Nicosia left. He was clearly shaken, there were no goodbyes and – it appeared to Scot – the row was unresolved.

Mustafa was also shaken, his usual confidence gone. He beckoned Scot into the office. 'Tell me, Scot, who gave you that man's name?'

Scot hesitated, and then opted to tell a formal version. 'An American named Richard Xanadu Jordan, whose business card gives him the title Associate Cultural Attaché at the American Embassy in Athens'.

'I don't think he just suddenly gave you this piece of paper with the name scribbled on it?' Mustafa eyeballed Scot seeking the circumstances in which an American diplomat would hand over such information to an acquaintance.

'Well,' said Scot hesitantly, 'he'd some trouble with the Cyprus police. He felt he'd been let down by his diplomatic colleagues in Nicosia, I gather.'

'I understand,' said Mustafa in a tone of extreme gravity. 'This cultural attaché is clearly a spy. And there's only one thing more dangerous than a spy, and that's a disillusioned spy.' He looked out his window as he mulled over the situation. 'But something has developed from this mess. There is a chance I have a lead on the whereabouts of Alexander. But life is like a game of chess, and I have to think out the options.'

'Maybe you should tell the police chief?'

Quick as a flash, Mustafa raised a finger and waved it in front of Scot. 'No, this must be between us for the time being at least. No one else must know. Maybe you could share your news with Ana, as she will not tell a soul. She's very good at keeping secrets. You go back to the hotel, enjoy yourself and I'll ring when I have a solution.'

Scot protested, but Mustafa gave him no option other than returning to the hotel. It was about five in the afternoon when Mustafa rang. 'Come over to my office, and bring your passport.'

When he arrived, Rasool was in a much better mood – the wind was back in his sails. 'How would you like to go for a long drive?'

'Why? Where?'

'Iraq … along a trail used by smugglers.' The Syrian then explained he believed Alexander had been abducted by a criminal group of smugglers. He clearly differentiated between smugglers who were making 'honest' money by defying sanctions against Iraq, and a 'criminal' element who sought bigger profits. 'Evidently, there has been a newspaper article published in Beirut, which said Alexander is a spy—'

'The *Beirut Underground* … I've seen the article.'

'Because of this, this stupid band of criminals believe the Iraqis will pay a lot of money for this English spy.'

'But I'm just a humble trader,' Scot said, realising at once he was falling into Mustafa speak. 'Why do you think I could rescue Alex?'

Mustafa then went through a detailed plan. He was waiting for a call from Baghdad, but he believed he would get the go-ahead. 'Your job is quite simple. All you will have to do is collect Alexander and accompany him back to Aleppo.' Then, almost as an afterthought, he said: 'It's a very pleasant drive. Very few people in the world have enjoyed such a trip.'

'But I have no visa for Iraq?'

Mustafa scoffed. 'You won't need a visa at the border as you will not cross at a border post. However, just in case Iraqi authorities question you, I will get you a visa. That's why I asked you to bring your passport.' Mustafa then asked what Scot understood about the circumstances of Alexander's dismissal from the British Army.

Scot told him what he knew. 'I even wrote the story for a London newspaper.'

The news cheered Mustafa. 'I didn't ever know the details exactly, but that is even more reason why you should make the trip. You will be able to be a first-hand witness to the unfortunate circumstances. Your presence will make Alex feel secure … instantly.' Mustafa added he'd call by the hotel once he'd spoken to Baghdad.

Scot found Ana in the hotel room, and filled her in on developments.

'No, don't go to Iraq. It's too dangerous to go on the smuggler's route. Anyway, I'd miss you.'

He hugged her. I'd only be away a few days, and when I return we could go back to Cyprus.'

Even that suggestion didn't enthuse her. 'Let Mustafa send someone else.'

'Well, we'll talk to Mustafa and find out the details, then decide.'

They didn't have to wait long. The old telephone in the room rang. Mustafa was downstairs in the bar. They went straight down. After arranging drinks, Mustafa handed Scot his passport. 'There's a new valid visa inside, and an entry stamp with tomorrow's date for good measure.'

'But visas take weeks to obtain?'

Mustafa patted Scot on the back. 'In emergencies like this, Baghdad approves the special issue of visas.'

'But not entry stamps—'

'Special circumstances demand special arrangements.'

Scot looked doubtful. 'So you spoke to Baghdad? Mr Kareem?'

'Yes, and he sends his kindest regards. In fact he was very interested in what you told me about the circumstances under which Alexander left the army.'

'I don't understand?'

'Well, Ahmad Kareem is sending a senior Iraqi in the Antiquities and Tourism Department to liaise with you just near where Alexander is being held. Mr Kareem said you met this man last time you were in Baghdad.'

'Adnan Bashir? But Kareem doesn't know I met him. I went alone as it was a personal visit.'

Mustafa snorted as if he was dealing with naïvety personified. 'Ahmad Kareem was probably worried about you and – let us say – provided protection for you. He's very good like that. Always worried his foreign friends will get into trouble.'

Ana looked concerned, but didn't interfere.

'But I don't understand why the Iraqis are being so helpful?'

'Humanitarian reasons, I guess. Also, Mr Kareem believes Alexander would be anti-British after his unfortunate experience with the army, and would have military experience to judge the impact of British bombing against Iraq for more than ten years since the '91 Gulf War.'

'I don't think so.'

'I think so,' said Mustafa. 'If he weighs up correctly the options he has—'

'Ana says someone else should go. Why don't you go?'

'Me? And leave the phones unmanned? The telephones are Alex's – and your – lifeline. If any trouble occurs, I can contact Kareem, and hopefully you. Any case I get car sick.'

Scot didn't know what to think. 'So what's the plan?'

'Come to my office at 7 a.m. tomorrow. I shall arrange a car with a driver very experienced in travelling to Iraq. You shall not regret it, Scot, it's a very nice drive and you will see a lot of this country and the Euphrates that very few people see. It will be a lifetime experience.' Mustafa finished his drink, and bid farewell. 'And have a very good night together.'

They did.

18

Still savouring the sweet moisture of Ana's lips, Scot
arrived at Rasool's office on the dot of 7 a.m. to find
Mustafa sealing more boxes containing cartons of
cigarettes and whisky. On one of the boxes, he stuck a
small sticky label 'Urgent'.

'These are your protection. If the Syrian police or any
people causing trouble stop you, you can give them a
carton of cigarettes. But for the love of God, don't open
this box marked "urgent". It is a special present for
Ahmad Kareem.'

'Four boxes of cigarettes, and two of whisky … You
must think we're facing a lot of trouble?'

'No, my friend. The driver gets most to sell in his
village, and others nearby. Otherwise, why would he drive
from Iraq to Aleppo? As you'll see not many people wait
on the road for passing taxis.'

'How will we get back to Aleppo?'

'Same driver! He makes the trip very regularly.'

'Full-time smuggler?'

'Full-time businessman!' Mustafa spoke firmly as if
discouraging anything that might link him to illegal trade.
'Anyway, if everything goes to plan, and Alex comes back
with you, surely his life is worth a few boxes of
cigarettes?'

Scot remained silent.

Mustafa looked at his watch. 'The driver will be here
shortly.' Then he had an afterthought, or what was timed
to appear an afterthought. He reached into a desk drawer

and retrieved two stainless steel pens. 'These are added protection for you and Mohammed.'

'To write confessions?'

'My friend, these are not what they seem. They're pistols. They used to be made in America, but these days I think someone else makes them. Best to be close to the target.'

'No, I don't carry guns.'

'There are scoundrels near the border, throughout *Al Jazirah* in fact. For your safety, I insist.'

'No.'

'You have met my friend the Chief of Police. You think a friend of the Chief of Police would advise you to take something if it were not advisable?' Before Scot had a chance to speak, Mustafa was demonstrating the gun. 'Straighten the pen fully, bend it to re-cock, straighten it, bend it a second time to re-cock it a second time then straighten it fully again.'

'I couldn't do it.'

'Wait, watch carefully, there's more … Unscrew the barrel, load a new bullet, and screw the barrel back on.'

'And ask the scoundrel to be patient?'

Mustafa shook his head in disgust at the flippancy. 'Don't show Mohammed. He may know they're very valuable. In this matchbox I've put eight point-22 calibre bullets.'

Scot could see Mustafa had made up his mind, and nothing would change it. It would be easier to take the pens, and hide them. 'Thanks.'

'Well, you shall see a lot of Syria not seen by the modern tourist. I'm quite envious.'

'Not too late, I'll stay and man the telephones.'

Mustafa ignored the remark. 'Mohammed will be waiting, so help with the boxes.'

Weak at the knees with trepidation, Scot carried a box down the stairs behind the Syrian. A man of indeterminable age – perhaps about thirty-five – was standing smoking and leaning against a battered dark green Dodge. It would have been someone's proud possession in the late 1970s. It had Iraqi number plates, and tyres that had seen better days. Mohammed, who was dressed in black trousers, a blue shirt, and a white *keffiyeh* head-dress, stubbed out his cigarette and opened the big boot. Mustafa kissed Mohammed on both cheeks then introduced Scot.

'*Ahlan Wa Sahlan,*' welcomed the driver.

'More boxes!' Twice more Scot followed Mustafa up and down the stairs until the cargo was loaded. The Syrian tapped the box marked 'Urgent' and winked at Scot. 'This one is best at the back of the boot, so you don't forget it's the special present.'

'Mohammed knows exactly where we'll meet Adnan Bashir?'

'Exactly. I've told him exactly.'

Mohammed took the driver's seat, and Scot – throwing his clothes bag on the back seat – shook Mustafa's hand.

'We'll have a party when you return.'

Or a wake if we don't, thought Scot. Suddenly, he glimpsed Ana waving from the balcony of the hotel. Jumping from the car, and waving both hands vigorously, he ostentatiously threw a kiss. 'Love you, love you'.

The engine of the old Dodge came alive with a smooth rumble. Mohammed, smiling broadly, steered the car into the traffic. They were on their way. Pictures of the Iraqi and the Syrian presidents adorned the dashboard, and served as a continual reminder of the foolishness of the trip. There was heavy traffic through the centre of the city as people made their way to work, but after less than thirty minutes, Mohammed was able to accelerate as the old

Dodge passed the city's airport. The asphalt road, with occasional potholes crossed a flat cultivated plain, punctuated by mounds, or *Tells*, where one settlement had replaced the previous, time and time again over the ages. Also, there were villages of conical-shaped mud sugar-loaf or beehive houses in which the farmers of the areas lived.

Smoking continuously, Mohammed listened to the radio tuned slightly off the channel. As reception deteriorated the further they travelled from the town, he leant across and fumbled in the glove box in front of Scot. He retrieved a tape box, and handed the box to his passenger while he started the cassette rolling. It was somehow surreal as the old Dodge ironed out the undulations in the road as 'Whiter Shades of Pale', 'Sounds of Silence' and 'Unchained Melody' played.

'Good Mister?' There was a glint in his eye, and he slapped Scot on the leg.

'Very good, Mohammed.'

Indeed, it was. As donkey carts were overtaken along the agricultural road, it was like seeing Syria from the comfort of an ageing capsule; like a film with a totally inappropriate soundtrack, which ironically seemed right. It was a trip back into nostalgia when things seemed stable and more predictable. Certainly more predictable! *Nineteen sixties are coming back again, 1960s want to dance with you . . .*

After an hour or so, the highway came close to the Euphrates River, which had flowed south from Turkey, and the giant Lake Al Assad. The road followed the river east towards the city of Deir Al Zor, more than 300 kilometres from Aleppo. It was well after 1 p.m. Mohammed was tiring so they broke the journey at a small restaurant on the corniche along the river. There was a long way to go, but for Scot the trip no longer seemed so foolish. Syrian beer had never tasted so good.

Mohammed got talking to another Iraqi driver, apparently getting up-to-date intelligence on the border area. The drivers drank sweet tea, and ate kebabs in flat bread, as they exchanged tips. The waiter – eager to practise his English – was Scot's company.

'You like our city? It is very, very nice with new houses.' The waiter pointed to the suspension bridge, which had been built in 1924 by the French. 'So beautiful it is by night with many lights.'

When Mohammed had eaten and gathered the required information, the Dodge headed off again towards Iraq. Beer had settled Scot's qualms. It was late afternoon as they approached the last Syrian town before the border, a small settlement with a police and customs post. Mohammed didn't enter the town, but took a sandy track to the south. The smugglers' route was slow, but clearly well used.

'This Iraq, Mister.'

After another few indeterminable kilometres the track swung north again. It was almost dark as they rejoined the main road and Mohammed switched on the car's headlights. A trap was revealed. Not a hundred metres ahead was a police car, which had been hidden in the darkness. But now, with its identity revealed and its quarry trapped, the flashing blue light began its torment. There were two men in uniform. One waved his arms above his head signalling to stop. The other aimed a revolver straight at the old Dodge. Scot's heart pounded. 'Police … Syrian or Iraqi?'

Mohammed mumbled 'Iraqi'.

The Dodge came to a halt behind the police car. The policemen slowly circled the car like vultures. Then the one who'd been waving talked to Mohammed, while the officer with the revolver shone a torch into Scot's face. He shouted: 'English?'

'No Australian ... *La Australie.*'

The policeman aimed his revolver at Scot's head. He spoke slow stilted English. 'I do not think *Australie*. I think English.'

Mohammed tried to help, as much for himself as for Scot. '*La*. Mister Scot *Australie.*'

'Passport,' the policeman wielding the gun said abruptly.

Scot fumbled for his passport, and with a trembling hand passed it over.

First the policeman held it upside down. Then – maybe prompted by the photograph – turned it and nodded slowly as he studied the passport. Scot waited apprehensively for the dubious entry stamp to be noted. Instead, the policeman's tone warmed a little as he said in a surprised way to his colleague '*Australie*'. Then to Scot, he said with intense concentration, 'Welcome ... I have cousin in Australia. Sydney.'

The policeman who'd been talking to Mohammed went to the police car and switched off the flashing light, then returned ordering the boot to be opened. They all went to the back of the car as the policemen flashed the torch around. The one with the Australian connection opened a box of cigarettes and removed four cartons, two of which he handed to his colleague. He then opened the box of whisky, and - after placing the revolver back in its holster - took a bottle. He appeared to have finished. Then, as an afterthought, flashed his torch around the boot one more time. The torch caught the box at the back, with its seals and stamp marked 'Urgent'. The policeman drew a penknife out of his pocket and reached towards the box.

'*La*, *La*, No, No,' Scot said, reaching out to stop the policeman.

'Why?' The policeman cocked his head as he spoke.

'That is a special box for Iraq's Interior Ministry.'

The policeman leered at Scot as if he were a fool. Leaning towards the box, his blade poised to slash the seals, it was Mohammed's turn to intervene. Scot gave the driver no chance. Why would the policeman take any notice of a taxi driver reduced to cross-border smuggling? It didn't make sense, but he did. The policeman looked directly into Mohammed's eyes almost cowering in the face of a revelation. There were few words exchanged, but the policeman began to nod reverently at the driver. Then he exchanged a word of explanation to his police colleague. The policemen now appeared as nervous as Scot felt.

As if to regain lost pride, the policeman with the Sydney connection played out one final charade. Holding the torch near his waist, and shining it upwards, he illuminated Scot's face and his own. 'One hundred dollar customs fine.'

Scot didn't think twice. He removed a hundred-dollar bill from his shirt pocket and handed it over.

The ordeal was over. The police waved the Dodge onwards. Heart pounding, Scot indicated thanks to the driver. As the car gained speed, Scot wondered why Mohammed had such clout with the police. Could he be an Iraqi agent while masquerading as a smuggler?

And what was in the sealed box?

It was around 10 p.m. by the time they reached their destination – a small settlement of mud walls and weathered concrete. The Iraqi drove into the garden compound of a small house and a weathered old man obviously known to Mohammed ushered them inside. He offered sweet tea and biscuits, before showing them to a small room with two narrow and basic bunks. Scot was ready for rest, but a meowing cat outside the window kept him awake. Mohammed, however, snored, exhausted after the long drive.

Morning came early with a rooster signalling daybreak. Scot hadn't slept much, but anxiety overrode tiredness. For another hour he just lay under the single woollen blanket until Mohammed woke. Feeling grotty, the Australian left the room and went outside to the garden and lit up a cigarette. In the daylight, the garden revealed its rustic splendour. There was a fig tree, an orange tree and a stone well. A mud-brick wall surrounded the compound. The Dodge looked safe, a gate having been closed. The cottage, while basic, was built of light coloured mud bricks. A red flowering creeper clung to the wall. Scot walked to the well and wound the handle. A bucket came up and rolling up his shirtsleeves, he washed his arms and face.

Near the back door of the house, there was a wooden table with two chairs. The man who'd greeted them the night before appeared and smiled broadly. He carried a third wooden chair from the house. Then Mohammed appeared, carrying a tray with a saucer of *hummus* and another of *babaganoug*, some flat bread, cucumbers sliced into four, a sliced tomato and some olives. There also was sweet tea. 'Morning Mister Scot … Break … Fast.'

With vegetation stretching well beyond the compound towards the Euphrates, it was easy to imagine the town's history as a staging post before the arrival of motor vehicles. They ate and drank with barely a word being spoken. Scot's anxiety lifted with the warmth of the silent hospitality. Mohammed was his friend, having delivered him safely to his destination.

After eating, Scot went inside for his battery razor and shaved by the well. Splashing more water from the bucket over his face and neck, he felt invigorated. Mohammed was ready to leave. His friend smiled profusely as Scot handed him $50 and a carton of cigarettes. It was probably more than necessary, and mean foreigners would blame him for raising the stakes of staying in the town, but bugger it. Scot wasn't intending to return – and even if he did – wouldn't regret it. He knew that. He was grateful for the hospitality – and the security.

Mohammed drove towards the river. There were lush crops everywhere on the fertile plain beside the Euphrates. Near the river there was a small restaurant with tables under a vine, and the car stopped. Scot opened the door and hopped out. From beneath the vine emerged Adnan Bashir, a straw hat protecting his balding head from the sun.

'I knew we would meet again,' he said, recalling their discussion in his Baghdad courtyard. Dressed in a lightweight tweed sports coat and cotton slacks, and dragging on a pipe, he looked every bit the archaeologist and academic, and nothing like an *apparatchik* of the Baghdad regime. They shook hands as if they were the closest of friends. 'Coffee?' After signalling to the waiter, Adnan Bashir delved into a satchel and retrieved a large manila envelope, and turned to Scot. 'I'm told you know a Mustafa Rasool. Could you give him this?'

The envelope was securely bound with tape. 'From?'

'Kareem,' replied Bashir.

Scot followed Adnan Bashir to a table under the vine. Mohammed joined them. Cats gathered around the table. A four-wheeled drive pulled up behind the Dodge, and out of the rear door Alexander Belfort-Smith emerged, looking tired and anxious, but not unwell.

'I think this is what you came for?'

They both went and greeted the Englishman. The Iraqi introduced himself to Alex with sadness, or respect for his own dead son, but it took some time for the connection to be comprehended. And, as Alex looked at Scot, he appeared even more confused. 'I'm sorry, why are you both here and where are we?'

'It's an Iraqi version of *This is Your Life.*' Scot's joke fell flat.

'What are we all doing here?'

'We're going home to Cyprus via Aleppo.'

'I knew nothing of this,' Alex said. 'I thought I was going to some sort of interrogation or court. I thought that's why I was ordered to shower and shave.'

They went slowly towards the tables under the vine and drank tea. Alex slowly comprehended the situation and Adnan Bashir's relationship with his Baghdad friend. But bafflement still figured prominently in his demeanour. It took time for him to turn to Scot and ask about Dimitri.

'He's well, but worried. He's coping well with the restaurant.'

Alex nodded and showed the first sign of a smile.

Scot offered cigarettes. Bashir declined, but Alex looked at the packet for some time before responding. 'Think I will.'

A police car pulled up behind the four-wheel drive and two officers approached Adnan, obviously aware of his senior position in the government. Mohammed then approached Adnan with the box marked 'urgent'. The archaeologist turned bureaucrat appeared to know about the box, and perhaps what it contained. He thanked the driver and placed the box under the table. Scot tried his damnedest to appear not to notice. After a further exchange, Mohammed left with the Dodge, Adnan explaining he'd gone to buy petrol.

Another car pulled up. This time a television crew emerged and after a couple of minutes started filming the scene at the table. They then joined the gathering, the cameraman placing his equipment on the table, and his colleague, who Scot guessed was the reporter, looked at the two foreigners and spoke in a matter-of-fact way. 'Which one is the English spy?'

Scot looked at Alexander, whose blood was rapidly draining from his face.

'I'm English, but I'm not a spy.'

Adnan eased the strain a little by speaking gently to the reporter in English. 'Be polite my friend, Mr Belfort-Smith is a guest of our country.'

Then another vehicle pulled up. This time it was a small van. First two wheelchairs were set up, and then three children on crutches were helped from the van, and another two were carried to the wheelchairs. A small crowd began to gather. For the sleepy little town, this was obviously a big day.

An army officer, who'd arrived with the children, approached the table and spoke to Adnan before turning to Alexander. He stretched out his hand as if for shaking. He spoke in stilted, but clear English. 'Major Belfort-Smith I am pleased to meet you.'

Adnan looked somewhat embarrassed, Scot felt puzzled, and Alexander looked stunned. He reluctantly stood and limply held out his hand for shaking. 'But I'm not Major Belfort-Smith, I'm just plain Mr Belfort-Smith, Alexander Belfort-Smith.'

Scot felt that if he were not sitting well inside Iraq with a dubious entry stamp in his passport, he would burst into laughter. But as his own safety was at stake, and with Alex looking extremely anxious, he suppressed any thought of humour.

Adnan tried to help by offering Alexander some gentle advice. Quietly, he said: 'Just play along and you'll be out of Iraq this afternoon.' Scot nodded support.

The television crew stood up and went to the roadside near the children. The Iraqi officer spoke in a firm, but not demanding tone. 'Major Belfort-Smith, would you follow me please and meet the children.'

They all got up and followed the officer. For Adnan and Scot it was easy enough. They were merely spectators. And the children? They were props for the television. One had a badly burnt, but healed face, two were missing arms, another had a missing foot. The last, standing with the help of crutches, had a thigh hanging, his leg having been amputated above the knee. They all looked well fed, and the horrific injuries had clearly occurred months if not years before. They looked puzzled rather than sad.

The Iraqi officer introduced Alexander to the children one by one, and then stood beside the Englishmen in front of the children. The reporter moved close to Alexander, and the cameraman focused on the small gathering.

Scot turned to Adnan. 'Where are these children from?'

'Several places, I believe, a couple from the city of Mosul.'

The camera started to whirr, a red light flashing. The reporter began more with a statement than a question. 'Mr Belfort-Smith, as a person trained by the British Army you must feel ashamed of your country's aggression when you see the severe wounds suffered by these children in the years since Britain's and America's invasion of the Iraqi homeland in 1991?'

Scot held his breath, realising Alexander's reaction could determine whether or not he went free today – or ever. Time seemed to stand still, until Alexander began his response. He spoke slowly, apparently considering every word with care. 'Like any caring person, I can see these children have suffered horrendous injuries. They look well cared for which is clearly a tribute to the doctors and medical staff in Iraqi hospitals and nursing homes.'

So far so good, but there was more to come. 'Mr Belfort-Smith, do you wish to condemn the actions of the British government in harming these orphaned children?'

The children were by now looking around puzzled and bored with the incomprehensible discussion that was taking place in front of them. One waved at the camera from his wheelchair.

'It is terrible when children are injured – whatever the cause may be – and especially unfortunate if they are caught up as innocent casualties in war.'

'How do you feel when you see these young victims of British imperialism?'

The question was more succinct and more difficult to answer. To question the cause of the injuries, or to deny his country's involvement would be futile. The rules of the game could not be changed. Iraq held all the cards. Scot drew in a deep breath. Alexander looked at Scot as if wishing to try out his response before proceeding. But of course he couldn't.

'I have been the victim of British government policy, which was unjust, and unworthy of any democratic and humane government. That policy led to my discharge from the army. It was a British policy criticised by the European Court of Human Rights. I feel sympathy for anyone who is the victim of inhumane government policy and decision-making anywhere in the world.'

'Thank you, Mr Belfort-Smith. We hope you enjoyed your visit to Iraq.'

The camera kept whirring, and Alexander turned to face the children again. One by one he kissed each of the little faces, until he came to the child with the badly burnt face. He hesitated, then kissed the little girl and hugged her. He then turned to face Scot and Adnan with tears streaming down his face. The cameraman caught the scene.

Was it the children, Scot wondered? Or a reaction to the ordeal being over? Or having had to revisit publicly the end of his army career? There was no way of knowing.

Whatever the reason, Scot and Adnan tried to escape the emotional impact, and together turned away from Alexander and slowly walked back to the table.

More coffee arrived and Scot's head was spinning with thoughts. The cause of the children's injuries was uncertain, and would never be established, nor the Iraqi claims substantiated. They could have been *collateral damage* from the regular British and American bombing of Iraqi military and communications installations. Those attacks had gone on for more than ten years after the 1991 Gulf War, which removed Iraq from Kuwait. The children's injuries could just as easily have been the result of car accidents, or other mishaps. Maybe the Iraqi officer and Adnan pondered that question too. And one would have to be naïve to believe the Iraqi television audience would be devoid of sceptics. War was a dirty and cynical game, and anyone playing had to accept the risk of sinking into the quicksand of inhumanity. For Scot, Alexander had played the interview without fault. Some would criticise him for putting his own freedom – and perhaps survival – ahead of criticising Iraq's cynical use of public relations, even its human rights record, including the use of nerve gas against its own Kurds. But critics would be well away from any personal threat. And anyway, direct criticism of Iraq would never go to air.

Scot was about to pass on his feelings to Adnan, who he'd liked since their first meeting in Baghdad. The civility of his courtyard where they'd shared coffee, their mutual compassion for each other's personal loss and tragedy, drew them together. Even the Iraqi's tweed sports coat and archaeological background were simplistic touchstones of civilisation. At the last second, Scot bit his tongue. After all, Adnan was a senior bureaucrat in Baghdad. Any enthusiastic suggestion that Alex had performed well could prompt the Iraqi to suggest the TV crew extracted more explicit criticism of Britain. It was unlikely, but possible. After all Adnan Bashir's continued survival could depend upon complex domestic political considerations.

The use of the children? Of course it was cynical, bordering on obscene. But almost all Western politicians used children. Around the world they kissed kids in shopping malls in the run-up to elections. Those western children didn't vote, it was their parents who were being charmed. For the children who were now being loaded back in the van, they'd probably enjoyed a rare day out. They'd seen the countryside. They'd been the centre of attention. They had something to talk about. For a day at least, they were made to feel useful. The event would have been a distraction from depressing reality.

Alexander sat back, silently enjoying the tea. He raised his eyebrows seeking Scot's approval. With a smile and a nod of the head, he received it. It was not a time for words. They could come later.

The children had left. The television crew was packing its gear. The policemen said farewell to Adnan. The Iraqi army officer joined the table. Tentatively, he engaged Alex, talking army ranks and military history. They touched upon the toys of war. They said nothing that was not public knowledge or the subject of basic textbooks used by armies around the world. Scot watched the Iraqi as he talked, and thought about issues the Iraqi could never venture an opinion upon for fear of being misinterpreted in a country stifled of free speech. Or only if he were reckless or suicidal! A decade or so of sanctions and bombing by US and the British would have drawn hostility from anyone linked by an officer's uniform to the regime. The sanctions and the bombing would amount to a serious attack on the country's sovereignty. Iraq's failure to comply with UN resolutions and its past use of chemical weapons would hardly sway this Iraqi's hostility. What would he make of American and British sabre-rattling in the Gulf? Did he fear war? Would he be prepared to die for a despotic leader? As Scot saw it, he was probably mortgaged to the regime: his house, car, television – his lifestyle – supplied by the army. Like so many Iraqis, this officer – just like the Americans and the British who couldn't pack up their Gulf-based armour without losing face – was trapped in the quicksand of the Middle East, a political quagmire.

It was a *Boys' Own Annual* type of encounter between Alex and the Iraqi. When the Iraqi rose to leave, Alexander stood and shook the Iraqi officer's hand.

With the stranger having left, Adnan turned to Alex. 'My late son often talked about meeting you in Paris. About the galleries and restaurants you visited. About walking along the Seine, and the squirrels in the Bois de Boulogne. He found it hard to believe you were in the army. He said you weren't military at all!'

Alex turned to Adnan with a wry smile. 'That's what the army thought too, in the end!'

A gentle smile crept over Adnan's face. 'Although my son did well as an artist in Baghdad, he found life restricting. I think he would have preferred to live in Europe. And so would I, of course.'

'Did he die peacefully, or did he suffer?'

'For more than a year, he had good days and bad days. He lost weight and looked drawn. The bad days became normal.' After a hesitation, Adnan added: 'I believe our mutual acquaintance kept you informed of developments, my son's decline.'

Scot noticed Alexander nodding an acknowledgement. He didn't speak. Was it that Alexander merely understood the suffering Adnan's son would have gone through, or acknowledging that 'our mutual acquaintance' had kept him informed? And who was this acquaintance?

'The end, when it came, was a relief, but it left me feeling very alone. I still miss him,' Adnan said.

Alexander returned to the earlier point Adnan had made. 'Why don't you leave Iraq, and live in Europe?'

Adnan smiled at the foreigners. 'Because I'm an Iraqi, I have a family to consider. It's where I belong. Most of us are trapped by our place of birth.' He looked sagely towards Alexander, then Scot. 'Foreigners like you take freedom for granted. The currents of the Tigris control our world.'

Then, as if wishing to change the subject, the archaeologist suggested they might like a walk around the village. In other circumstances it would be interesting, but not today. Adnan understood. The Dodge returned with a refreshed Mohammed. He looked happy. Maybe he'd off-loaded the cigarettes and whisky at a good price. They decided it was time to leave on the long journey back to Aleppo. They thanked Adnan and said farewell. There was relief all round.

The Dodge pulled away, and Mohammed played his tape. *Nineteen Sixties are coming again, 1960s we want to dance with you.* This time, the driver turned to Alex in the back seat, and asked: 'Good, Mister?'

'Very good, Mohammed.'

By mid afternoon, they'd retraced the route without incident. Perhaps no one, including the police, thought a car travelling from Iraq would have anything of value on board. After an exhausting and emotional morning, and the stress of the illegal border crossing, it was decided to stay overnight in Deir Al Zor.

'You could ring Limassol, Alex. Dimitri will be very relieved to hear your voice.'

They checked into the Furat Cham Palace Hotel. The city is beyond the reach of most tourists. There were other foreigners though – mainly oil experts exploring the region. Three East Europeans were interested in the condition of the road beyond the city, fuelling speculation their cross-border business involved more than cigarettes and whisky. Scot offered Mohammed a room in the hotel, but he insisted he'd stay with a friend. He'd return at 8 a.m.

Before going to their rooms, Alex enthusiastically accepted Scot's suggestion of a beer. It was the first he'd had for some time. Although safely back in Syria, Alex was still concerned about his safety. He recounted his abduction from the centre of Aleppo.

'Until I leave the country, I won't feel really safe. There were just two men. I think I'd recognise them, but I don't know. For some reason, they had some mad idea I'd be worth something to Iraq. I struggled, but I lost consciousness. I woke up and there were three desert tribes people of some kind judging by their clothes. We were in the middle of nowhere in the desert. In retrospect, there was a funny side to it. Once the men made contact with some Iraqi officials, it took some time for them to be persuaded I was of any value at all. They seemed to think I was just a bloody nuisance. Finally, some Iraqi was persuaded I might be of value.'

'Always nice to be wanted.' This time Alexander understood the quip. He was recovering.

'But I'm at a loss to know why they thought the Iraqis would want me?'

Scot told him about the list published by the *Beirut Underground*. Alex looked genuinely bewildered, but it could have been feigned puzzlement. And confirmation was not expected. A clue might come one day, but not today.

Scot thought of Ahmad Kareem in Baghdad, but – not wanting to divulge to Alex the extent of his contacts in Iraq – spoke of Adnan instead.

'The Iraqis are full of surprises. Adnan's a very kind and gentle man, nothing like you'd expect from a senior bureaucrat in Baghdad.'

Alex thought for a while before responding. 'All governments and regimes, whether good or bad, have good and bad people within. They can only function with the good ... That's as true for Western democracies as it is for dictatorships.'

After finishing the beers, they went to their rooms, both relishing the idea of a shower.

'I'll try and ring Dimitri. I hope he's pleased. After all, it's been quite a time now.'

'He'll be pleased.'

19

As they approached Aleppo the next day, Alexander was repeatedly mentioning how pleased Dimitri had sounded. Annoyance was fermenting. After all, Scot had predicted Dimitri's reaction. They had been through Alex's disappearance together. They'd shared the hassles, the frustrations, and the interrogation by Richard Xanadu Jordan. Scot was also envious. While Alexander had successfully dialled Limassol, he'd been unable to contact Ana. 'She's not in her room,' the hotel's telephonist said repeatedly.

There were other frustrations. Alexander had so far given no clear explanation of the reason behind his trip to Aleppo. Scot was beginning to accept Rick Jordan's belief that the Englishman had not been on Debbie London's trail at all. She was just a decoy.

But a decoy for what?

As Alexander droned on about Dimitri yet again, Scot thought of Ana. He could almost feel her soft skin as he planned their evening together. However anticipation was dampened by the expectation Alex would hang around. And Rasool, justifiably pleased with his role in the rescue, would expect to be involved in a celebration. Resentment grew as Scot assessed the inevitable.

'So why did you travel to Aleppo in the first place?'

'Debbie London. Thought I explained that. I hoped to get a lead on her whereabouts.'

Scot was far from convinced the story was so simple. 'What's Rick Jordan's role in all this?'

'We go back a long way. From what you told me about his concern about me, I guess he was worried about an old mate.'

'There seem to be a hell of a lot of old loyalties being acted upon. You worry about Debbie, and Jordan worries about you. I find it all a bit hard to believe.'

Alexander didn't respond.

But Scot wouldn't let go. He'd seen the passing scenery already and didn't mind annoying Alexander. 'You go back a long way with Jordan? To a time when you were involved in intelligence in Washington?'

'I was in Washington, yes. But there are things I can say and others I can't, due to Britain's Official Secrets Act.'

'So *Beirut Underground* had it right? You are a spy?'

Alexander didn't answer. And Scot had spent all the energy he had to pursue the matter. There was silence between the two for the remaining hour of the trip. Mohammed – perhaps sensing the tension – turned on the radio. It was mid afternoon by the time they passed Aleppo airport, and the run to Baron Street was quick. The Dodge stopped outside Rasool's office.

Scot looked across at the hotel, in the vain hope Ana would be waiting on the balcony. Dashing across the road, he explained he'd return to Rasool's office shortly.

'Good afternoon,' said the man at reception handing over the room key. Entering the room, he looked around in disbelief, jubilation turning to heaviness. All Ana's belongings had gone. Damn Rasool, he'd sent her on another mystery errand.

Tired, miffed and impatient, he sullenly left the hotel and walked across to the trade consultant's office. There, he found Rasool, Alexander and Mohammed, celebrating the Englishman's safe return. Rasool was basking in glory, but generous when Scot arrived.

'This, Alexander, is the real hero. Who else would chase across international borders for the sake of a friend? Only a very good friend!'

'Where's Ana?'

Rasool let a sombre look creep across his face. 'A cousin has been taken seriously ill in Belgrade and she's returned home.'

'So suddenly?'

The Syrian nodded, handing Scot an envelope. 'She left you this.'

As he tore open the envelope, excitement drained from his body, the vacuum being filled by gloom.

> *Dear Scot,*
> *My dear cousin is dying. I received a telephone call from Belgrade an hour or so ago. Although I will miss you every minute, I must return to Serbia. I am uncertain where I will stay for the first couple of weeks, but will contact you in Limassol. Love you so much and thank you for our friendship.*
> *Love Ana.*

Scot looked up at Mustafa. 'When did she leave?'

'Last night.'

'So she may be in Damascus still?'

Mustafa shook his head slowly. 'No, she went by road into Turkey. She'd be beyond Ankara now. She'll ring you from Belgrade, and she'll be back again soon.' He then added an unconvincing prediction. 'I'm sure of that.'

Scot remembered the envelope. 'A letter for you Mustafa ... from Ahmad Kareem.'

As Rasool read, his lips twitched, and his head shook in disbelief. He looked towards Scot. 'Suppose you wouldn't like another trip to Iraq?' The question was rhetorical. 'You took them as much Viagra as was possible

– enough for the whole regime. Now they want something else. They're too demanding! These sanctions must end. What is it you people say: "Give an inch and they'll take a mile"? Well, they're trying to take a mile.'

'So the sealed box contained Viagra?' A smile crept across Scot's face. 'And you marked it urgent!'

Rasool nodded, while Alex looked puzzled. He, for once, was out of the loop, and Scot wasn't intending to let him in.

'Well, Alex, through no fault of your own, you're late for lunch. I suggest we all go to my favourite restaurant. I'm sure they're still holding the booking.'

With Ana gone, Scot followed reluctantly.

In a hotel bed alone once more, Scot dozed rather than slept, thinking of Ana, hoping she was safe, and planning a trip to Belgrade. An ache of loneliness had returned. As dawn broke, he showered, and walked the street pavements – more for distraction than exercise.

A shoeshine man, clad in flowing *dishdasha* and *keffiyeh*, pointed at Scot's shoes as he walked past a tarnished, but elaborate brass box. The teasing and glinting eyes of the weathered old man caught Scot's.

'Shoes too dirty, sir!'

Scot looked down and agreed. As he stood, one foot on the step of the box then the other, a nearby newspaper stall grabbed his attention. There was a screaming headline, but it was the black and white picture that caught his eye. Next to the Arabic newspaper, there was the English language *Syria Times*. The picture was the same, and the headline read: HOTEL MURDER. But it was the picture, an unmistakable image of the man seen arguing with Mustafa Rasool on the day before he'd left for Iraq, that held his attention.

'Thank you, sir,' said the shoeshine man as Scot passed over more money than he'd expected.

Buying a copy of the *Syria Times*, he studied the story.

> *Police are investigating the murder of an Aleppo man found shot dead in a hotel used by tourists in the northern Syrian city. The man, a local businessman known to police, was lying in bed when shot by a small calibre gun. His clothes were found in a heap beside the bed.*

> *The police said last night they were searching for the murderer and the point-22 calibre weapon. Hotel maids discovered the body when routinely cleaning the hotel room. They believed the man was killed the previous evening.*

The mention of a point-22 calibre weapon rang alarm bells. The pen pistols that Mustafa Rasool had given him were point-22 calibre. Rasool had said that himself, hadn't he? And Mustafa had been seen arguing with the dead man. Scot walked briskly back towards the hotel and across the road to Rasool's office. He hurried up the stairs two at a time. He hammered on the door. It was locked. At 7 a.m., it was too early.

During an unsettled breakfast in the hotel, he considered the tack he'd take with Rasool. He'd merely return the unused pistols, and judge Rasool's reaction to the story. Returning to his room, he rummaged through his baggage, found one pen pistol hidden amongst his underclothes. But the other pistol? He went methodically through every item of clothing, even his sponge bag. It was nowhere to be found. His baggage had been in the Dodge when Mohammed had gone to sell the cigarettes and whisky. Surely, the driver wouldn't have stolen it?

Nothing in the bag had looked disturbed. Over dinner in Deir Al Zor, the bag was left in the room. But again, there was no sign of the room having been entered or the bag's contents rifled. Anyway, no one would have expected him to leave money in the room. And they wouldn't have known there'd be pen pistols in the bag. Even if they'd been found, why take one but not the other?

Returning to Rasool's office, Scot found Mustafa sitting at his desk reading an Arabic newspaper.

'Puzzling murder, isn't it?'

'Puzzling!'

Mustafa looked up with a welcoming smile. 'Morning Scot, sleep well?'

'Not well.'

'She'll return. You'll hear from Ana.'

Drawing the gun out of his shirt pocket, he handed it to the Syrian. 'I'm afraid I can only find one, but you gave me two, didn't you?'

'Two, yes.'

'I'll look again, but I shouldn't have taken them at all. They weren't necessary.'

'Look again, if you can. They're expensive, as I explained, but the cost is not important. You rescued Alexander after all.'

'Did you say these guns use point-22 calibre bullets?'

'Maybe, but I know very little about guns.' The self-confessed shady trade consultant gave an angelic smile, feigned of course. 'I think I'm what you call a pacifist.'

Scot pointed to the newspaper. 'The *Syria Times* says police are looking for a point-22 calibre gun.'

'Very common calibre, I believe.'

'But I saw you arguing with the dead man?'

Mustafa looked directly at Scot. 'You Europeans see two Arabs shouting at each other, and think it's an argument. But there are arguments and arguments, and shouting is a cultural trait of ours. It's misunderstood often. We're very emotional people, and often argue with our closest friends. We don't argue with our enemies. We, my dear friend, understand that shouting and argument is not the best way to defeat our enemies.'

'I know, I know, but it looked a pretty serious dispute to me.'

'I have told our friend the police chief about my meeting with the poor man. I thought the police would wish to know all his movements in the days before the tragic murder. Also, I have conveyed my deepest condolences to his family. His father is such a dear friend of mine. I didn't mention to his father about his son's role in the abduction of Alexander, or about the missing credit card. Why worry the poor man? Let the dead rest in peace. Let Allah be the judge.'

'But was he? Involved in the abduction?'

'Definite, my dear Scot, definite.'

Scot looked at the Syrian, feeling certain he knew more about the man's murder than he was letting on. But he was in Aleppo, where his word would count for nothing against a businessman who shakes the hand of the president. And the gun he'd lost? That wouldn't look good, whatever jurisdiction.

'Are those guns legal?'

'I'm sure they must be because I paid good money for them. And now I have just one.' He shook his head at Scot and pursed his lips. 'You could ask our friend the police chief. As you know he speaks English. He'd know whether they are legal or not.' A sickly grin crossed his face, as he reached for the phone. 'Do you want to ask the police chief? I have his direct number.'

Scot shook his head, turned, and headed from the room.

'Where are you going?'

'To find Alex. See how he slept, and make plans to return to Cyprus.'

As the airliner descended over Larnaca Bay, its undercarriage locked into place. Lower and lower, over fishing boats just below, the plane skirted over the rocky shore before touching down on the runway. Scot felt relief at returning home. In the next seat, Alex smiled. The short flight from Damascus delivered them back into a familiar world and away from Mustafa Rasool and the intrigue that surrounded him.

Scot's relief didn't last long. After clearing immigration and customs, he glimpsed the newspaper of a departing traveller. Finding a news-stand, and fumbling for change with trembling hands, he bought the *Cyprus Daily*. 'NICOSIA, ALEPPO MURDERS LINKED,' screamed the headline.

> *Cyprus and Syrian police are investigating a possible link between the recent murder of a Syrian man in the Nicosia Grand Hotel and this week's slaying in an Aleppo Hotel.*

> *Both murders were committed with a point-22 calibre weapon. Cyprus police believe the gun could have been a pen pistol or another small gun easily concealed by the murderer.*

> *'Both murdered men were Syrian and both were murdered while naked and lying in bed,' a Cyprus police spokesman said.*

The victim of the Aleppo murder was seen chatting in the bar of the Nicosia Grand with the man murdered just days later in the hotel.

Police are trying to identify a mystery woman seen with the two men in the Nicosia Grand. They appealed for the woman to come forward to police. Anyone knowing the whereabouts of the woman has been asked to ring the police.

'At this stage, we are not treating the woman as a suspect in the murders, but she could provide vital clues to the crimes,' a police spokesman said.

A fuzzy image of Ana taken from the hotel's security camera was published alongside the story. Scot's mind was working overtime. Go to the police and clear her name? As certain as night follows day, that would point the finger no matter what the police said about the woman not being a suspect. And Scot himself? He'd have some explaining to do. How did he meet her? 'Well, I had to deliver twenty-thousand dollars in cash to her.' Where did this money come from? 'I'm a small trader, and it was given to me by Syrian and Iraqi connections.' Why was the money being paid to this woman? 'I don't know exactly.' Where is this woman? 'In Belgrade, or on her way to Belgrade?' What is her address? 'I don't know.' Shit!

'You ready?'

Startled, Scot spun around to see a beaming Alex.

'Great to be back in Cyprus, isn't it?'

Scot nodded and tried to smile.

'You all right?'

Scot's mouth opened, but it took time for a word to emerge. '… earache.'

'Aircraft pressurisation. Sometimes suffer myself, but not today.'

After getting into a taxi to take them to Limassol, Scot handed Alex the newspaper. 'They're linking the murders. The two men I saw in the Nicosia Grand after your credit card was used.'

Alex studied the paper. 'Wonder if the woman killed both the men?'

'Doubt it.'

'Why?'

'What I mean is I haven't a clue.'

'Well, she'd have to have been in Aleppo, and the police don't seem to know whether she's left Cyprus.'

'Exactly.' Scot breathed more easily as Alex handed back the newspaper. He knew about Ana, but hadn't seen her. Dimitri was the only person who might link him to the fuzzy picture in the newspaper. Maybe he wouldn't recognise her. With the laser beams flashing on the dance floor at the time, the chances were he wouldn't.

'Dimitri will be getting the restaurant ready for lunch. You must come in for a drink.'

'No, I'll go straight home to the apartment. Let Dimitri welcome you home. I'll come around later.'

'I insist! You've done so much. If it wasn't for you, Dimitri and Mustafa, I'd still be languishing in Iraq.'

As the taxi continued along the motorway little was said. Small talk was on the agenda, rather than substantive discussion. That was being left to the committee arguing inside Scot's head. Maybe it would be better to face Dimitri immediately. He'd be distracted by Alex's return. Amidst heavy traffic the taxi crawled to Club Downtown. Scot paid the driver, and they carried their baggage inside.

Dimitri dashed from the back of the restaurant and hugged Alexander. Scot felt very much a voyeur, a spectator, a courier of relief. It was a role he savoured.

Then Dimitri stretched one arm out and around his neck, and they all came together like a Maypole. Round and round they went until Dimitri tripped on a chair and the chain of limbs uncoupled.

After regaining his breath, Dimitri dropped a bombshell.

'Alex, that woman Debbie you were looking for has turned up. She was here in Limassol with her parents until a day or so ago.' Turning to the bar, he added, 'I have her Kurdish friend working for us.'

As Scot approached the bar, Dimitri overtook him, Alexander in tow.

'Alex, this is Sami.' The two shook hands across the bar, Alex showing a little surprise. 'Sami is Debbie London's friend, but she went to London urgently. So he's working here part time.'

Scot asked Sami for a beer. Dimitri filled Alex in on developments regarding Debbie. As he took a first sip, he heard Dimitri mention something about a court, and turned for elaboration.

'Yes, she's had to go to London for a court case. Much secrecy, and poor Sami was left with nothing to do.'

'What sort of court case?' Scot listened, but the answer was vague. 'So where are Debbie's parents?'

'Think they're still at their hotel, but maybe London.'

For Scot, Alexander's reaction to the latest news about Debbie was astonishing. He showed no surprise. Either he was preoccupied with his own return, which was quite possible, or knew more about developments surrounding Debbie than he was letting on.

Dimitri, lonely for so long, kept talking. 'Scot, by the way … the police I made contact with? Remember?'

Scot responded tentatively, fearful of what might follow. 'Yes, I remember.'

'They say the man murdered – the one who used Alex's credit card – was a drug smuggler. The Syrian police knew him, they said. The other man killed in Syria was a criminal too. Both of the men were on a list the Americans have. What is it? The Drug Forcement Body?'

'The Drug Enforcement Agency.' Alex impatiently corrected Dimitri.

'That's it.'

'And what about the woman?'

Scot stopped breathing as he waited for Dimitri's response to Alex's question.

'The one on the television and in the newspapers?'

'Yes,' said Alex.

'The police don't know if that woman was involved. But they think the murderer was a woman ... because both men were naked.'

Alex spoke with slow, deliberate drollness. 'Well, they would think that. They're so predictably homophobic.'

They all laughed, even Sami, whose small English vocabulary was unlikely to grasp the comment.

Emboldened, Scot suggested the murders were likely the result of a drug syndicate feud.

'Turkish,' Dimitri said. 'They say the murders were the work of Turkish drug kings because pen guns have been found smuggled into Turkey.'

Alexander expelled a puff of cynical despair. 'The Cyprus police appear to have used the latest in forensic prejudice! Blame the Turks, and rule out the possibility the men were gay.'

Dimitri cocked his head, and gently rebuked his partner. 'No Alex, the police are very thorough and it's known by everybody the Turkish have very big and bad drug kings. You wouldn't know.'

Scot noticed Alex pursing his lips, and decided to push the envelope of mystery surrounding the Englishman just a little further. 'Dimitri's right. Turkey has a big drug problem.'

Alex gave the sigh of someone impatient with amateurs, or was that just Scot's imagination? 'I know, I know.' Alex spoke as if he wanted the subject dropped.

They sat for a drink, but as soon as it seemed reasonable to do so, Scot got up to leave. 'Better get back home, and check things.'

Alex and Dimitri followed him to the door, thanking him profusely. 'Come back for dinner,' Dimitri said. 'We'll have a proper celebration.'

20

As Scot approached the apartment block, he'd one niggling concern. Had Nikos seen Ana? She'd used the security phone, but that didn't mean a thing given Nikos's irregularity. Even if Nikos recognised the fuzzy picture, Scot decided to respond vaguely.

'Good trip I hope. Welcome back to Limassol.' That was all Nikos said as Scot passed.

In the apartment, the answering machine's flashing light was ignored. Walking on to the balcony, Scot reflected how much time and effort was wasted worrying. If Dimitri hadn't recognised the photograph, which had also been on television, why should he worry?

Something puzzled him though. Surely the police would have known from Ana's *friends of friends* the identity of the woman? No, he wasn't going to the police. They'd combine all the circumstantial evidence, and more than likely come to the conclusion there was enough to issue an international arrest warrant. He refused to convict Ana, whom he missed madly. What he didn't know for certain, he didn't have to believe. It was increasingly unlikely he'd ever know for sure.

Returning to the phone, he pushed the button on the answering machine. 'Hello, Scot, could you ring me? It's Matthew York.' There were five messages altogether, three of them relating to business. Finally, the machine played a message from Lilly London. 'Love to catch up again, we'll be here until the weekend. Ring us at the hotel.' Well, it could have been last weekend she was referring to, but unlikely seeing her message was the last.

Lifting the handset, Scot was about to dial. But he hesitated, put the phone down, and slumped in the chair. While Lionel and Lilly would shed light on Debbie's surprise departure for London, and Matthew might let more slip about Alex, heaviness had descended. Back home now, there was time to think. Recent events rushed to fill the vacuum left as bustle departed. Travel, either business or pleasure, was an escape from reality, everyday problems. It postponed the need for taking stock of developments. One day's problems could be deferred with an airport check-in, or something similarly mundane. That's why his life was so appealing. Just like the Bedouin of Arabia looking for new food and water for their goats and sheep, yesterday's problems could be forgotten with today's hassles. For Scot, it was time to face reality. That wasn't pleasant, and why seeing the Londons or Matthew held no appeal. Their talk would throw more pieces on the table, complicating the puzzle not solving it. The facts as he knew it were that Ahmad Kareem in Baghdad paid Mustafa Rasool in Aleppo. But for what he wasn't certain. In turn, Rasool paid Ana for something that was clearly more than carrying cigarette boxes. You don't pay US$20,000 for something a casual labourer could do for a fraction of the cost. He revisited the words 'in turn'. No, he had no real reason to believe Kareem had any connection with Ana. Sure, some of the money Kareem had asked him to give Rasool in Aleppo had been handed back for payment to Ana. That only vaguely linked Kareem to Ana as it was not known whether anyone had directed the payment, or whether Rasool was acting off his own bat. There was the phone call Rasool had taken in his office before lunch with Scot, and Larnaca and American dollars had been mentioned. But it was not known to whom Rasool had been talking. It was evidence that would be dismissed by most courts. Nevertheless, Scot's gut feeling was they were linked. Why? He didn't know.

The next painful question involved Ana. Even its consideration caused a mixture of hurt, anger, and loss. He tried to imagine he was still a journalist and not emotionally involved. The facts were compelling that Ana, or Rasool, were linked to the two murders. She knew both murdered men, and Rasool had access to point-22 calibre pen pistols. She was paid a lot of money for undisclosed work. She'd been in Cyprus at the time of the first murder, and Aleppo when the second man was killed. Maybe Rasool's real motive in sending him to Iraq had been to remove him from Aleppo, and away from Ana. The Aleppo murder may have been planned already. The idea that an old acquaintance would make Alex feel instantly secure could all have been a smokescreen. Scot shook his head in horror at his own gullibility.

The *Beirut Underground* wouldn't hesitate to link Rasool and Ana to the murders, but most newspapers might shy away in fear of litigation. However, Alex had a point, even if it was an unlikely, flippant one. The murdered men could have been gay, or bisexual, which would broaden the motives and the suspects. But assuming Rasool had paid Ana to kill the two men a question remained: why? Because they'd been involved, either directly or indirectly, in Alex's abduction – a kidnapping apparently aimed at getting a ransom from Iraq for handing over a British spy? Unless Mustafa Rasool was some crazy Good Samaritan seeking to root out evil in the world that would hardly be a motive. But Alex did know Rasool, and their relationship may only superficially be dubbed a restaurant customer and proprietor friendship. Maybe there was more to it. Assuming the *Beirut Underground* was correct in naming Alex as some kind of intelligence agent of Britain, the US, or both, could Rasool also be an agent? With his dubious business connections, penchant for flashing money around, and links with weapons favoured by criminal elements, he may never be suspected. In intelligence parlance, he'd be hidden in *plain sight*. And with his police contacts, and suspicious business associates, he could be a mine of information. Could Kareem, be linked? His position in the Iraqi Interior Ministry indicated he was involved in Iraqi intelligence. But it would be quite another thing to imagine him as an agent of Britain and America. Then something was remembered. Kareem had served in London. Could Britain or the US have recruited him? Unlikely, but it would explain his help in securing Alexander's exit from Iraq. Was he a double agent? Helping Alexander would certainly maintain his credibility in London. But why would he get Scot to play banker if he had good contacts in Britain?

The web of intrigue winding within Scot's mind then caught Adnan and his son. Were they somehow involved too? No, this was becoming stupid. Speculation upon speculation was leading nowhere. It was just putting off the central topic: was Ana an assassin? Scot looked around the room. Although he'd known Ana for such a short time, she was everywhere. At the balcony table enjoying his home-cooked dinner. Sitting in the chair when Dimitri had rung about the break-in. On the telephone ringing Rasool. In a modest dress preparing to leave for Syria, and in leather jeans at the Nicosia Grand. Scot thought of her in bed. But it wasn't the sensual satisfaction they'd shared that was foremost. It was her whimpering in the midst of a nightmare. He remembered that because he cared for her so much. So suddenly, she'd become a key part of his life. The nightmare was during the first night she'd stayed. They'd been dancing. He'd thought it must have been linked to the bombing of Belgrade during which her father died. It was before he'd read about the murder in Nicosia, but after the murder had been committed. She'd been working that morning. That's why she couldn't come for lunch. His head shook vigorously, automatically, as if it couldn't take anymore. So he lifted the phone again and dialled Lionel and Lilly.

'Wonderful to hear your voice,' Lilly said. 'Lionel and I have been wondering every day when you'd return. We hoped we wouldn't miss you.'

Lionel came on the line. 'Good to hear you, old chap. Now I want to see you again, would you be free tonight?'

Scot explained about Alexander's return, but didn't go into details. 'I've been invited to a celebration at the restaurant, but you'd both be welcome.' Scot expected Lionel to make an excuse, but the reaction was quite the opposite.

'That sounds splendid, but could we meet at your apartment?'

They jumped at the idea of coming for drinks at the flat, and then going on to Club Downtown. After their criticism of Alex, Scot was surprised they were so keen to attend the welcome-home party. But surprise was becoming a quantifiable commodity for Scot. It was like the Richter scale. Across the graph paper it rose quite gently for a while, then suddenly turned sharply upwards. Lionel's surprise was somewhere just as the graph started to turn upwards. On the other hand, speculation about Ana was up high in the danger zone where lives were shattered. The thought switched him into problem deferral mode. So he dialled Matthew York at the British High Commission.

'Extremely fortuitous you rang today,' Matthew said upon answering. 'I'm coming down to Limassol this evening for a bash being given by a shipping group.' He'd heard about Alexander turning up, but didn't know the details or if he'd returned to Cyprus. 'You say there's a party at the restaurant? Would I be welcome?'

'Yes, I'm sure.'

Matthew said he'd be at the restaurant around 9 p.m. He accepted an offer to kip overnight at the apartment.

Having dealt with the recorded messages, Scot slumped back in his chair, suddenly exhausted.

Then the phone rang.

'So you're back.'

There were none of the courtesies common in telephone calls. But the heavy accent, and the abruptness, made that unnecessary. 'Good to hear from you, Boris,' said Scot, meaning exactly the opposite.

'We have an appointment with the developer tomorrow. It is settlement day. My lawyer has looked at the transfer documents, etcetera, etcetera, and has declared them to be correct in every detail. So now Ahmad Kareem can at last become the owner of his dream home in Cyprus.'

'Things seem to have happened more quickly than I thought,' Scot said.

'Often do, here on Cyprus,' the Russian said. 'It's the way they like to do business. At least, when they know I'm helping things along.' He then hesitated before adding: 'The Cypriots know we Russians like to act quickly. Not like the British they have to deal with who have to – as you say – weigh up all the options, seek opinion after opinion, and then come to the conclusion they could have made in the first place. Very frustrating for the poor developers.'

Scot remained silent.

'So if you could have a bank cheque for the balance ready by say midday, I'll pick you up. And we can have everything signed and sealed within an hour.'

'I'm not certain I have enough money in the account.'

'I think you'll find you have,' Bragonov concluded.

Scot sat stunned, then went online to check the balance in the account he'd opened for Kareem. Sure enough, another large deposit had been made. This time it had been transferred by a Russian bank.

As darkness fell over the bay, Lionel arrived alone, explaining Lilly would follow shortly. They settled on the balcony sipping beer. 'You must be delighted Debbie's turned up.'

'We're both delighted, of course. It's been a hell of a worry.' Lionel then commented on the sea view, but there was something else on his mind. 'I'd like to clear the air before Lilly arrives. Alexander's dismissal from the Army had nothing to do with me.'

'You leaked the story?'

'Yes, yes, I acknowledge that.' He looked at Scot as if begging to be believed. 'The whole process was already in train when I gave you the story. I had nothing to do with bringing about the process. In fact, I disagreed with the policy.'

'So why'd you leak the story? That's what I've never understood.'

Lionel looked at his watch, perhaps thinking Lilly was about to arrive. Maybe he wanted this whole subject wrapped up and closed before the arrival of his wife, who'd almost certainly disapprove of Lionel's treachery. 'To be honest, I suppose I have to admit, I was a bit jealous of Alexander. We had a few problems, nothing serious, but matters that made me look less than totally on top of things. We all slip up from time to time, and I'm no different. I thought the story would come out anyway.'

The security phone rang. Scot got up and went towards the door.

Lionel followed him. 'You do accept all this don't you?' He pleaded for an answer.

'Of course I do. As far as I'm concerned, the matter's closed.' Scot then answered the security phone. 'Lilly, come up.'

'Thank you,' Lionel said as he returned to the balcony and Scot waited for Lilly. They joined Lionel, Lilly placing a plastic shopping bag on the balcony floor next to her handbag. They were eager to hear all about Alexander, and his return to what Lionel termed 'the land of the living'.

Scot filled them in to exclamations of much astonishment, and then asked about their news. 'I hear Debbie has had to go to London for a court case?'

The Londons looked at each other, then Lilly spoke. 'All a bit hush-hush, actually. How'd you hear?'

Scot explained.

'I see,' she went on. 'Dimitri's been very helpful. It gives Sami something to do, and somewhere to stay. He's staying with Dimitri – and Alex now – for the time being. It takes a load off our mind.'

Lionel added more explanation. 'You see, we have to return to the UK at the weekend, as much as we like it here.'

'But the court case? What's that about?'

Lilly hesitated, apparently assessing what she could say. 'Well, Debbie is in no trouble—'

'Quite the opposite,' Lionel butted in. 'She's a star witness for the government.'

Lilly looked at her husband sternly, as if he was saying too much. 'I wouldn't say a star witness, but she's important to the prosecution in a serious case.'

'She certainly got VIP treatment from the High Commission,' Lionel added, clearly to Lilly's dismay. 'They couldn't do enough for her, an official even came from London to accompany her back. They flew First Class.'

It was Lilly's turn again. 'Well, the upshot of all this is the High Commission says it's highly likely Sami will be able to get a visa for the UK once the legal matters are over.'

'If he wishes,' said Lionel rather hopefully.

Lilly turned to Lionel, shaking her head in apparent disbelief. 'I think it's pretty clear he wishes, Lionel!'

Scot couldn't resist making mischief. 'Well, it'll be nice for you Lionel, being able to introduce Sami to your mates at the local ... Or maybe your club? Are there many Kurdish members?'

Before Lionel had a chance to bite, Lilly said it would be quite a relief once things settled down. 'Debbie's already talking about getting a *proper* job and using her qualifications.'

It was now Scot's turn to look at his watch. 'We should make a move shortly.'

As they walked to the Club Downtown, Lilly said in a confidential way that it would be best if Scot kept to himself what they'd told him about the court case. 'Dimitri doesn't know as much detail as we've told you. In fact we only learned as much as we did because Lionel was going on and on about Sami's – how shall I put it? – suitability. Debbie finally told us the little we know because she wanted her father to be proud of what she'd done, and that her time in northern Iraq had been far from wasted.'

For Scot, the whole discussion had raised more questions than it answered about Debbie.

Club Downtown was buzzing. Dimitri was near the entrance welcoming people. He settled them at Scot's usual table and brought another chair after learning Matthew York would be joining them. He whispered in Scot's ear. 'Don't mention Richard Jordan to Alex. He's a bit funny about what happened to him with the police. Says he's a nice man, which he isn't at all.'

Scot acknowledged the advice, and Dimitri parted with a wicked smile, and glinting eyes. Sami – looking very pleased with himself – arrived with the menus, and took drink orders. He wore sandy-coloured traditional Kurdish trousers – tight around the waist, very full around the thighs and narrowing to tight around the calf muscles and ankles. With a blue cummerbund around the waist, he wore a tailored white shirt covered by a colourful waistcoat. Matching the waistcoat the ensemble was topped off with a cap – *tarboosh* in Turkish – similar to a fez. The image was Kurdish chic, but unlikely to be seen anywhere in Kurdistan.

'Good man, brandy with soda for me.' Lionel then mouthed 'large' to Sami, as if everyone else at the table was blind and stupid.

Some change in attitude, thought Scot, as he assessed everything he'd learnt in the past couple of hours. With Debbie now safe, Lionel had felt it necessary to clear the slate regarding the leaking of the story about Alex. The developments involving Debbie would take some time to digest. But Dimitri's warning about the sensitive subject of Richard Xanadu Jordan provided instant amusement. He'd previously wondered whether the Cypriot would even mention to Alex the embarrassment the American had suffered at the hands of the police. He'd have liked to be a fly on the wall when Dimitri revealed the trouble he'd caused.

There were a lot of people Scot hadn't seen before. Many greeted Alex, kissing him on both cheeks, or hugging him, or both. Clearly, they were part of a circle of friends that the pair kept separate from their restaurant regulars. But as Club Downtown was open for lunch and dinner seven days a week until the early hours of each morning, perhaps they were the late crowd. Finally, Alexander broke away from the group, which had formed on and around the dance floor. As he came to the table, he acknowledged Scot, but effusively greeted the Londons.

'We've heard all about your horrific adventure,' Lilly said, hugging Alex. They talked about their happy times at Episkopi together, and Alex asked how Lionel liked the restaurant.

'Splendid.'

Matthew York arrived just as the orders were being served. Although he hadn't met the Londons, he said he knew 'exactly who you are'.

'You may have met Debbie, our daughter?' Lionel looked wide-eyed and hopeful.

'Haven't met her personally, but, of course, some of my colleagues know her very well.'

Lionel caught Scot's eyes, and let his head fall slowly and rise again as if to say 'Told you she was important!'

Another chair was brought to the table, and in turn Alexander and Sami joined the gathering. Lilly made a point of introducing Sami to Matthew as if the Kurd would need as many friends as possible at the High Commission. After a good dinner, a lot of wine, and even more small talk, the gathering broke up around 11.30 p.m. Scot and Matthew, who was carrying just a briefcase, walked to the apartment.

Matthew accepted the offer of a nightcap on the balcony. The snippets of news and gossip Matthew disclosed with little prompting wakened Scot from drowsiness.

Matthew had seen a transcript of the Iraqi television report of Alexander's impromptu press conference before being freed from Iraq. The transcript had been compiled by the British Broadcasting Corporation's monitoring service, and was therefore not classified information. 'The report described Alexander as an intelligence officer employed by Britain in a war on drugs. According to the report, Baghdad decided to release him because of the regime's own war on drugs. The report was slanted to pander to the Iraqi people.'

'Could the Iraqis be right?'

'All I can say is the Foreign Office does have a Drugs and International Crime Department.'

'During his time in the British Army, he spent some time with intelligence liaison in Washington,' Scot said.

'That I didn't know, and it may not mean all that much anyway. You have to realise, it's a bit out of my work agenda. I don't know how they recruit people for that sort of work.'

'Alex does have some rather spooky American friends,' Scot said as he topped up Matthew's brandy. Elaborating, he told him about meeting Rick Jordan with Alex in Kakopetria, and Jordan's run in with the Cyprus police.

Matthew said he'd heard about the police incident. 'There was huge amusement for days on the diplomatic circuit about that.' He then stared out to sea blankly. 'Come to think of it, it was said at the time that Mr Jordan was employed by the US Drug Enforcement Agency. I thought that was just unsubstantiated idle gossip. After all, you hear all kinds of things on the G&T circuit.'

'But now?'

'Well, you say he was a friend of Alex's, then maybe Iraqi television was right. Perhaps he is involved in some way with either our people or the DEA. Someone thought he's an agent of some kind given the *Beirut Underground* cutting I sent you.'

Scot went into details about the meeting in Kakopetria. 'It went on for two or three days, it looked like a business meeting. And there was a third man, a Brad Birmington.'

Matthew looked directly at Scot. 'Wait a minute, I've seen that name mentioned in a press report from Syria. You say Birmington, not Birmingham?'

'Yes.'

Matthew was puzzling over something, as if sorting files in his mind. 'There was an American of that name shot dead by some gunmen on motorcycles in Latakia about two weeks ago. It wasn't given a lot of coverage, but it was reported in the Syrian press. I think the Syrian President expressed condolences to the man's family. That was the gist of the story.'

In a bid to keep Matthew talking, Scot offered some information he knew the diplomat would know. 'Well, the port of Latakia is often mentioned as a departure point for drugs going to Europe, and elsewhere.'

'Yes, not only for drugs from Lebanon, but Turkey as well.'

'Why wouldn't Turkish gangs use Turkey's own small ports?'

'They do, I suppose, but I guess they vary the routes to make it more difficult to track. Also, some pretty big ships sail out of Latakia, so perhaps that's why Syria is used. Also, of course, it means the involvement of Syrian elements, who want their share of the proceeds.'

Scot was piecing together what Matthew had said with what he already knew. If Brad Birmington was shot in

Latakia about two weeks ago, then that was just after Alexander had set off for Aleppo. Perhaps they met up on some kind of joint operation before Birmington was killed? Or maybe a rendezvous was foiled because of Alex's abduction? 'So what do you hear about the murder at the Nicosia Grand?'

Quick as a flash Matthew said what Scot didn't want to hear. 'The woman caught by the hotel security camera … She did it. Then she left Cyprus for Syria, and it's pretty certain she carried out the murder in Aleppo too.'

'Where's she now?'

'Syrian police can't find her. Think she may have left the country.'

Scot tried to give the impression he wasn't too interested in the case. 'Well, it's absolutely amazing the gossip picked up on the diplomatic drinks circuit. I should come up to Nicosia more often.'

'That's not gossip. It seems pretty clear a Syrian group directed the murders because the two men had got in their way.'

'Well, I saw the one killed in Nicosia passing himself off as Alex. You don't mean he ended up dead because he got in Alex's way.'

Matthew spluttered with amusement. 'Not my area and I don't know if Alex has a moonlight job with our people or the DEA. And Iraqi television is hardly an impeccable source. But whatever, I don't think people would get killed for stealing Alex's credit card.'

Scot smiled. 'It's the broader picture I'm wondering about. If Alex and Brad Birmington were involved – maybe with some kind of official Syrian help – in some anti-drug operation, then maybe these men got in the way?'

'As I said, I don't know how our people operate, nor the DEA, but I doubt they carry out assassinations – our people anyway!'

'But if they have Syrian partners, perhaps the Syrians do?'

Matthew shrugged as if not knowing. 'Maybe. Who knows?' He then looked at his watch, indicating it was time for bed.

So Scot attempted to extract just one more piece for the puzzle. 'So, what's all this about Debbie London going to London as a witness in a court case?'

'Well, that subject really is hush-hush, highly confidential. I don't know any more than that, and even if I did, I couldn't say.'

21

Sleep had come easily after the nightcap, but Scot woke at dawn piecing the puzzle together. Walking barefoot and quietly to the kitchen he boiled the kettle for tea. Carrying a tray with a teapot, a jug of milk and two mugs to the balcony, he wildly speculated about Alexander's moonlight job. It was too much of a coincidence for Brad Birmington to be killed in Latakia around the time of Alex's trip to Syria – and abduction – for them not to be involved in some kind of operation together. But why – if Alexander had all along thought the trip to Aleppo was risky – did he tell Dimitri to contact an Australian trader of all people 'if he got out of touch'? So much had happened it was difficult to get the chronology correct, but Alex had told Dimitri he, Scot Wallace, former journalist turned trader, had just met Rasool, so that was the course of action he should follow. Surely it would have been much more sensible to tell Dimitri to contact someone at the High Commission? Embassies and High Commissions were often asked to trace missing nationals. So why would it matter if Dimitri followed normal practice. It wouldn't imply Alex worked for the government.

The balcony door slid open.

'Morning. Slept like a top, you too I hope?' Matthew was dressed in his suit already, and looked ready to leave for Nicosia. He leant over the table, and poured a little milk and tea into the spare mug. 'Something occurred to me in the night. Nothing important, but you might like to know you were also caught by the hotel's security camera.'

'As you know, I was there having a beer. Watching. Because I thought it was the man who'd used Alex's credit card.'

'Yes, I know.'

Scot thought the implications through carefully, then spoke as if not being too interested at all. 'Do the police know my name?'

'Well they didn't, but they came to us because they thought you may have been a UK national. They played the tape to a small group of us – any of us available at the time – and I was able to put your name to the face.'

Breathing deeply to calm qualms rapidly building, Scot turned and looked towards the sea in case his face was displaying some nervousness. 'I haven't heard from them, the police.'

'I guess they didn't think it was that unusual for you to be having a beer in the bar.'

'No.'

'I didn't say anything about you having seen the murdered man using Alex's credit card, because by then they knew that.'

'So as far as they're concerned I'm just an innocent bystander?' As soon as he'd spoken, he regretted it.

'Well you are, aren't you?'

Scot turned to face Matthew directly. 'Of course.'

'After all the bits and pieces we discussed last night, I was just wondering whether you too were involved in the web of intrigue. After all, as a lone trader you have an excellent cover. And you did rescue Alex.'

Scot laughed off the suggestion. 'Wish I was. They'd probably pay me quite well, whoever they are.'

'Well, I must be off.'

'Love to Sophie,' Scot said as he closed the apartment door.

Glad to be alone, he remembered the last time he'd expressed good wishes to Sophie. It had been after the dinner at the Aegean Restaurant in Nicosia. Then, he envied Matthew going home with his wife while he returned for a night alone in a hotel double bed. Things he couldn't mention had changed since then. Ana had come into his life for a few frantic weeks of love. Loneliness had become a thing of the past. But it had returned as quickly as it had disappeared. And it had reappeared with an ugly companion – paranoia.

He felt paranoia about being caught by the security camera, about the police knowing his name. If they knew Ana had left for Syria, then they could easily know he did too. And what if someone else had seen him dining with Ana, or dancing at the Club Downtown? The implications were too dreadful to contemplate.

The pavement was hot and the sun burning as Scot waited outside his apartment for Boris Bragonov. The bank cheque for the settlement on Ahmad Kareem's villa was folded in his shirt pocket. He looked at his watch once again, irritable after the previous long day and night, and the hassle of getting to the bank early to arrange the cheque. And now Bragonov was late. The only thing keeping him waiting was the commission he was due to receive. Then the black Land Cruiser approached, lights flashing, horn honking.

'Sorry. Call from Moscow.'

The late morning traffic was heavy as they headed to the developer's office. 'Hope this doesn't take too long,' Scot said.

Bragonov shook his head slowly, and exhaled a brisk puff of peppermint breath, as if to say 'it's anyone's guess'. No word was spoken. No word was necessary.

Communication was through international body language. Then he spoke. 'My lawyer is meeting us, just to make sure things are in order.'

They were shown to the same conference room in which the deposit had been paid. The Russian's lawyer was waiting, sipping Nescafé. He was neatly dressed in a grey suit, white shirt and blue striped tie. With dark well-groomed hair and piercing blue eyes, Angelos was a picture of honesty. It was the image Bragonov wanted his lawyer to project. That seemed certain.

'Angelos, born Cyprus, raised England, but has lived in Limassol since becoming an advocate,' Bragonov said, in a way akin to boasting. 'Except for a year in Moscow where he learnt our language.' Then, as an afterthought, he said: 'And customs.'

Angelos elaborated: 'With the collapse of the Soviet Union, and close ties between the people of Cyprus and Russia, I decided there could be opportunities. And there have been ...' He then eyed Bragonov with the hint of a respectful, but somewhat sinister smile. It was as if the English school cricket captain had joined the local Hell's Angels – and was enjoying it.

'But you are Cypriot?' Scot asked, more out of respect than inquisitively. The lawyer's looks and Home Counties' English accent prompted the question.

'Of course, Mr Wallace.'

The developer entered the room, and shook hands all round. 'Ah yes, I know Angelos well. I have great respect for him as a lawyer.'

The relationship seemed a bit cosier than Scot had anticipated and wanted. But Limassol had a large Russian expatriate community, so perhaps it wasn't surprising the developer would know the lawyer, who was possibly the only Russian-speaking Cypriot advocate in the city. Certainly, Angelos would be one of very few.

Angelos handed the developer Kareem's new Power of Attorney document.

'This looks fine.' He then looked more closely at the document and shook his head with surprise. 'I see you're one of the witnesses, Angelos. So you made a special visit to Baghdad?' The developer's raised right eyebrow indicated it wasn't really a question. 'Weather good?'

'Sunny and politically hot,' Angelos replied.

After haggling over stamp duty liability, and whether or not Kareem was liable for the usual real estate transfer tax as he was not a resident, Angelos and the developer got down to a polite and convoluted argument about the real value of the property for purposes of the capital gains tax liable to be paid by the seller. The developer said it could be claimed the value of the swimming pool should not be included as it was not built when the property was first inspected by Kareem's representatives. He eyed Scot and Bragonov. It was an argument opposed by Angelos.

'Yes, I understand your client has problems, but Mr Kareem could be liable for more capital gains tax in the future unless the correct value is placed on the property at this stage.'

They finally agreed on a compromise which involved Kareem and the seller splitting the cost of the swimming pool thereby reducing a little the value of the property for capital gains purposes.

Angelos looked closely at the documents again – particularly the developer's charges. He shook his head in disbelief, either real or feigned. 'But you've charged eight per cent commission.'

'I'm a developer.'

'But in this case you're just an agent.'

'It's a new house, so I'm in a way the builder, seller, and developer.'

'No,' Angelos said, remaining cool. 'In this case you're merely an agent, so the maximum you're due is five per cent. And as you'll want more business from Mr Bragonov and his countrymen we'll make it three.'

Bragonov gestured to Scot, throwing his head back and giving a solemn wink, as if to say 'so you doubted my friend Angelos?'

That seemed to be the end of the matter. Scot handed over the bank cheque.

Bragonov spoke. 'Deed?'

'Deed, yes.' The developer hesitated, then added: 'Once the bank cheque has been cleared.'

'Cleared,' Bragonov shouted. 'It's a bank cheque!'

Angelic Angelos urged calm, directing a stare towards Bragonov.

But the developer pursued the matter. 'It looks like a bank cheque, I know, just like the Power of Attorney document looks real. But how do I know? I have to wait for the cheque to be cleared.' He then switched to charm mode. 'If you were the seller, my client, you'd appreciate my same diligent attention.'

With the business of the day done, the door to the conference room opened and the receptionist carried in a tray with a bottle of Champagne and four tall glasses. Bragonov shook his head as if he wasn't going to drink with the devil. Then, when he saw Scot, Angelos and the developer sipping a toast to the absent Kareem, Bragonov raised his glass, and without hesitation or courtesy, tossed off the contents. Kareem's villa deal was done. Or so it seemed.

22

As the weeks passed and the weeks became months, the pain of losing Ana subsided, but memories, hurt and puzzlement lingered. Scot found himself concentrating more on business than on the events that followed his fateful meeting with Ahmad Kareem in Baghdad. New business opportunities became something of an obsession as the threat of an American-led invasion of Iraq became reality. Scot's TV remained glued to war coverage as columns of armed forces pushed north from Kuwait, and Baghdad's key buildings were pounded from the air. Baghdad fell surprisingly quickly, Saddam Hussein giving way to looters, terror attacks, chaos and uncertainty. Some regime leaders gave themselves up, some were killed and others captured. Scot pondered the fate of Ahmad Kareem, Adnan Bashir and Sadeq Ramadi. Hopefully Sadeq would be able to slink away and retire peacefully. Adnan, archaeologist turned bureaucrat, may be seen as untainted and needed – especially in view of widespread looting of antiquities. Kareem was a different matter, however. As an official in Saddam Hussein's Interior Ministry and security apparatus, he could be a target of revenge, or of interest to the Americans. If it were not for the complex legal ownership of the villa, Kareem was a name that could be erased from Scot's contact book.

That's what Scot thought initially.

In the first month after Ana disappeared, snow had fallen on the island's Troodos mountains and Scot spent a relaxing couple of weekends with his friends in Kakopetria, talking by open fires in stone hearths and

sipping Cyprus brandy. On one of these occasions by the
fire at The Mill hotel, his long-time friend drank camomile
tea and reminisced about the foreign woman who'd
thrown a glass of water over her 'Arab' companion on the
balcony one summer lunchtime.

'I remember, I was sitting at the next table,' Scot said
cautiously.

His friend nodded sagely, but appeared to doubt Scot's
close proximity to the incident. He clearly thought Scot
just wished he'd been involved in the drama. 'Well, that
woman was a friend of the Syrian man murdered in the
Nicosia Grand Hotel. Her photograph was in all the
newspapers. I recognised her immediately. Maybe she
murdered him because he had another girlfriend.'

'Maybe.' Then Scot registered what his friend had
said. 'Did she?'

'No ... I don't know, but she may have.'

'Well, anything's possible.'

That had been the only time anyone had mentioned
Ana. He hadn't been linked to the *mystery* woman, which
was a relief. On the other hand, she'd failed to make
contact too. In the letter left with Rasool she'd promised to
make contact, but she hadn't. In view of her links with
murder and intrigue, he was concerned for her safety and
had contacted most of the entries of her family name in the
Belgrade phone book. That exercise produced no results.
No one had heard of an Ana who'd gone to work in
Cyprus and Syria after the death of her father during the
bombing of the city.

The first few weeks after his nightcap with Matthew
York had been filled with the dread of a phone call from
the police – or worse still – a heavy knock on the door.
He'd even rehearsed a response to police questioning.
'She was a tourist, I thought, and met her by chance at a
café on the beachfront at Larnaca. I got to know her very

well. She was attractive, officer, and we got on well. She even visited me in Limassol.' And if the police asked why he'd left for Syria just a couple of days after the woman? 'Must have been a coincidence.'

He knew there was a weak point in his rehearsed story. After the second murder in Aleppo, surely the staff at the Baron Hotel would have told the police that the woman had stayed at the hotel with an Australian named Scot Wallace. Hopefully, Mustafa Rasool had explained away that coincidence with his friend, the police chief. Rasool had said as much in a cryptic phone call. 'Just recently, I told a mutual friend of ours that like so many depraved Westerners, you are a habitual womaniser ... chasing any foreign woman you fancy.' Scot had been philosophical about that slur on his reputation. Amongst Rasool's dubious contacts, it could enhance rather than diminish their interest. Anything that made people remember his name was good for business.

'And how's your friend Ahmad Kareem in Baghdad?' Scot wondered how the Iraqi would cope facing American hostility.

Quick as a flash, Rasool retorted: 'Your friend too! And you'll be pleased to learn he's got a very suitable position with the new authorities in Baghdad. He had a quiet rest laying low in the countryside for a while, but then the American authorities learnt how knowledgeable he was and asked him to return to work.'

'But he must have been a member of Saddam's party?'

'Only because he had to be. That's what he told the new people.'

'And they believed him?'

'My friend, of course they did. Ahmad Kareem's a man of honour. Anyone can see that!' Rasool mentioned something else of interest. 'You know Alex and I are going to London together?'

'Hadn't heard.'

'I thought after what you did for Alex, he would have mentioned it to you.'

'He doesn't tell me everything.' Quite a lot Alex didn't tell, Scot thought once the call was over. And Rasool's trip to London seemed to indicate the Syrian was involved in Alex's covert operation. *So am I, Scot Wallace, the only one out of the loop?*

Scot recalled again the incident at The Mill Hotel, when Ana had argued with a companion. From that very first time, he'd stored a vision of the anonymous woman somewhere in his mind. It was something like a computer's clipart file, which had been retrieved once he saw her again at the Nicosia Grand Hotel. That time he remembered being physically drawn to the woman, an excitement that had exacerbated the feeling of loneliness pervading his life without Lisa. Was it true that one could anticipate meeting someone? The idea of the premonition of a liaison – a premonition with concrete signals – had seemed always to be something mystical, a fantasy. In this case, though, it had happened. He didn't regret the affair. Even her dark secrets were forgiven. In some ways Scot glorified her by equating her to a spy – or even intelligence chiefs – who couldn't share with their nearest and dearest details of their work. He was capable of such rationalisation because parts of his own life – his associates Kareem, Rasool and Ana and the web they'd spun – couldn't be discussed even with his closest friends. He might be implicated as an accessory to the two murders, and an associate of a shadowy group whose motives he didn't know. Scot consoled himself with the notion that if Ana had killed, it was for a greater good. After all, Rasool had links with Alex and he'd been involved somehow in a clandestine operation, which had led to the arrest in Britain of the leaders of a drug cartel.

Late one afternoon, after the Sunday papers arrived from London, Scot sat reading and drinking coffee at a pavement café on the esplanade below his apartment. An intriguing story dealt with revelations from the court trial of the drug ringleaders – five Middle East nationals, including a Kurd, and two Britons. They'd been behind the transhipment of drugs across Turkey and Syria, where they'd been loaded on to a container ship at Latakia. British police and drug enforcement authorities arrested the men after the ship docked in Liverpool. The prosecution alleged it was the biggest shipment of heroin and marijuana ever imported into Britain.

The part of the story that fascinated Scot dealt with Debbie London's role in tracking the drugs as they were transported to Latakia. At one point in the trial, she was described as a 'Legend' – one of a small group of Customs agents who live undercover for long periods in jobs often unrelated to the drug trade. They give evidence in open court just once because after that their cover is blown. Sometimes they're given new identities once the trial is over. Scot took the newspaper around to the Club Downtown, and showed the story to Alexander. Predictably, he didn't confirm or deny any part in the operation, but said, 'Yes, Debbie London certainly came up trumps.' That was all he said, although he did smile in a way that could be described as 'knowingly'.

There was something else. Scot asked how Sami was getting on at the restaurant? It was Dimitri who replied. 'Didn't you know? He's gone to London.'

Wandering back to the apartment, Scot fantasised that Lionel would have a new drinking mate at his local, and could be teaching Sami the niceties of cricket by now.

In a way, he was jealous. The Londons and Sami were all together, whereas he was alone. All the favours he'd done for Rasool and Kareem ended in nothing but intrigue

– and that was something he could do without. The mysterious bank account, the carrying of wads of money, the elevation of Rasool from a name casually met and forgotten to someone close, made him feel decidedly used: trapped in the quicksand of the Middle East. As he looked across the road and out to sea, he vowed never, ever again to do anything for the Iraqi or the Syrian. He'd never get involved, even if his business had to suffer. He'd learn from his mistakes, and never be trapped again.

Then the phone rang.

23

'Scot Wallace?'

Scot knew the voice immediately, and a sense of foreboding flooded his mind as he realised the call sounded local, not patched through Italy, or anywhere else for that matter. 'Speaking.'

'It is Kareem here, Ahmad Kareem, and I'm just around the corner from your flat.'

Scot had given up wondering, or indeed caring, how Ahmad Kareem would know exactly where he lived. Bragonov probably told him. The break-in while he visited Baghdad and the discovery of his diary on the pavement was just another mysterious twist in his recent life. Instead he tried to ignore the Iraqi's proximity to his apartment. In an offhand kind of way, he just asked: 'Staying in Cyprus long?'

But Kareem wasn't deterred. 'Maybe, maybe not … It could depend very much on you. I need to talk with you. Urgently.'

Scot gave in. Clearly the sooner he met with Kareem, the sooner he'd be free of the Iraqi. The title to the villa could be transferred to Kareem. And that would mean being free. 'Where would you like to meet? At a restaurant, or meet for a coffee?'

'Best at your flat, Scot. There'd be more privacy. I'll be there in five minutes.'

Kareem announced his arrival with a firm knock on the door. The Iraqi's shaved head was a surprise, and it was debateable whether he looked more or less sinister than Scot remembered him from Baghdad. The one-time thug for Saddam Hussein had morphed into a lackey for the new Baghdad regime and the Americans. While other Saddam Hussein lieutenants languished in American-run gaols, Ahmad Kareem was a textbook case of survival of the fittest, or canniest at least.

'Big changes since last we met,' Scot observed.

'Stuff happens.' Kareem underlined his Rumsfeld jargon with the hint of a smile.

'Scotch?'

'Just a little ice, thanks.' Then, as Scot poured the drinks, Ahmed got straight down to business. 'I believe you have some money of mine. Could you introduce me to your bank manager? Maybe a good reference would be a help.'

'Surely the Iraqi government, or the Americans, would be better. They know you.' Maybe that was the problem, Scot surmised.

'They'd ask too many questions.'

Indeed they might! Whose money was it, and for what purpose exactly? Those questions certainly might be of interest in Baghdad. The amounts Kareem had sent were hardly insignificant, and Cyprus could be just one strand of the Iraqi's operation. There could be other accounts around the world.

'Anyway, I like the look of Cyprus. Maybe I'll stay. The villa sounds wonderful. Thank you for organising everything.' Then, after a short hesitation, the Iraqi added: 'We could get to know each other much better, maybe do some business together.'

'I work alone, but anyway, what about Baghdad, your job, your family?'

Kareem dismissed the question with a shrug.

'We can get your money tomorrow,' Scot said. 'Or do you want it sent to another bank?'

'I want to open an account here.'

'They might ask where the money came from.'

'I'll say I lent it to you and you're paying it back.'

Deeper into Kareem's mire, Scot felt himself sinking. The quicksand of the Middle East allows no escape.

'You should think about us working together. Not all the time, but on some special projects.' After a hesitation, Kareem added: 'You'd make real money.'

Scot just shook his head slowly.

'There are so many opportunities in this part of the world. As you say in English, the sky's the limit.'

There was still no reaction from Scot.

'Well, there'll be plenty of time to talk about business opportunities. We'll get the banking over … First things first. Tomorrow.'

At nine thirty the next morning, Scot met Kareem on the pavement outside his apartment. It turned out he was staying in a small hotel along the corniche. The banking turned out to be straightforward. On the basis of Ahmad Kareem's diplomatic passport issued by the Iraqi government, the bank opened the new account with few questions asked. Kareem quibbled a little with the exchange rate given for the American dollars, but that was with the bank rather than Scot. Much to Scot's relief, the bank manager was not in. After the account had been opened, Kareem suggested to Scot he wait outside. From outside the door Scot saw Kareem open a small document case he'd been carrying and hand to the teller about ten large bundles of bank notes. So the money trail from Baghdad was still open!

As they walked from the bank, Scot asked: 'Do all Iraqi government workers get diplomatic passports?'

'Probably. But I don't work in the passport division, so I wouldn't really know.'

'What do you do?'

'So many questions ... Like before under the old regime. Same type of job.'

Scot had never known Kareem's exact job at the Interior Ministry, just what he'd asked him to do. And as he thought back to their first meeting in Baghdad, the bank account, the Iraqi's relationship with Rasool in Aleppo, and the Iraqi's role in the release of Alexander Belfort-Smith, he guessed he wasn't ever going to learn much more. In the Middle East, there are many things you never really know. The point is no outsider knows. Some people appear to know more than others, or claim to, but often those claims are an illusion.

They sat for coffee at a pavement café. 'I must contact Mr Belfort-Smith. Maybe we could see him together?'

Without a word, Scot questioned Ahmed with tilt of his head.

'Well, I did arrange his release from Iraq. And that was against the wishes of many in Saddam's circle.'

'In that case, he may like to thank you personally.' Then, as an instantly regretted afterthought, Scot added: 'He's just got a British honour.'

'I know. For spying.'

'That's not what the citation said.'

Kareem scoffed a laugh.

'Anyway, have you spoken to Boris Bragonov?'

'Yes. He didn't tell you? We're all going to Kakopetria tomorrow to inspect the villa. Just the three of us. Boris said you'd know somewhere we could lunch.'

They then went their own way, Ahmad Kareem to his hotel and Scot back to his flat. Bragonov rang and arranged the trip to the mountains.

'Nine thirty on the dot I'll pick you up. And Kareem.'

Just after 9.15 a.m. the next day, Scot was waiting on the pavement for Boris Bragonov. He glanced at the front-page picture of the *Cyprus Daily*. He recognised the face and read the caption. Sure enough, it was Adnan Bashir under the headline 'Iraq Seeks Cyprus Help'.

> *A senior official of Iraq's post-war Antiquities Department, Dr Adnan Bashir, visited the Nicosia Museum yesterday and said he believed it was one of the most important museums in the Eastern Mediterranean and Middle East region.*

> *An expert of international renown, Dr Bashir is visiting Cyprus to learn first hand from Cypriot officials the most effective way of tracing looted antiquity objects.*

> *'After the American invasion of my country, many objects of great importance were taken illegally from the museum in Baghdad. We want to get them back,' Dr Bashir said.*

> *He said archaeologists and museum officials around the world admired how Cypriot museum officials had never given up the hope of recovering antiquities stolen after Turkey's invasion of part of the island in 1974.*

> *Dr Bashir will also be seeing church officials and learning from them about their quest to recover church objects that disappeared during and after the invasion.*

'He's in Nicosia, and staying at the Centrum Hotel.' Scot swung around to see a smiling Ahmad Kareem.

'Spoke to him last night,' Kareem added. 'Says he hopes to come down to see the Limassol Castle. But time might beat him.'

There was loud tooting from further down the street, and they looked to see Bragonov's land cruiser, lights flashing, approaching.

'For me, today is so exciting. It's like a dream come true.' Kareem was dressed in light-olive-green slacks and off-white shirt with green stripes. He carried a small black bag.

Bragonov, dressed in black slacks and shirt and sporting a gold chain around his neck, leapt from the vehicle and profusely greeted his two passengers. 'Let's get going.'

As they sped up the mountain road, there was no music. Instead Bragonov and Kareem, who was sitting in the front passenger seat, discussed some business opportunity. The Russian turned around and faced Scot. 'You should join us in this venture. It's what you call a once-in-lifetime opportunity.'

'Look out, Boris,' Kareem shouted.

Bragonov turned back to face the road as the vehicle hit gravel beside a thirty-metre drop. He corrected direction successfully, and boasted. 'I'm experienced with these roads from my time in the Caucasus Mountains.'

Kareem faced the Russian with an uncertain look, but said nothing. Scot remained silent. Bragonov hit the CD player, and disco rock blared out.

Well, if it helps him concentrate, it was worth the discomfort, thought Scot.

They reached the road down to Kakopetria in under an hour. Kareem marvelled at the pine trees beside the road. 'It's even better than I dreamed.'

After driving through the village, they took the road to the villa, through the avenue of fig trees and under the pergola of grape vines.

'For years, I haven't seen such lushness, such greenness,' Kareem enthused.

Bragonov unlocked the villa's front door, and uttered a welcome in Russian and Greek.

Kareem responded in Russian, then broke into English. 'So this is my house. Everything I want,' he said as he looked into every room, every cupboard. 'Electric stove.'

'Reliable electricity too – mainly,' Bragonov said.

At the French doors overlooking the granite-paved veranda leading to the swimming pool, Kareem became mildly agitated. He pointed a finger towards the orchard at the side of the granite paving. 'What is this? The local militia?'

Oblivious of the audience, a swarthy man dressed in jungle greens was aiming a rifle into a tree.

'Local hunter,' Scot offered.

Exasperated, Bragonov unlocked the doors and strode out on to the paving. 'This private property.'

The hunter swung around in fright, as the black-clad Russian strode towards him. 'Sorry, going.'

But Bragonov wasn't going to be put off by an apology. He grabbed the hunter by the shoulders and shook him so hard his rifle discharged and fell to the ground, and his head nearly followed.

'It's okay, Boris, I'm used to guns,' Kareem said. 'And he's probably a neighbour. I'll have to live with these people.'

The hunter scurried away.

Boris then headed to the swimming pool. 'Oh my God. That son of a bitch developer. I'll have his balls.'

Scot and Kareem looked at the pool. The rough concreting was finished, but tiling had not even begun. The filter system hadn't been installed.

'It won't take them long to finish,' Scot said.

'But it's meant to be finished. We'll go straight back to Limassol and get that developer,' the Russian said.

'Scot's right, it won't take long,' Kareem said.

'I don't settle for second best like you two. We'll go straight back to Limassol. And I'll get the deed too. The cheque would have been cleared.'

'I'd rather lunch first,' Kareem said.

'I know just the place,' Scot said as he directed a silent Boris down to the village, to the Village Pub with a balcony draped in red and pink geraniums. They took a table overlooking the promontory where two mountain streams rushed together and became one.

The sound of the water was calming for Scot and Kareem, but not enough for Boris. 'This water gives me idea. I'll drown the developer.'

A fair woman hovered beside the table. 'Can I get you drinks? Wine, beer?'

'A very large brandy,' Boris demanded.

'You're driving,' Scot said.

'I'll drown you too.'

24

The next day began with an early phone call from Boris Bragonov. He insisted Scot go with him and Kareem to see the developer. 'My lawyer Angelos will be in attendance,' Bragonov said formally. 'We'll lay down the law, as you say. We'll scare the daylights out of the developer.'

For Scot, problems involving the villa were becoming tedious, but now Kareem was on the island he wanted his name off the title. So he reluctantly agreed. 'I think it's best to be polite, though. Cypriots can interpret anger – loss of temper – as weakness. They can think they have the upper hand. Best to be calm, polite.'

Bragonov guffawed down the line.

There was tea and coffee waiting in the developer's conference room when Scot arrived. Bragonov was sitting heavily in a chair. He raised his chin momentarily to acknowledge Scot's arrival. Kareem, deep in thought, was looking out the window towards the car park. It was only angelic Angelos who made Scot at all welcome. He smiled and shook Scot's hand. As the minutes ticked by, Bragonov started tapping his watch.

Thirty minutes after the appointed time for the meeting, the developer entered. 'Welcome gentlemen.'

'The swimming pool's not finished, and where is the title deed?' Bragonov responded loudly.

Pope-like, Angelos lifted his hand in an attempt to calm the small, assembled congregation. 'My client – along with Mr Kareem and Mr Wallace – has some concerns.'

'And rightly so,' the developer responded, completely robbing the wind from the lawyer's sails. 'And let me say right from the outset how pleased I am to meet at last Mr Kareem, of Baghdad and Kakopetria.' Shaking Kareem's hand, he added: 'I trust you had a good trip.'

'Our concerns are—'

The developer cut the lawyer short. Obviously he was well practised in controlling hostile clients. 'Number one,' he said, crossing off one finger with a finger of the other hand. 'The pool has been delayed because the tiles have been held up in some European port. The builder is most apologetic. It's out of his control.'

'And what port is the title deed in?' Bragonov sneered. 'I thought I'd made myself clear about the deed. We want it now.'

Angelos again raised a calming hand.

'You see,' Scot said, 'now that Mr Kareem is on the island, I would like my name taken off the deed. It was an interim measure only, you know.'

The developer responded: 'Your wishes shall be done, Mr Wallace.'

The lawyer asked gently to see the deed.

'Unbeknown to me,' the developer said, 'my assistant deposited the title deed in the bank for safe keeping.'

It was Bragonov's turn. 'Collateral for another mortgage, I suppose. I've heard enough.'

'No, for safe keeping.' Although responding to the Russian, the developer addressed the lawyer with a smile. 'As soon as I was informed about this meeting, I sent my assistant to the bank. But the bank has sent the deeds it holds to Nicosia, where it has an even safer safe than it has here.'

Bragonov stood, and strode towards the developer. 'Twenty-four fucking hours. That's all the time you have.'

He punctuated every word by lightly punching the developer's chest. 'Not a minute more.'

Once home, Scot dialled Adnan Bashir's hotel. He wanted to pick Adnan's brains about Kareem, so arranged to drive up to Nicosia and have dinner with the archaeologist. 'I'll meet you at your hotel, say 7.30 p.m.'

After parking in the dry moat outside Nicosia's Venetian walls, Scot arrived at the Centrum Hotel just a couple of minutes late. Leading Adnan around the corner and into the renovated Laiki Yitonia area behind the hotel, Scot found a restaurant. It was grotto-like with vaulted ceilings. 'It's not bad here.'

'After Baghdad, every restaurant looks fine. Nightlife is somewhat crippled in my home city.'

After ordering dinner, Scot steered the conversation towards the subject of Kareem. 'He seems to be planning to settle here, in Cyprus.'

After showing initial surprise, Adnan Bashir said: 'He's restless. A lot of us are restless. We've faced so much change so suddenly.'

'Money? Does he earn a lot, or does he have family wealth?'

'Well, I …' The Iraqi hesitated. 'By the standards of many Iraqis, he'd earn a good wage, but he'd not be wealthy by standards in the West. Family money? Maybe they'd own some property, farmland. But who'd buy it?'

The question was rhetorical.

'Is he a close friend of yours?'

'I wouldn't say friend, but he's been helpful over the years.' A mistiness came to Adnan's eyes. 'When my son was in London, I sent money to the Iraqi company Kareem worked for, and he was able to pass it over to my son,

Adnan. So he was helpful. I believe my son introduced Kareem to Alexander Belfort-Smith.'

'But you didn't mention this when you met Alex after his release in Iraq. You were talking to Alex, but you didn't mention—'

'We had ears. Remember the Iraqi army officer? Under Saddam we learnt to keep things to ourselves, especially things related to foreigners. Silence was the best course.'

'How did Alex know about your son's illness?'

'Maybe Kareem kept him informed. I don't know.'

Scot scanned the restaurant, and then whispered. 'Is it possible Mr Kareem did some work for Alex, for the British?'

Adnan sipped at his wine, and stared directly into Scot's eyes in a bemused kind of way. 'I wouldn't know, but Kareem was in our Interior Ministry. He knows his way around. But to work for the British would have been highly dangerous under Saddam.' The Iraqi fell silent for what seemed a few minutes, before speaking again. 'But maybe if he'd good contacts in the West, it wouldn't have been so surprising. The West helped us – even encouraged us – during our war with Iran. Many of us were surprised Kareem was offered a good job in the new American administration. So I suppose it's possible he had some connections the Americans respected. But I wouldn't know.' Bashir fell silent again, now almost tortured in thought. Then he spoke, almost philosophically: 'Kareem is good and bad. There are stories his team was at the museum when it was looted. They said they were keeping order. But who knows? Kareem was helpful to me, but who's good and who's bad? The currents of the Tigris control our world.'

25

Back in Limassol, Scot took a call from Boris Bragonov around lunchtime the next day. The Russian was furious his twenty-four-hour deadline for the developer to hand over the title deed hadn't been met.

'I am going to escape Limassol, and relax. I can't wait around here and take no for an answer.' For added emphasis, Boris declared word by word in a manner akin to a computer-generated response: 'Boris Bragonov does not take no for an answer.'

'Where?'

'Where what?'

'Where to relax?'

'I'm going to a beautiful monastery I know in the Troodos Mountains. I have stayed before when stress gets me down. I pray, I walk. There are many mountain footpaths. It is most relaxing.'

Scot had never thought of Bragonov as in anyway religious. Sure, he sometimes wore a gold cross dangling from a neck chain, but that appeared no more than a fashion accessory. Scot's mind boggled at the idea of Bragonov sitting still and silent long enough to pray.

'Kareem too?'

'No, he's Moslem, as you know. He wouldn't get a sense of spiritual peace in a monastery. Well, not like me anyway.'

After the call, Scot slumped back into his desk chair, chuckling inwardly. Pity the poor monks, he thought. It was not until the next morning that Boris Bragonov was given another thought.

Sipping coffee on his balcony about 10 a.m., Scot heard police sirens in the street below. Looking down, two police cars and a police van were speeding along the esplanade, blue lights flashing. They stopped right outside the apartment block, and six armed policemen jumped from the vehicles, and ran into the building.

A minute or so later, there was a heavy knock on Scot's door. As soon as the lock was released, the police pushed the door open, stormed in, and encircled Scot. One officer pointed a revolver at Scot's chest.

'Hands on head ... Hands on head,' one officer shouted. He then carried out a pat search down the lone trader's body, under his arms, around his chest and waist, between his legs, and around his socks and shoes.

'You Mr Scot Wallace?' It was another officer with braiding on his uniform indicating some kind of rank who spoke.

'Yes.'

'Handcuff him,' the officer ordered, before facing Scot. 'You're a suspect in a murder, a brutal murder.'

After cautioning Scot, the police led the way to the lift. They didn't say another word as the lift descended. Nikos's jaw dropped as the police led the way out of the building and bundled Scot into the van behind the two patrol cars.

At a police station, painted white with blue windows and adorned with Greek and Cyprus flags, they locked Scot in a cell. He had company. It was Ahmad Kareem.

'What the hell's happening?'

'Been a murder,' Kareem said. 'The developer's been murdered.'

'And they think we did it?'

Kareem nodded, then rocked his head as if indicating more vagueness. 'Well, we're suspects. Just suspects.' After a moment of silence, the Iraqi added: 'They let me ring Angelos, Bragonov's lawyer. I had his card. He's on his way.'

'Ridiculous! Why do they think we'd kill him?'

'The title deed.'

Scot shook his head in disbelief.

As they sat silently in the cell, they heard Angelos arrive. He was chatting at length to the police, weaving his charm as effectively in Greek as in English. A policeman led him to the cell. With a sheath of papers in hand, he was let in, and the door locked heavily behind him. The policeman left the cell area.

'To cut things short,' Angelos began, 'our developer's body has been found dumped in the car park opposite his office. His private parts were found stuffed in his mouth.' With some understatement, he added: 'It's all most unpleasant.'

'But why we here?'

'Mr Wallace, the police have spoken to the developer's receptionist who said her boss had had a very unpleasant meeting with three men and me two days ago. They said threats were made against the developer about the title deed. Your names are on that deed.'

'Bragonov set a deadline, that's all,' Scot said.

'I know, I know,' the lawyer said tapping Scot on the shoulder in a comforting sort of way. 'Things will all be sorted out.'

'Where is Boris?' Kareem asked.

'They can't find him.'

Scot remembered: 'He's staying at a monastery in the mountains.'

'Where?' Kareem spoke, acutely surprised.

'He's praying,' Scot replied with the hint of a smile.

Kareem shook his head in disbelief. 'For us, I hope.'

It was the lawyer's turn. 'The police heard about the monastery from Bragonov's office, but don't know which one. They're trying to locate him because they say assassinations were carried out in a similar way during the Soviet years.'

'I remember a case in Beirut,' Scot offered. 'In the eighties I think. A threat was made against the Soviet Embassy. A member of the group who'd made the threat was found dead with testicles in his mouth. It was said to be a warning, and the threats did stop.'

Kareem offered insight. 'In Baghdad we used to sometimes—'

Angelos lifted his hand. 'Mr Kareem we don't need a history lesson.'

'Soviet advisers taught—'

Again Angelos lifted his hand then covered his mouth, more urgently this time. 'This is why they want to speak to Bragonov,' Angelos said. 'Because he's Russian. But his mobile is off, and there are many monasteries in the mountains. They are visiting them one by one.'

'How long will they hold us?' Scot asked. 'They have no evidence we were involved; that I was involved.'

'Nor me,' Kareem added with a tinge of outrage.

'I think they may arrange bail for you two, if you can tell me what you were doing last night,' Angelos offered. 'They believe the developer was kidnapped when he left his office at about eight o'clock last night. Murdered somewhere else, private parts cut off, then dumped back in the car park late in the evening when the streets were quiet.'

Kareem said he'd been at a fish restaurant until late and had a receipt to prove it. He was alone, but had talked at length with the restaurant owner.

Scot said he returned from Nicosia after staying one night, and then had been in his flat. He'd done some internet banking and had printed receipts. That would prove he was online.

'The date it would, but the time?'

Scot answered Angelos. 'Well, the bank might be able to…to tell the time. And Nikos, downstairs at the apartments, may be able to confirm I didn't leave my flat.'

Angelos nodded, and said he'd investigate. 'Mr Wallace, Boris didn't say which monastery he was visiting, did he?'

Scot shook his head.

About an hour after Angelos left, a policeman brought to the cell two kebabs in pitta bread and two Cokes. After the policeman left, Scot said: 'I'd kill for a Scotch.'

Kareem eyed Scot suspiciously. 'So … for just a Scotch?'

'I mean I'd like a Scotch.'

As dusk fell, the policeman returned, delivering another two kebabs in pitta bread, this time with sweet mint tea. Around 10 p.m. another policeman returned with two mattresses. He took the prisoners, one by one, to a bathroom, and then said good night.

Around 10 a.m. the next day, Angelos arrived. 'I have good news. The police are letting you go, but you are not allowed to leave Cyprus. You may be needed for further questioning.'

'Great … Why?' Scot stood and combed his hair.

'It seems that after the news of the murder became known, police headquarters was inundated with phone calls. There were more than fifty anonymous callers, mainly British sounding, but others with German accents, and others speaking Greek. Some claimed to have murdered the developer, others said they wished they had, and all said he deserved to die. Their stories were all the same. The developer had withheld title deeds to properties they'd bought, some as long ago as five years.'

'So what are the police doing?' Scot asked.

'They're tracing the calls if they can, one by one.'

'Bragonov?' Kareem asked.

'They found him in a small monastery, praying with a senior monk. The monk said Boris was an old friend, who'd arrived for two days of contemplation during the afternoon of the murder – hours before the killing.'

26

After Scot's release from the cell, the police – according to the local newspapers – seemed to conclude the developer's killer could be any number of disgruntled clients. They believed the killer had adopted old-style Soviet assassination methods to confuse the investigation. There was press speculation that the assassin disliked the large number of Russians settling in the Limassol area and aimed to have members of that community blamed for the slaying. The police visited Scot once, but were not aggressive in their questioning. They cleared Scot to leave the country whenever he wished.

After his release from police custody, Scot started receiving nuisance phone calls. Perhaps it was a coincidence, but his name had appeared in the local press – along with Ahmad Kareem's – and his number was in the Limassol phone book. Bragonov's name didn't appear in the newspapers as he'd never been arrested. The nuisance calls were either long silences, or heavy breathing, or raucous laughter – or a combination of all three.

The developer's killing had meant Scot's name had never been taken off the title deed to the Kakopetria villa, and he started to get bills relating to insurance and rates. In fact, there seemed little chance the situation would change anytime soon, as the deed still hadn't been handed over, and the developer's firm refused to deal with Scot, Bragonov or Kareem. Angelos had been to see the firm's lawyer, but the deed was still safely in a bank vault somewhere. To put it mildly, Scot was pissed off with the situation. *How did I let myself become involved?*

It was a couple of weeks before Scot saw Kareem again. One night about eight, Scot walked into the Club Downtown for a quick dinner and a chat with Alex. Sitting at his regular table were Ahmad Kareem, Alex and Boris Bragonov. Kareem was talking and the other two laughing raucously. They then saw Scot and Alex beckoned him across.

'Listen, Scot, this is Ahmad Kareem, an Iraqi, and he's telling us about the final days of Saddam Hussein,' Alex said. 'It's killingly funny. Despite the brave statements, the whole of the regime was scared witless as the Americans bombed Baghdad. According to Ahmad Kareem, there was more shock than awe.'

'I know Ahmad and Boris, but how …?' Scot looked towards Alex.

'Oh, I just met Ahmad. He introduced himself because he had something to do with my release from Iraq. He says—'

'I know,' Scot said. 'So it's a coincidence he should meet you in Limassol. You hadn't met before? Maybe in London?'

Alex and Kareem caught each other's eyes, heads tilting in apparent, or feigned, puzzlement. 'I don't think we met in London, did we Ahmad?'

Kareem shook his head slowly.

'Boris looks after investments for some oligarch,' Alex noted. 'But I think you know that. Ahmad and Boris are planning a business together. I've asked them to my celebration party tomorrow night. I've told them they'll have to join in a toast to the Queen's health.'

Not for the first time, Scot felt excluded from Alexander's world. After what he'd heard from Adnan Bashir about Alex and Ahmad meeting in London, he felt he was on the periphery of Alex's loop. Perhaps Bashir was wrong, but that seemed doubtful. Visions of the weekend in Kakopetria when Alex had his two American mates sprang to mind. Birmington was dead, and the real Rick Jordan remained as illusive as ever. There were some things he was never going to learn about Alexander, Ahmad, or the cast of players surrounding them. Things he was never going to know for sure, anyway.

Scot was left to eat with Kareem and Boris. Alex returned from time to time to chat in between serving other customers. As Ahmad Kareem topped up the wine glasses, he lent across to Scot. 'Boris and I think you'd be a great asset to our business. We would like you to join us.'

'We need someone like you,' Boris added. 'Someone calm to counter my impetuous temper. My lawyer likes you.'

'I'm a loner. I work alone, so I'm just not interested. Anyway, I don't know a thing about your plans.'

Kareem and Boris looked at each other, shaking their heads slowly with frustration. Their attitude indicated they thought Scot a stupid naïve man, who was turning down the offer of a lifetime. Ahmad Kareem finally spoke.

'Boris manages investments in Cyprus on behalf of a couple of Russia's richest men, so we have capital. No problem about that.'

'And you, Ahmad?'

'Some people in Iraq have expressed to me a similar interest in investing in Cyprus.'

'Well, good luck to you,' Scot said. 'Cyprus has a vibrant business sector, so you may do well. But they're good at business, the Cypriots. They may have all the profits and deals tied up already.'

'Exactly,' Kareem said, quick as a flash. 'That's why we want you to join us. You know people. You can provide introductions. You know how Cyprus works. You know how the Limassol port works. Because you've lived here.'

'You've lived here, Boris. You know people, and how things work. And Angelos can help you.'

'But you have contacts in the ports, in the shipping companies,' Boris replied.

'What are you shipping? Arms, drugs?' Scot didn't expect an answer. 'If your trade is legal, you just go to a shipping company or agent and they'll do the rest. Simple as that.'

Boris and Ahmad shook their heads dismissively.

'Anyway, for me, the longer I live here the more I know how much I don't know,' Scot said.

Boris countered. 'You're too modest. You have so much stored in your head you make us feel like children.'

Scot took a giant gulp of his wine. 'No, sorry, I'm not interested.'

Boris noisily slid his chair back, and left the table. Ahmad Kareem drew a brown envelope from a plastic bag and handed it to Scot. 'No hard feelings, but you might like this memento of our association.'

The envelope was of the same kind he'd delivered to Mustafa Rasool after his trip to Baghdad. Scot slid a photograph from the envelope. It was blackmail. It was a photograph of Ana and Scot eating at the restaurant on the Larnaca seafront.

'Rasool told me he'd introduced you to a very nice girl,' Kareem said. 'So it's nice to have this to remember her by.'

'It's blackmail!'

'Why?'

'You must know the police would be interested in this.'

Ahmad Kareem snatched back the photograph and the envelope.

It was no use fighting over the picture. There could be many other copies. It was no use making a scene either. Shouting and punching would make things worse. The police would arrive. They'd likely see the picture.

Boris returned to the table. 'So Vodka nightcaps all round?'

'Not for me, I'm off. Ahmad said your oligarchs are paying. Thank them for me.' Scot avoided looking at Kareem as he left the table and the restaurant.

Alex hurried across the restaurant and caught Scot on the pavement outside. 'Everything okay? I'd hoped to talk more.'

Scot didn't respond.

'Well, I'll see you tomorrow. At the party. You won't mind toasting the Queen?'

'Wonderful party,' Kareem said as he led a reluctant Scot to the door. 'Alex so much deserved the Queen's award. He does so much for Britain. It was good to have old friends around to celebrate his contribution to the Great Britain.'

Scot listened but didn't respond. But he did note the term 'old friends'. So Kareem and Alex had known each other longer than two days. And how would Kareem know what contribution Alex had made to, as he put it, 'the Great Britain'?

Just before reaching the door, an extremely mellow Brit grabbed Scot's arm. 'You're Scot Wallace, aren't you? And you Ahmad Kareem, I think?'

The pair nodded.

'Well, heartiest congratulations,' the Brit said. 'You're heroes in my community. Your names have been toasted night after night amongst my friends. That developer refused to hand over title deeds belonging to many of us. He deserved to die. I just wanted you to hear my congratulations personally.'

'But we didn't—'

Scot cut Kareem short. 'Don't waste your time, Ahmad. He won't believe you.'

Just outside the door, Kareem whispered his secret. 'I've been granted British citizenship, a British passport. I'm now British, and a member of the European Community. I'm so happy. So I have something you want.' The Iraqi handed Scot the envelope he'd seen the evening before.

Scot looked inside. There was a photograph and a negative.

'Now I'm British, I thought it just wasn't cricket to keep it.'

Scot nodded thanks, then folded the envelope and buttoned it securely in his shirt pocket.

Then, the clunk of a motorcycle gear could be heard. The bike started roaring, and suddenly the machine was accelerating towards them.

Everything went blank.

27

By the time the ambulance reached the hospital, Scot was conscious.

'Keep calm,' the paramedic said. 'A bullet just grazed the side of your stomach, but you've lost some blood. You've suffered severe shock and trauma, so you must remain quiet and still.' The paramedic put a cold damp towel on Scot's forehead.

Scot looked across the ambulance to the other bunk. 'Kareem, how's he?'

The paramedic moved the towel across the forehead. 'Just be calm, relax. No more talking. It will exhaust you.'

At the hospital, Scot was checked out by a young doctor, and taken on a trolley for X-rays and scans. Once in a bed, he was given two injections, and some tablets. They must have been sleeping pills as he slept until daylight. Tea was brought, and later some watery porridge. After drinking the tea, he fell asleep again.

Just before midday, Scot woke to find a silent Alexander Belfort-Smith sitting in the chair beside the bed. 'So you've woken,' Alex said gently.

'Kareem?'

'He was dead when they lifted him into the ambulance,' Alex continued. 'But the medics didn't say anything then. A bullet went straight through his heart.'

Scot raised his eyebrows.

'He was clearly the target. You were just unlucky.'

But as the days passed, it became clear the police saw the facts less clearly. They initially had a theory that Scot had lured Kareem on to the footpath and stood there so the gunman could identify the Iraqi.

'We think the gunman just grazed you with a bullet so we wouldn't be suspicious,' an officer said aggressively. 'But you seem to crop up in all our murder investigations. First there was the developer, and now this. A bit of a coincidence? Best to tell us what you know.'

'From a speeding motorcycle, the killer just grazed me?' Scot protested. 'Bloody good shot.'

After a while, the police seemed to go cool on this line of investigation. They remained suspicious, however, because Scot's name was on the title deed of a Kakopetria property along with Ahmad Kareem and Boris Bragonov. 'You gained a lot by Kareem's death and now the disappearance of Bragonov,' they observed. Scot's response that he'd never seen any title deed of the house cut little ice with them.

A month after Kareem's assassination, investigations continued, but as far as Scot knew there were no firm suspects. Or too many! Ahmad Kareem hadn't lived long enough in Limassol to make many real friends, and no one appeared to mourn his passing. Except, of course, there were some regrets he was gunned down in the centre of the city around midnight. It wasn't good for tourism, the mayor pointed out in a press release.

Boris Bragonov disappeared completely, never to be seen again in Limassol. Mustafa Rasool didn't bother to travel from Aleppo for Kareem's funeral, and didn't give the impression over the phone he was too upset about the Iraqi's death.

'Much blood, Scot? Well, those who live by the sword have to expect to die by the sword,' he said. 'I'm packing my bags for London. It will be good to see Alexander there.'

Nikos, at the front desk of Scot's apartment block thought 'it must have been interesting' to be so close to the murder. 'Something to remember,' he added.

And Dimitri predictably believed the murder was the work of Rick Jordan. In fact, he rang the police to give them the lead, but they didn't seem to believe the American was involved.

Such was Ahmad Kareem's extraordinary life – from loyal Saddam official to confidant of the new American-backed Iraqi government – that the assassination became a gossip picnic. Everyone had a theory. All were backed up by so-called authoritative sources, such as the American Embassy, the British High Commission, Russians living in Limassol, and even the Embassy of Israel. Some people said the Kurds could have been involved because of Kareem's work with Saddam's regime. Others said it was the result of differences between Iraqi Sunni and Shiite Moslems. In short, everyone had a theory, and everyone was in the frame.

Especially Scot. Even four weeks after the killing, the police still had further questions. At least, they called them further questions, but in fact they were the same old queries put differently. 'No they were both wearing helmets and it was night, so I couldn't identify the two on the motorcycle.' 'I don't know what type of bike it was.' 'At least one – the driver – was wearing a leather jacket.' 'It was a powerful bike, yes.' Scot was getting weary of the inquiries, but realised the importance of remaining cool, polite.

Alexander felt somewhat responsible for Kareem's death having invited him to the party at short notice, or else regretted the murder had taken place right outside his restaurant. So, he arranged and hosted a memorial service in the restaurant. Most of the people who'd attended the OBE party returned, plus a few others. It was more a

second party than a funeral, but at least during the formal
proceedings people were suitably solemn. Alex asked Scot
to say a few words, and finally he agreed to read the
Twenty-Third Psalm, which some thought inappropriate
for a Moslem. Despite protesting he hardly knew anything
about Mr Ahmad Kareem apart from his account number,
Kareem's bank manager, after some persuasion, agreed to
say a few words in lieu of an oration. He spoke of the
Iraqi's distinguished career, and how he felt certain he
would be missed by so many. Then everyone moved to the
bar and toasted the deceased. The police mingled.

A few days later, Scot was having a quiet drink and a
cigarette alone on his balcony. He was holding the
envelope Kareem had given him just before he died.
Finally, he slid the photograph out and a kaleidoscope of
thoughts was unleashed. Taken from a slight angle, it was
a clear image of Scot and Ana at the Larnaca beach
restaurant. It was not taken by chance. It was a professional job. But how did the photographer know they
would be sitting at that restaurant? It was a random choice.
Or was it? Ana certainly guided Scot to the restaurant, and
that particular table. So did Ana know the photographer,
or was she the target of the cameraman? But for Ana, the
image was hardly incriminating. At the time the picture
was taken, it was not incriminating for Scot either. Only
the later murders in Nicosia and Aleppo, and Ana's
apparent link, made the picture a problem for Scot. But
with Kareem dead, the chances of another copy of the
photograph ever coming to light seemed remote. Anyway,
as he'd already rehearsed, he would tell the police he met
Ana by chance and liked her. There was nothing unusual
about that on an island attracting two million tourists each
year.

Scot looked at the photograph again. It captured Ana
just as Scot remembered her. Kareem had been right, in

one respect. It was a nice memento of the relationship. Scot, though, didn't need a reminder like this. There were too many other issues surrounding the affair that a photo couldn't capture.

With Rasool going to London to meet Alexander, and Kareem having been granted British citizenship so suddenly, it seemed to Scot the pair were linked to Alexander's undercover work. If Adnan was correct and Alex and Kareem had met years before in London, could the Iraqi have been a British agent all along? Scot knew he'd never know for certain.

But it did trigger a thought. Were the murders in Nicosia and Aleppo – killings Ana was associated with – carried out on behalf of British and perhaps American intelligence? If so, was Ana now in Britain too? Had she been given citizenship as a reward? But he couldn't ask Alexander or anyone else. It would be too risky. Because, if those killings had nothing to do with Western intelligence then he'd merely draw attention to his link with the Serbian woman police still wanted to question.

Alone on his balcony, Scot's lips briefly touched the picture, then he placed it back in the envelope, and held it over the ashtray. He set fire to it with his cigarette lighter. As it burned, he said goodbye to Ana, Ahmad Kareem, and Mustafa Rasool. Never again would he be trapped in a Middle East quagmire like the Americans, British, French, Australians, and others.

For Scot, it was time for a new start. He breathed in the salty air, and felt free.

The security phone rang. It was Nikos asking Scot to go down to his desk. Scot caught the lift and found Nikos beaming enthusiastically. 'There's someone waiting for you, Scot. We're drinking coffee.'

Scot looked into Nikos's office, where a slim young woman with long dark silky hair was waiting. 'You Mr

Scot Wallace?' She spoke with a charmingly stilted, but alluring, voice.

Scot nodded.

'Mr Rasool in Aleppo told me to contact you, Mr Wallace. I'm from Romania, and he says you're very kind, and would like to help me. Would you?'

For quite a few seconds, perhaps minutes, Scot just stared in disbelief. Nikos beamed encouragement as if it were his business somehow. Finally, Scot bent down and picked up the woman's battered suitcase. 'Come up for a drink. There's no harm in talking.'

Postscript

The Middle East is a trap for players, big and small. From the time of the Crusades, major powers have been snared in the Middle East.

Ever since the Second World War, the United States, Britain, France and the Soviet Union have intervened in the area militarily or through documented intelligence operations. All major powers compete selling weapons in the Middle East.

Their allies, including Australia and Canada, have become embroiled in military adventures in Iraq and Afghanistan and have contributed troops and police to peace-keeping missions in the area.

According to an Egyptian saying, those that drink from the Nile always return. Perhaps it's the same for the Tigris, Euphrates, Barada, and Jordan rivers, and the snow-fed streams of Afghanistan.